THE ROTTING ROOM

Viggy Parr Hampton

First edition, April 2025
ISBN Paperback: 979-8-9898755-4-2
ISBN Hardcover: 979-8-9898755-6-6
ISBN Ebook: 979-8-9898755-5-9
Book Design by Nuno Moreira, NMDESIGN

THE ROTTING ROOM

Viggy Parr Hampton

For my Dad, who besides being one of the most moral and ethical
people I know, also possesses an attention to detail and commitment
to historical accuracy that made this a better book.
I didn't take 105% of your edits like you asked, but I took at least 70%.

A Cold Night for Alligators

A determined CDC epidemiologist goes rogue to tackle a
mysterious outbreak in Savannah, only to find himself entangled
with a pair of urban explorers and a dangerous, tortured soul in
an abandoned theme park where dark forces stir.

Much Too Vulgar

Disturbed pre-med student Keely Rexroth is unable to take
'no' for an answer when she is denied entry into a prestigious
research program. As her ambition curdles into dark mania, she
embarks on her own curriculum of twisted experimentation,
fighting to keep her secrets from a campus priest who is too
perceptive for his own good. If she can't get what she deserves
on her own merit, she'll eliminate her competition.

Sisters of Divine Innocence Horarium

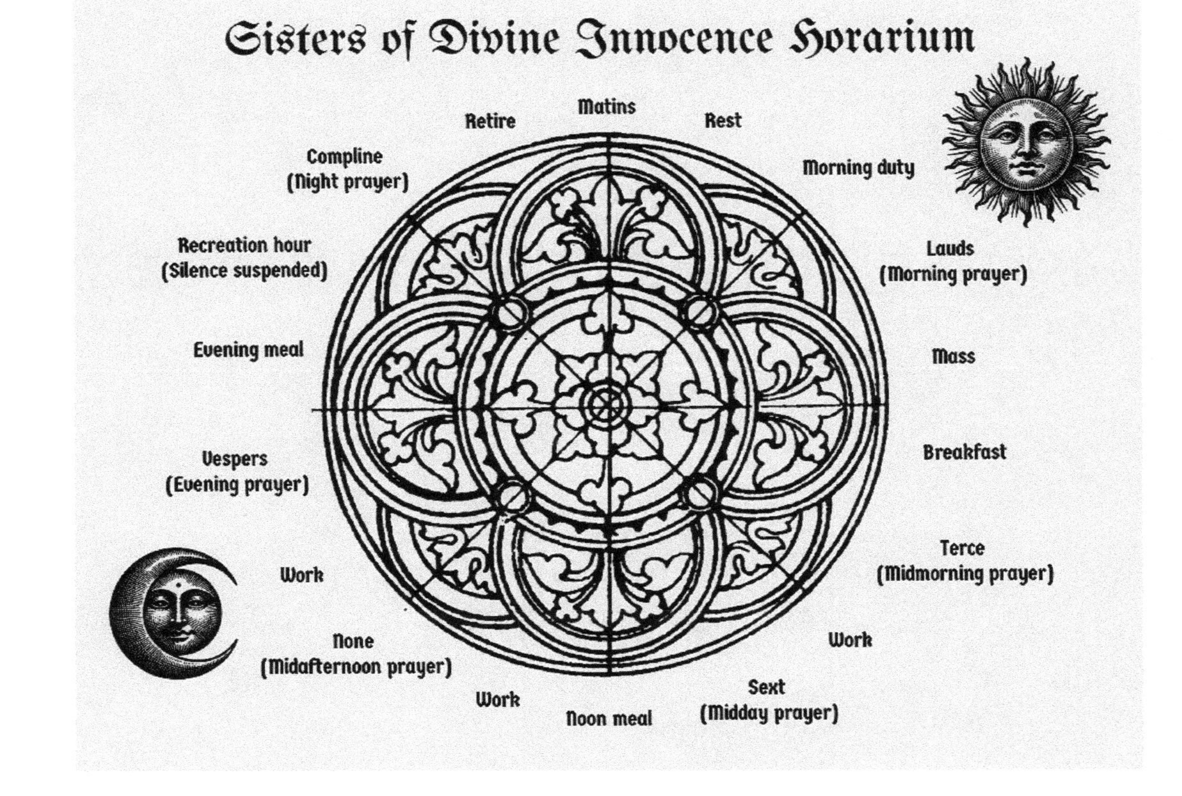

CHAPTER ONE

Sister Rafaela

A scream bubbled in my throat like bile as I stared into the face of a rotting Sister. Her black, withered eyes, her brown teeth jutting from shriveled lips, the yellow-gray paper of her flesh, so mottled it looked burned—I had never before seen something so gruesome, even during my time with the Rafaelites, which I sincerely hoped to forget. I made the sign of the cross, shuddering.

"Sister Rafaela," Mother Superior said, her tone authoritative. It sliced right through my terror, my breath dying in my throat. Her face was weathered and mapped with deep wrinkles, and she seemed to look down on me, even though she was considerably shorter. "I must acquaint you with this chamber, seeing as your Rafaelites, to my knowledge, do not incorporate this practice."

I pulled in another breath to respond, but Mother Superior put up a gnarled hand to stop me. I glanced frantically around the room, which was cavelike and warm, moist with the pungent smell of death, and lit by candelabra mounted into niches in the rock. The low light illuminated the rough stone chairs, only one of which was occupied, lining three of the four walls. Each chair was bordered by heavy stone armrests and contained a large void in its seat, like a privy. "Sister, this is the chamber of divine decomposition for the Sisters of Divine Innocence. We bring our dead here to complete the cycle of their earthly lives. In this room, we can pray and encourage them as they begin their ascents into Heaven to be with God the Father Almighty." Her dark eyes glittered with something that could have been rapture or ferocity.

I crossed myself again. My hands felt jittery, like the butterflies that used to flit around the garden of the Rafaelite abbey where I dwelt before the trouble happened. The dead Sister's face held my gaze with defiance. Her mouth was open, as if she were yawning—or screaming.

A *drip-drop* broke the silence, and my entire body convulsed.

"Oh, one more thing," Mother Superior said, as if sensing my discomfort. "As the divine spark leaves the bodies of our beloved Sisters, so, too, do their bodily liquids."

Acid rose in my throat in place of a scream this time, but once again, I swallowed hard against it.

Mother Superior continued, "We collect this holy essence."

There was a beat of uncomfortable quiet. When my voice finally emerged from between my lips, it was squeaky. "For what purpose?"

Mother Superior smiled, and her teeth looked sharp in the low light flickering from the candelabras. "It erases sin," she said.

Before I had time to respond, Mother Superior turned swiftly on one heel, heading for the small doorway. When I began to follow, she held up one wrinkled palm.

"Do not follow me, Sister. This is your first night, and you must pay your respects to Sister Faustina." She gestured to the withered figure on the stone chair. "You must become acquainted more intimately with the customs of the Sisters of Divine Innocence. You have missed the evening meal, so you must pray here with Sister Faustina until matins. After that, one of the Sisters will show you to your cell."

The triple toll of the bells, which coordinated every facet of our lives, punctuated her orders. Our recreational time was over. In my terror, I briefly forgot myself, forgot my vow of silence that went into effect during all hours of the day except for our one hour of recreation, our time in the confessional booth, and our few spoken prayers during services.

"But Mother—" I blurted, unsure of what I could possibly say to allow me to follow her out of that room, away from the rotting husk of Sister Faustina.

She silenced me with a hard stare and a sharp shake of her head. Without another word, she turned on her heel and slipped through the door, closing it behind her.

A sickening panic constricted my chest as I stood near the entrance, my eyes locked on Sister Faustina. I shivered, even though the chamber held an unpleasant warmth. The scents of char and ash filled the air, as well as something passably sweet, like pressed flowers crumbled to dust. In that moment, I acutely longed for my old abbey in which I had lived with the Rafaelites, the only home I'd known since my birthplace, back in Barcelona—despite the horrors that had befallen me there.

The Sisters of Divine Innocence had agreed to take me in, even though they must have known about the trouble with the Rafaelites, the way the abbess had perverted the rituals of God. Finding a new home to continue my spiritual work had surely been evidence of God's mercy. I needed to be grateful. God had given me the chance to find my way back to Him. Squandering that chance would be the gravest of sins.

I took one small step toward Sister Faustina, my hands clasped in prayer. *Hail Mary, full of grace. The Lord is with thee. Blessed art thou amongst women, and blessed is the fruit of thy womb, Jesus. Holy Mary, Mother of God, pray for us sinners, now and at the hour of our death. Amen.*

The *drip-drop* sound filled the room again. The dull grain of a wooden bucket, underneath the chair and behind Sister Faustina's shriveled, blackened feet, came into view in the low light. I fought the gorge that threatened to rise up into my throat yet again. My stomach no longer rumbled with hunger.

Such a thing as a chamber of divine decomposition was entirely new to me. I did not feel bathed in holiness as I moved closer to Sister Faustina, but I knew I needed to do as Mother Superior instructed. I shook with fear just thinking of disobeying her, of seeing her dagger-sharp eyes pointed at me, like blades quivering and ready to strike.

My knees popped as I knelt in front of Sister Faustina, a crackling sound that reminded me I was alive. Sister Faustina would never hear her knees pop again.

I closed my eyes and reached out one trembling hand. My fingers alighted on a papery stretch of flesh. Sister Faustina's skin was cold despite the warmth of the room, and the pressure of my touch released an animal smell that reminded me of my father's farm outside of Barcelona.

Before additional thoughts could set my blood to rushing again, I grasped the corpse's spindly hand in mine. She felt so delicate, so vulnerable.

There I stayed, gripping the dead Sister's hand, sending silent prayers to God the Father and thinking about the series of occurrences that had led me to this moment, to this stagnant room. Rosary beads slipped through my sweaty fingers, one after another, until the bells tolled again and a knock on the door startled me out of my trance.

The knock announced the Sister designated to gather us all for matins, aptly named the Caller. As I followed her out through the narrow doorway and into the church, I looked back at Sister Faustina. I wiped my sweaty hand on my white scapular, leaving a black smear, and stared into her empty skull, her eyes having dripped out of her body some time ago. I searched and searched, but there was no holiness to be found there.

CHAPTER TWO

Sister Rafaela

If the Caller found my presence in the chamber of divine decomposition odd, she did not show it. Perhaps my initiation was a matter of routine, something all new Sisters experienced. There was some comfort in that feeling of solidarity, and I leaned into it like a beggar grasping for a crust of discarded bread.

The Caller padded quietly past the altar of the church, and I followed. My feet felt heavy, as though I were wearing leaden slippers. I turned back just once, the thought of Lot's salt-encrusted wife springing to the forefront of my mind. The small, pointed door to the right of the altar still reached out for me, its particular scent following me like a curse.

I was so entranced by the beauty of the church, with its gilded cornices and lush red velvet pews, that it took me a moment to notice the sea of heads bowed in prayer in front of me. It being the middle of the night, the Caller remained silent as she led me to an empty seat in the pews. The Rafaelites had practiced silence as well, but not like this. In this abbey, silence was almost tangible, its virtue irreproachable. The Rafaelites had spoken when necessary; it seemed as though the Sisters of Divine Innocence failed to speak even when necessary. It would take time for me to adjust, of course.

As I nervously settled into my seat, I stole a glance at the Caller. She was far taller than Mother Superior, with a brusque liveliness. My mind formed a picture of her face, which I expected to be round and lovely with youth and God's light.

That was not so.

When a shaft of moonlight through the windows illuminated her visage for the briefest of moments, what I saw framed by her veil was jarring. Silvery, still-healing scars, made brighter in the white light, crisscrossed the features of her face like rivers on a merchant's map. Between the healing knots of skin were great red, raw patches. Pity overwhelmed my heart, and I looked away. What unfortunate circumstance must have befallen the Sister? I sent a quick prayer to God for her, and comforted myself with the reminder that her suffering only brought her closer to God. In a way, perhaps she was even more fortunate than the unscarred.

The Caller moved quickly into her own pew, joining the rest of the Sisters of Divine Innocence. I looked around me, expecting puzzled stares but receiving nothing. They must have known of my arrival, for they all remained as they were, heads bowed, immobile as statues.

We prayed in silence. Back in Barcelona, the Rafaelites had held matins, too, but everything felt different here. That is what I wanted— to feel different, to look different, to *be* different. The Rafaelites had never been the right fit for me, but my father's warm friendship with the Archbishop of Barcelona had dictated my life since before I could speak. Archbishop Orriva believed the Rafaelites would suit me just fine, and the abbey desperately needed the money my father would donate for the Order's acceptance of his daughter. That exchange should have been a dark omen from the beginning: a holy order placing such high esteem on gold, making it outshine the spiritual enlightenment we were there to achieve. We were not closer to God because we had heavy golden chalices or solid silver pitchers. We were not holier because we knelt on cushions filled with the finest goose down, or because we slept on soft mattresses in comfortable, well-appointed rooms. Despite my privileged upbringing, I had never cared much for material things, preferring instead to look to God and live modestly.

Studying the church more closely, with its gilt and velvet, I grew even more uneasy. Had I been rescued from one sinful situation only to be thrust, unknowingly, into another?

I tried to refocus my treacherous thoughts and concentrate on my prayer, but my mind kept wandering into the past, a lonely traveler. I trusted my father, I trusted Archbishop Orriva, and I trusted God the Father, but the Rafaelites had fallen away from God's light. I had always thought Abbess Cecelia Maria had understood God's requirements of us, but when the sacrifices began, something soured in my heart. What could I say? Where could I go? Abbess Cecelia Maria knew what God wanted. I followed along despite my misgivings, because I knew I was just a poor sinner throwing myself on God's mercy. I did not know better than the abbess, and to think so would have been to break my vow of obedience and stink of pride.

When Archbishop Orriva finally visited the Rafaelite abbey after a long absence, he saw how Abbess Cecelia Maria had perverted and twisted the will of God. She had blood on her hands, as did we all. Archbishop Orriva, his face a mask of horror, had banished the abbess and many of the Sisters. I do not know what became of them, and I do not wish to know.

Archbishop Orriva spared me excommunication, by the grace of God. He recommended the Sisters of Divine Innocence instead, in this abbey atop the hill where I now prayed. I trusted the Archbishop—he must have had some insight into God's plan for me, so I knew I must acclimate myself to this isolated place, this place where Sisters knelt before their own dead to be closer to the Almighty.

The bells tolled, and I whispered a prayer to God for my wandering mind—*O my God, I am heartily sorry for having offended thee.* The Sisters filed out of the church and through the doors, and Mother Superior silently directed me to follow the scarred Sister yet again. Without a word, she led me through the cloister, where the wind howled through the bare, peeling trees and set me to shivering. My hand still felt sticky where I had touched the rotten, greasy skin of Sister Faustina.

A stone doorway rose out of the darkness, and the scarred Sister stepped through it. Once inside, the coldness of the dormitory floor seeped through my thin slippers, and I fought to control my complicated feelings—I missed the warmth of the Rafaelite abbey, but I also knew that warmth came only from the Devil and his hell-fires, which had infiltrated the Rafaelites like a plague.

Rows of small stone cells passed by on my left and right; they looked different from the cells I had left behind in Barcelona—more austere, more appropriate. A smile of relief spread across my face as I walked. Finally, the scarred Sister stopped in front of an open door and waved me inside. The low light did her scars no favors, turning her pleasant expression into an impossibly gruesome smirk.

The room held a thin straw mattress upon a wooden bed frame, a narrow table, and a chair. A large earthen jug of water sat atop the table near a shallow basin, and when I caught sight of it, my thirst ignited. I turned to nod gratefully at the scarred Sister, but she was gone, having closed the door of my cell without making a sound.

Despite the exhaustion of my travel, the anxiety that had grown within me since meeting Mother Superior, and spending so many long, dark hours in the chamber of divine decomposition, my eyes were wide open, and my mind raced. Unwanted images of my past flickered through my thoughts—first the bloodied nanny goat stretched out upon the altar, then the milk cow gutted from neck to tail, finally, the—no. I couldn't let my thoughts drift too far into that dark place. The Rafaelites were best left behind. It was time to embrace God's plan for me in this new abbey, which was so far from the corrupting influences of the city. I would fully recommit myself to my vows here and now, and God would grant me easy rest for my fidelity.

I took several sips from the jug, slaking my thirst. A nightgown had been laid out for me atop my bed, and a smile of gratitude lifted the corners of my mouth. I stepped out of my habit, which held the smells of my long journey, as well as the chamber. I peeled off my scapular, stained with remnants of Sister Faustina, and removed my veil, coif, and tunic. With eager hands, I hoisted the nightgown into the air and up over my shorn head, where my cold, nervous sweat had begun to dry. As the nightgown slipped past my nose, I recoiled. That smell was familiar— slightly sweet, with a rotten core, like a bad apple.

Like Sister Faustina.

I was unable to choke back my bile; I gagged uselessly, bent over double, struggling to be sick in silence. Finally, a thin stream of yellow saliva dripped from my lips. Perhaps missing the evening meal had been a blessing from God—I could contain myself, at least somewhat. It wouldn't be prudent to make a mess of myself now, just as I was settling in to my new home.

What I was now sure was Sister Faustina's nightgown was soft and worn from years of use. The fabric was thin and almost bare around the elbows and knees, and I couldn't help imagining the nightgown draping over her emaciated body as she drew her last breath.

Hail Mary, full of grace.

Anger at my own ingratitude blossomed behind my eyes. How selfish was I to be repulsed by a gift of charity the Sisters had bestowed upon me? God provided for me through his agents on earth, and I must be grateful. Did I expect a newly sewn gown of velvet, perhaps edged in golden thread? Did I expect freshly woven cloth, just for me? My own greed was emerging; I had been as yet unable to purge it, even though I thought I had left it far behind me. I needed to try harder; perhaps wearing Sister Faustina's gown would expand my capacity for humility and empathy.

I lay down on the thin mattress. It accepted my weight by emitting a puff of air, which held the same fragrance as the nightgown. I closed my eyes and breathed deeply, trying to find the grace in the scent of a holy life well lived instead of ignorant disgust. Behind my eyelids, Sister Faustina's empty skull stared into me from the darkness. I wondered if Archbishop Orriva knew about the chamber of divine decomposition, if he was privy to any secrets that weighed heavy on his heart. With my fingers pressed to my temples, I squeezed the uncomfortable questions out of my head. My new life could not begin with doubts creeping into my mind, doubts which were insidious and damning. I would not break my vow of obedience, and if Mother Superior deemed the chamber holy and good, then it was. I needed to place my trust in those who knew better.

I was still performing penance for my unwitting but unholy sinning with the Rafaelites, and I refused to add anything more to my burden. In fact, I would visit the chamber of divine decomposition often, to familiarize myself with its purpose, its smell, its feel. I would search, and I would find the holiness that lived there. I would find my way back into God's good graces.

The wind howled as I drifted to sleep. I felt calm and peaceful, happy in my decision to uphold my vows with vigor.

That night, Sister Faustina crept into my dreams. Her empty eyes blinked, her dry jaw clicked, and her skeletal hands beckoned, shedding snowfalls of dead flesh when her fingers rubbed together.

I thanked God the Father when the bells awoke me a short while later for morning duty, putting an end to my interminable first night with the Sisters of Divine Innocence.

CHAPTER THREE

Sister Rafaela

I washed my face in the basin and dressed quickly. When I opened the door of my cell, the scarred Sister was standing there in the hallway of the dormitory, her creased face expressionless. I bowed my head in deference, and the Sister turned swiftly on one heel and walked away. She must have intended for me to follow her, so I hurried to match her pace. The other Sisters were emerging from their cells, many clutching golden candleholders, the flickering light making their faces seem ghoulish.

O my God, I am heartily sorry for having offended thee. It would not do to have such superstitious thoughts crowding my mind, nor to let my eyes trick me into seeing unholiness where none existed.

The scarred Sister, with me at her heels, walked outside, through the cloister, and turned into a small structure I had not noticed the evening before. The building was made of a hard, blistered wood, and reminded me of a house I had seen in Barcelona as a child that had burned; after the fire had spent itself, the home was a charred husk, blackened and evil-looking. All who had lived there had been burned alive.

No, no, I was getting carried away again—there was no evil in this place. I tried to assure myself that everything at the abbey of the Sisters of Divine Innocence was holy, but the notion felt hollower the more

I pushed, so I stopped. Instead, I distracted myself by staring at the uneven stones lining the cloister, counting how many paces it took to reach that black building, which perched like a raven on the hill.

Without turning around, the scarred Sister entered the building. I followed.

The smell hit me immediately. I recognized it instantly, for it clung to my own skin from my night with Sister Faustina—the sickly sweetness, the rotten undercurrent. I looked up and around, trying desperately to find the source of the stench. All I could see were shelves upon shelves of small glass bottles, each filled with a brown-green liquid. The color reminded me of my neighbor Josef Querida's well-water, which was undrinkable ever since his fattest sow fell through the wooden covering and was left to rot at the bottom. There was no easy way to remove the detritus of death, no matter how hard one might try.

The glass, though—so much of it! I'd never dreamed one place could contain such an abundance of something so scarce and expensive. If I had not been already aware of the abbey's wealth, the almost ostentatious display of glass was irrefutable proof. The abbey may have played at modesty, but that was belied by this display. Whatever was inside those bottles must be enormously valuable to be worth the glass needed to encase it.

Straight ahead were two rows of long wooden tables, which stretched almost the entire length of the room. Empty glass bottles were crowded in the center of the tables, along with piles of corks and several funnels. Wooden buckets had been placed at intervals on the floor. The ceilings arched high overhead, higher than I would have imagined from the outside. Everything was dark despite the freshly lit candles perched on every available surface. The profusion of flames seemed irresponsible given the building's charred exterior. One would think those candles had caused problems in the past.

There were others in the room, too—other Sisters. Their faces were cast in shadow from their veils, and they glanced up only briefly as I entered with the scarred Sister before returning to their work.

The scarred Sister seated herself on a bench at one of the tables, and gestured for me to do the same. She did not say anything, it being our time of silence, but I knew she meant for me to join in the work. I watched her intently as she hefted a wooden bucket from the floor to the table. She placed a small funnel into the open mouth of a glass bottle and plucked a heavy-looking ladle from within the bucket. Delicately, she dipped the ladle into the bucket, filling it completely, then tipped it toward the funnel, stopping at the precise moment when the little bottle would take no more of the green-brown liquid. She replaced the ladle in the bucket and stoppered the glass bottle with a cork before pushing it to the side and repeating the process again—all without spilling a single drop.

I took a seat at the bench opposite her; I could smell a similar wooden bucket at my feet. My duty was clear.

I set to my work reluctantly, praying to God the Father to guide my hands. Despite my prayers, my hands trembled, for I knew that particular smell that permeated every bit of this black cavern that felt far too much like the interior of some scavenger's hungry stomach. My time in the chamber of divine decomposition had embedded the stench in my memory forever, but surely there was another explanation for the provenance of the brown-green liquid. I scolded myself for my curiosity; if I was meant to know, then I would be told. Still, I wondered if this liquid was indeed that 'holy essence' collected in the chamber of divine decomposition, and why it was being bottled so. It was clearly very valuable... perhaps because, as Mother Superior had insisted, it erased sin? This did not make much sense to me—only God the Father had the power to erase our sins—but I hoped that after the evening meal I could ask one of the Sisters, if it was in God's plan for me to do so. Until then, I would be silent.

Silence did not trouble me. Throughout my childhood in Barcelona,

I had always followed my older brother Sebastian, mostly without question. Where he went, I went—or at least tried desperately to follow. When he gave me a task, I performed it without complaint. Sebastian had my father's trust, while I had my father's heart. We both knew and accepted this fact about our little family, which would have been bigger had our five younger siblings not died in infancy. Mother had named them all, and Archbishop Orriva had completed the baptisms before each was interred in the family crypt. Mother could not bear the thought of not being reunited with her babies in Heaven. It was that desperation, more than the fear of eternal damnation, that powered Mother's religiosity. She might not have recognized this fault of hers, but it was always so clear to me, even more so after I received a convent education. I tried not to pity her, and instead demonstrated my filial love by praying for her soul whenever I could.

My hands quit their trembling, and I grew accustomed to the task before me, filling bottles as swiftly as the other Sisters. I had always been good with my hands; I had helped my brother build a small fort on our land, at least until my Father put a stop to it, telling me that working like that would roughen my fingers and was unbecoming for a lady of my status. I did not really understand what that meant at the time, but I did now. Sending me to the Rafaelites meant I received a good education, and I could shine God's holy light on my family through the act of my devotion. My role was important. I would safeguard my family's relationship with God and pray for our salvation, for it was heartily necessary.

My acute sensitivity to the stench had lessened, and I began to breathe deeply once again. I assumed the other Sisters had also become accustomed to the penetrating scent. I lifted my eyes to God, thinking there must be some divine purpose in it.

As I grew comfortable in my work and my vision continued to adjust to the darkened room, I could make out three other Sisters besides the scarred one and myself, all filling bottles as well. For a moment, just a brief moment, a shiver of unease crept up my back, because every one of us had started that hour of work with a full bucket, and I could see the dull sheen of liquid in at least a dozen other buckets lined up against the wall, opposite the shelves of jars. I chided myself for my fantastical imagination. The liquid was not what I suspected from the smell; it could not be. Still, my thoughts wandered in sinful directions. Sister Faustina had been the only one in the chamber, but surely that little woman couldn't have produced that much… juice.

Dear God the Father, please keep death at bay. Please keep it from following me here, and guide me ever after into Your loving embrace, and let me bask in Your holy light. Amen.

My father always told me the regimentation of a religious life would comfort and sustain me, guiding me away from the fanciful imaginings and, at times, uncomely behavior to which I had been prone, like building the fort with my brother. He explained that the silence, the unvarying schedule, the proximity to God's holiness—all would contrive to rid me of any darkness that followed me into this world. All humans sinned. It was not enough that we were a pious and observant family or that we did good works. Greater penance was needed, of course.

A sharp shake of my head drove my troublesome thoughts away. There I was again, lost in imaginings of the past, like a young girl mooning over a handsome boy. Could I be any more disgraceful? *Glory be to the Father, and to the Son, and to the Holy Spirit.*

Whatever the provenance of the contents of the small bottles, it was not as though their existence was a completely foreign concept. The Rafaelites had sold goods, as well. Their product was a small, crunchy, marzipan confection dotted with crushed almonds. We baked them every morning before the sun rose, and by nightfall we had always sold them all, exchanging confection-filled tins for coins through the small grate in the cloister wall. Patrons from all over Barcelona, all over Spain, would line up at our grate to purchase our sweets. We took pride in them—which was perhaps our first mistake. I did not realize it in time; I was not even aware sin was creeping into my own heart until it was too late. I breathed a silent sigh of relief, because here with the Sisters of Divine Innocence, I sensed no taint of pride. There was something else, maybe, something that sparked my unease, but whatever it was, pride was not a part of it.

When the bells tolled to signal the end of our morning duties, I copied the actions of the other Sisters: replacing my bucket under the bench; placing my filled bottles in a small box at the end of the table; upturning my funnel in a dull washbasin near the door. I followed the others out the doors and into the chilly air. The moon hung fat and heavy in the sky, and I pulled my woolen habit more tightly against myself.

The sun was just beginning to filter God's divine light into the sky when Mass began, led by a young priest with a shock of dark hair. As his deep and melodious voice, tinged with a foreign accent I could not place, performed the Latin service, I focused my attention on praising God the Father, Christ, Mother Mary, and the Holy Spirit, asking for forgiveness for my sins and those of my family, and praying for the needy, for the lost children, for the men in battle, for the women with child. I thanked God for shining His divine light upon me.

So enraptured was I in the sacrament that I did not take full stock of the young priest until he slipped the Host between my lips. My eyes rested on his hands, which were pale and beautiful, with long fingers and clean pink nails. Unintentionally, my gaze floated upward from his hands, crawling over the soft shine of his vestments and coming to rest on his gentle, unlined face. What beauty I found there! He looked so much like the portraits of Jesus I had seen, with his thick dark beard, his long sharp nose, his soulful, heavy-lidded eyes. Yearning filled me to the brim, but before it could spill over into something sinful, I forced it to evaporate, as if boiled away by the heat of my religious fervor. In its afterglow, a sense of peace pervaded my being, along with a profound certainty that I would be safe from sin with the Sisters of Divine Innocence and this young priest to guide me.

As I turned to walk away and out of the church, the scarred Sister appeared before me as suddenly as an apparition, her countenance firm, her finger pointing. I turned to see what she was indicating; on the opposite side of the altar from the entry to the chamber of divine decomposition was a small, intricately carved wooden confessional. I had failed to notice it before, so delicately did it blend with the decoration of the church walls.

Fear flooded my lungs like cold water. It had been far too long since my last confession.

I had much to confess.

CHAPTER FOUR

Father Bruno

The path to the abbey of the Sisters of Divine Innocence was rocky and uneven, peppered with large divots that would easily lame a horse or a break a carriage's wheel. The early morning light was thin and floury, barely allowing me to see where I placed my feet. Every morning, as I walked to the abbey from my parish in the village, black dread crept over me like some skulking animal. Every morning, I prayed to God the Father, asking for tolerance, asking for him to use me as his vessel for good works, asking for him to banish the dread from my heart. Every morning, I failed—for the dread never lifted, it only grew darker and more suffocating as the abbey atop the hill came into view.

There was no choice for me but to carry out God's will; the Sisters of Divine Innocence required a priest for their daily Mass and confession, and I was the closest one, appointed by Archbishop Orriva himself. So why my sense of overpowering dread? There was nothing particularly awful about the Sisters; they attended Mass wreathed in holy meekness, devoted to their prayers and to the glory of God. When they came to confession, they recounted their venial sins methodically, as if counting them off on their fingers. They performed their penance and went about their duties, only to repeat the process again the following day. They were quick and efficient, dry and soft-spoken. There was nothing wrong with them—besides the smell, of course. That slightly sweet, bitter, sour odor clung to all of them like sticky perfume. It was not like any other odor I had smelled before, and when I left the abbey after confession each day, I felt the smell following me, trying to cling to me, too. Fortunately, the walk back down the hill to the village in the fresh air cleansed me before I reached my own parish church.

Today, the abbey again loomed over me, gloomy and hulking. Dear God, what was I to do with these dark thoughts? This abbey was a place of unchallenged holiness, surely? I of all people should understand how holiness could hide behind the roughest of facades—the poor, the sick, the stinking, the damaged. Especially the damaged! My mind went to Sister Leonella, the poor woman, whose face had been badly burned as she tried to save a fellow Sister from a fire. That God should leave her scarred for an act of heroism seemed unjust, but of course—that was not for me to decide. Such questioning of God's plan was a sin in itself, something I would have to reveal at my own confession. I sighed, weary, as I reached the church doors.

Once inside, the cloying odor assaulted me, tunneling into my nostrils and leaving me nauseated. How did the Sisters endure it? I supposed if one lives with something long enough, one learns to deal with it. Or, perhaps, they had grown to find it appealing?

By the time I was dressed in my vestments and at the altar of the abbey's church, all of the Sisters were present in the pews, their veiled heads bowed. I performed the Mass as I had hundreds of times, then I began the sacrament of the Eucharist. The Sisters lined up before me, red tongues darting out to take in the body of Christ before tasting of His blood from a silver chalice. I saw Mother Superior, the poor scarred Sister Leonella, Sister Cecelia, and the others.

Then, a new face, one I did not recognize. The Sister now before me was young, not too far from my own age of thirty years, if I were to guess.

Her hair was hidden beneath her veil, but I could see her dark, almost black eyebrows and inky, heavy-lidded eyes. My breath caught briefly in my throat because she was so unexpectedly, ethereally beautiful. I coughed softly into my hand to hide my consternation, then placed the Host on her tongue, which accepted the offering eagerly. I next handed her the silver chalice, from which she sipped daintily, her alluring eyes fixed on mine. Her thick eyelashes looked soft, and I wondered what it would be like to touch them. As I pulled the chalice away from her lips, my skin began to perspire beneath my vestments, and I felt feelings stirring in me that warred against my vow of chastity.

This new Sister blinked up at me, oh so slowly, then retreated. I could barely concentrate as I placed the Host on the next Sister's tongue. Who was that new Sister? Where could she possibly have come from? Most of all, why did she affect me so? I felt temptation knocking against my ribs, and I focused on my breathing to quell my impure thoughts. My own confession could not come soon enough as guilt seeped into my stomach and settled there, heavy and rancid.

Such disgraceful feelings had not been aroused in me in such a long, long time—not since my childhood in Albania, when, on the cusp of manhood, I became lost in the forest.

No, no—I would not think of such things. Not now, not during the holiest of Sacraments. How had a glimpse of a single Sister led my thoughts to stray so far, and to such dark places? Shame engulfed me, far worse than any odor the Sisters could exude. My cheeks burned as I completed the Eucharist, lifting the silver chalice to the final Sister's cracked, gray lips.

*　*　*

"In the name of the Father, the Son, and the Holy Spirit."

I could tell from the gravelly voice that Sister Leonella was now kneeling in the penitent compartment of the confessional booth. Her vocal cords had been damaged by exposure to the smoke from the fire, and as a result she spoke with a husky intonation that was instantly recognizable. My heart wanted to pity her, but then I remembered how God favors the meek. Sister Leonella would be handsomely rewarded in Heaven for her sacrifice, perhaps doubly so after the suffering she experienced here on Earth.

"Hello, Sister," I said. "'The Lord lifteth up the meek, and bringeth the wicked down even to the ground.'" I always offered Sister Leonella a piece of Scripture relating to meekness or illness, to remind her of the reward that awaited her in God's eternal glory.

"It has been one day since my last confession. Forgive me Father, for I have sinned."

"Continue, Sister," I said, my vestments rustling as I adjusted myself on the hard bench.

Through the grille separating us, Sister Leonella's scratchy voice drifted in tandem with that inescapable, earthy smell. "This past evening, I was not as welcoming to the newest Sister as I could have been."

My ears perked up upon hearing of the newest Sister—surely Sister Leonella was referring to the heavy-lidded beauty who had so enraptured me against my will. Without meaning to, I leaned closer to the grille, intent on capturing every word, every bit of information possible.

Sister Leonella continued, "Forgive me, Father, for I have judged this Sister based on rumor alone, instead of leaving all judgment to God the Father."

So this new Sister had something of a checkered past. How interesting. *Damn it, Bruno,* I chastised myself, *You cannot let your thoughts stray to this woman. She is a bride of Christ, and your soul can abide no more sin.* I gulped, hoping Sister Leonella could not hear it.

"I was slow to awaken when the bells tolled for morning duty. I lay on my mattress and felt pity for myself, because my wounds were hurting. I was slothful and self-indulgent, and I am ashamed."

I felt shame myself at being so uninterested in her small sins; all I wanted was to hear more about this new Sister, despite myself. I waited for Sister Leonella to continue, but she remained silent, waiting for me.

"Anything else, Sister?"

Her raspy breathing came through the grille, and her throat caught once, twice, as though she were trying to get something out, but could not bring herself to do so. Finally, she said, "I am sorry for all of my sins."

I was sorry she said no more about the newest Sister, but I ferociously suppressed my curiosity and gave Sister Leonella her penance and her absolution. After her gravelly "Amen," the hinges of the confessional booth creaked, and Sister Leonella departed.

Several minutes passed, and fevered thoughts rattled around in my head, bouncing off of one thing and on to the next, frantic in their marked avoidance of the newest Sister. Happy images of my Albanian childhood flashed in my mind's eye, feelings of freedom that only the really young can appreciate.

My thoughts were just beginning to veer down the path of that Albanian forest I so feared when the confessional door hinges creaked again, and the swish of wool announced a new penitent.

"In the name of the Father, the Son, and the Holy Ghost."

My eyes narrowed. The Holy Ghost? All of the other Sisters favored Holy Spirit, not Holy Ghost. My heart raced in my chest.

"Hello, Sister," I said, not bothering to correct her. After all, her greeting was not technically incorrect, just disfavored. Different. Foreign, even.

It appeared I was about to engage with the newest Sister.

I searched my mind for an appropriate verse, landing on, "'Let no man, when he is tempted, say that he is tempted by God. For God is not a tempter of evils, and he tempteth no man. But every man is tempted by his own concupiscence, being drawn away and allured. Then when concupiscence hath conceived, it bringeth forth sin. But sin, when it is completed, begetteth death.'" My own words surprised me, the verse piercing so deep into the latent desires of my own soul that I squirmed on the wooden bench. There was a sharp intake of breath from the other side of the grille.

"It has been three months since my last confession. Forgive me, Father."

Now I was positive—this was the newest Sister. Three months was far too long to go without the sacrament of confession, especially for a member of a religious order. Where had she been? What had she been doing all that time?

"Please relay your sins, Sister," I said, trying and failing to stifle the tremor in my words. Her own voice was mellifluous and thick, like honey. I wanted to drown myself in it. Instead, I tugged on my beard, hoping the sharp pinches of pain would bring me back to myself.

On the other side of the grille, the Sister sighed heavily. "I come from Barcelona," she began. "I was… a member of another religious order there. The Rafaelites. My father named me after Saint Rafaela, so he thought the Rafaelites would be a good fit for me, a place I could be closer to God and receive a pious education."

Ah, so I had learned her name at last: Rafaela. The syllables coated and warmed my tongue, like rich melted butter. My fingers found my beard again, and I pulled—harder this time.

Sister Rafaela sighed again, clearly weary. "There were… many unholy happenings at the Rafaelite abbey."

When she said nothing more, I prodded her gently. "Go on, Sister."

Her voice was shaky. "We—we baked special confections to sell, with marzipan and almonds from Andalucía. We all took far too much pride in our bakery, in the quality of our product. Pride was only the first sin."

She paused, and I could hear her ragged breathing. I was about to urge her to continue, when she said, "But it was certainly not the last."

Now my own breathing became stilted, and the overwhelming scent of the abbey was suddenly even thicker and more cloying in my nostrils. I did not want to think of that stench permeating Sister Rafaela, clouding her luminous eyes, settling over her fair skin like a pallor. Most of all, I did not want this benighted place to claim her. I knew from painful experience how quickly darkness could plunder the soul.

She gulped, the sound loud as a church tower bell in the silence. "Father," she said, having regained a measure of composure. "I have been thinking often, since I left the Rafaelites, about my childhood." Another loud gulp. "There were… things… that happened. Or, I suppose, that I thought happened. I was told I was mistaken, but I have had much time to reflect since my last confession, and now… now I am not so sure I was wrong, after all."

As a priest, I had already heard many tales of horror—abuse, forced sexual gratification, self-harm, blasphemy, and the like—and I naively assumed I was immune to shock.

Alas, I should have braced myself. When Sister Rafaela began to speak, the fetid air seemed to freeze, to preserve the environment in which we sat to prevent even the slightest eddy of atmosphere from curtailing Sister Rafaela's confession. As her tale unfolded, my hands were clasped so tightly around my crucifix that small beads of scarlet blood welled up between my fingers, but I was powerless to loosen my grip. I was frozen along with the atmosphere.

"You see, Father," Sister Rafaela said, her tone becoming more casual, more familiar. "I was born to a wealthy nobleman in Barcelona with vast land holdings. My mother was the daughter of another landed nobleman, so she had only ever known wealth and privilege. She was… how do I say this… quite enamored of her life, quite happy with the station God had furnished her. I used to think that was because she was grateful to live in God's holy light as a good woman, but I do not believe that anymore." She paused, collecting herself. "I have a brother, Sebastian. He is older than me, and, I think, he was meant to be my mother's only child."

In a rush of teary emotion, Sister Rafaela poured out the rest of her tale as a waterfall tumbles to a pool below. I was caught in the crush and pressure of the water. My hands gripped the crucifix even tighter, piercing my flesh more deeply.

"You know, Father, not every woman is content to bear children year in and year out. Not every woman aspires to be a mother. I think this was the case with my own mother. She bore Sebastian, the firstborn son, and she was happy with him, mostly because my father was happy and she felt she had fulfilled her marital duty. She had given him a perfect son. But then, you see, shortly after bearing Sebastian, she discovered she was pregnant again, with me. I know she bore me, too, for here I am, but I have come to believe that I was simply lucky, that my mother had not yet marshaled the will to fight my existence. You see, I was not my mother's last child, but I was the last child who survived. Mother bore several more babies after me, but none lived. Yes, she acted distraught, she feigned distress, with tears and prayers to God and entreaties for the souls of her baptized infants in Heaven, but, dear God, I know what I saw!"

Blood from several small cuts along my palms was now running in rivulets through the creases of my fingers, soaking into my vestments.

"I saw her kill one of the children! I saw her push Margarita under the water of the washtub basin, and hold her until there were no more bubbles breaking the surface. I—I saw how flat Mother's gaze became, how static her countenance, as though the Devil himself was holding her hands to the little babe's head!"

Sister Rafaela stopped, her breath overtaken with loud, echoing sobs. Something in the frozen atmosphere thawed, and I was finally able to unclench my fingers. As I flexed my hands, more blood dripped from my skin to my vestments. My hands looked gruesome, as though shot through with stigmata.

Through her wailing, Sister Rafaela confessed her most closely held sin. "And I—I said nothing! My mother knew I was watching, and she told me I did not know what I saw. But she was wrong. She was wrong! I know what I saw, and I said nothing!" She wailed again, the sound deafening in the tight confines of the confessional booth. After a moment, she quieted and said with pained resignation, "These are my sins, and I am heartily sorry."

I would have asked further questions, or offered some sort of additional comfort, but I could sense a tightening in the air that presaged the tolling of the bells. Sister Rafaela would be called away shortly.

I gave Sister Rafaela her absolution and her penance, but both felt hollow. Inside my chest, my heart broke for the child Rafaela had been, the child who had seen far too much of human cruelty.

*　　*　　*

I understood Sister Rafaela far better than I had expected to. In at least one way, we were the same. I, too, had seen my share of cruelty at an age far too tender. Worst of all, it came from those who should have shown the most kindness.

It happened in Albania when I was twelve years old, nearly a man. My mother, who was preoccupied with my new baby sisters, sent me to the village to fetch something—what it was exactly escapes me now. It is possible I never really heard what it was she wanted, given my young age and my pure excitement at being given free rein to go into the village, like the grown man I would soon become. Merrily, I trotted off in the direction of the market.

I knew then, even as a child, that cutting through the thick forest to get to the village was dangerous. My mother and father and older siblings had all warned me of the forest, of how easily a person could get lost in its dark depths. Then, of course, there was the threat of coming across a bear, or, perhaps even more worryingly, a thick, sharp animal trap set by one of the villagers. They were well concealed, and others had fallen prey to the snap of a bear trap while walking through the woods.

I knew all this, and yet I still headed into the greenery, so dark within that it was almost black, even in bright daylight. My eagerness to go into the village outweighed any caution I might have exercised.

Venturing into the forest was my choice—so all that happened after was my fault.

Being in the forest by myself was a wondrous experience, at first. Birds chirped high overhead, a song just for me. Small insects flitted about my head, tickling my cheeks and brow. I laid my hands against thick trees just to feel the roughness of the bark. The world around me hummed with life and wonder, and I was so enraptured that I failed to see the gnarled root jutting from the ground. My foot caught against it and I fell, sprawling into the undergrowth.

Had I fallen just a pace or two in either direction, I would have been all right, and nothing bad would have happened—but it was God's will that I fell where I did. When I connected with a jagged root jutting from the hard ground, my right wrist exploded with pain. All I can remember is the blood—so much of it, and such a deep scarlet, almost like Communion wine.

When I awoke, the first thing I noticed after the pain in my wrist was the scent of cooking in the air. Despite my discomfort, my stomach rumbled violently, and my eyes opened on a strange domestic scene. I was lying on a straw mattress pushed against a wall. I was in a large room, but the raging fire in the hearth kept everything cozy and warm. Over the fire, a pot bubbled. I was not in my home; I was not in my own bed. That was not my hearth, that was not my mother's pot.

The woman in the corner was not my mother.

I must have made a noise, because she turned to face me, her pale grey eyes kind and wrinkled at the corners. Her nose was long but straight, almost masculine. She wore a simple dark dress.

"Hello, little one," she said, smiling.

I opened my mouth to protest her appellation, because I was nearly a grown man, but only a sour croak vaulted from my throat.

"Shh, shh," she said. She stepped toward me, placing one knobby hand on my forehead. "You still feel rather warm."

I said nothing, but the loud rumbling of my stomach filled the room.

"Ah, hungry, are we? That's a good sign. I've got some broth going, that will be just the thing."

My head began to spin when I pulled myself up to sitting. "Where am I?" I managed to ask.

"You are in my home," she said, stirring the contents of the pot with a long-handled wooden spoon.

Of course I was not in my own home, I had already worked out as much. "How did I get here?"

She pulled the spoon out of the pot and slurped. She made a satisfied clucking sound with her tongue, then returned the spoon to the pot. "Almost ready," she said. Then, as if just registering my question, she added, "You took quite a nasty tumble out there in the forest," she said. "I was looking for mushrooms when I found you. You had cut your arm rather badly. You had lost quite a lot of blood."

I must have blanched or gasped, because she let out a small laugh. "Oh, worry not, little one! I fixed you right up, bandaged up your wound. And now you are awake, we will get some good food into you and you will be good as new before you know it."

I slumped back onto the straw mattress as I pondered her answer. I remembered hurting myself, and of course, all the blood—but everything between that moment and now was empty. Something new occurred to me, and a shiver made me convulse. "How long have I been here? My mother must be so worried about me!"

She let out another small chuckle and stirred the pot again. "Be calm, little one. It has been only a few hours. It is still light out yet, but the sun will be down soon. I think it is best if you stay the night here, get your strength back, and then I will take you back to your mamma in the morning."

Despite my confusion and fear, the woman's warmth comforted me. I let myself relax again. Since my mother had given birth to the twins, she'd been far less attentive to me. Where she used to shower me, her only son, with affection, all her love was now reserved for the baby girls. That was to be expected, of course, but I still missed her hand on the back of my head, her arms protective around me, even though I was nearly grown. Being cared for by this woman almost made up for everything I missed from my mother.

We passed awhile in contented silence, the only sounds the hissing and bubbling coming from the pot. When it was ready, she again made that satisfied clucking sound and ladled a generous portion of broth into an earthenware bowl. As she carried it over to me, she blew on it. "I would not want this to burn your little mouth," she said, smiling down at me. I was so comfortable and grateful for her ministrations that I did not even bristle when she again called me 'little.'

When she reached me, she placed the bowl in my hands and helped me sit up properly. Holding the bowl, I noticed for the first time that my right wrist and much of my forearm was heavily bandaged in strips of grey cloth. A dull ache rippled just beneath the bandages.

She saw me examining my bandages and placed a hand on my head, where she ran her fingers through my hair. "It was a nasty cut, that one," she said. "But it's all taken care of now, little one. Just drink some broth and get your strength back."

She continued to scratch my head as I sipped the broth, first timidly, then, as the delicious liquid ran over my tongue, more desperately. I was ravenous, and I slurped with such abandon that broth ran down my chin. She laughed again. "Slow down, little one! You will make yourself sick, taking everything that fast!"

Not until the bowl was empty did I finally take it from my lips. I wished for more, but I did not want to be impolite. At home, there was never enough for extra helpings. My parents, after all, had five mouths to feed. We had to make do.

"What a good little one," she said, gently taking the bowl from my hands. Her fingers still ran across my scalp, making it tingle. "You know, you remind me of my little boy."

This surprised me. I had seen no evidence of another person living in the house, and the woman seemed too old to have a boy my age. "Where is your son?" I asked.

Her eyes, which were so pale and kind, clouded. "He has been gone these last ten years," she said, her voice barely above a whisper. "Fever took him away."

I was too young to have seen a loved one die, but I could still feel her pain radiating from her skin, even after all these years.

"I am sorry," I said. When she said nothing, only continued staring toward the hearth with tears shining in those pale eyes, I said, "Thank you for saving me."

She blinked away her tears and turned back to face me. "Give it not another thought, little one. In truth, it has been nice to have someone to care for again."

I smiled at her, but inwardly, my heart was breaking. I imagined my own mother, all of her children dead, living alone deep in the forest, with only herself for company. No little bodies to envelop in her arms, no salty tears to wipe away from plump cheeks, no suckling mouths hungering for the breast. The thought made tears spring to my own eyes, and I tried to blink them away as the woman had. Grown men did not cry.

"Why do you live out here by yourself?" I asked. After all, she could have chosen to live in the village, so at least she would not be all alone. I had only imagined the crushing loneliness she must be feeling for a slim moment, but it was already unbearable.

She smiled again, but it did not reach her eyes. "Sweet little one, not everyone in the village would understand me."

"What do you mean?"

She sighed. "With my husband and child long gone, I am on my own. Wherever I go, there is only me. I would rather have the forest for a companion than the judgmental eyes of neighbors who think my solitude is my own fault."

I did not really understand what she meant, being so young, but I nodded anyway. Looking back, everything was all too clear—that poor woman had no one left, and the villagers would have whispered about her, judged her, mocked her, even, for the simple fact of her aloneness. Back then, in that place—and even now, if I was being honest with myself—a woman on her own was something to revile, something to fear. This woman was lonely out of practicality, not out of preference.

I put my hand on her shoulder. That simple act seemed to let loose a flood within her, and tears spilled down her cheeks. She enveloped me in her arms then, rocking back and forth.

She held me like that, weeping silently, until I fell asleep.

I wish everything had ended there, for what came after has never left my mind, no matter how far I have traveled, how harshly I have punished myself, how much I have sacrificed. What came after left a permanent stain on my soul that I cannot seem to scrub away.

CHAPTER FIVE

Sister Rafaela

The bells tolled again as I left the confessional, and I joined the line of Sisters heading toward the refectory for breakfast. My hands were shaking, my heart thumping madly in my chest. For years, I had studiously avoided those painful childhood memories, suppressing them into the darkest corners of my heart and omitting them from my confessions. Something about Father Bruno pulled all that torment from me, called forth the anguish and forced me to confront what I had seen. My mother had worked herself into a lather admonishing me for my sneakiness, then berating me for my imagination, then condemning me for what she claimed were my lies. She had been so forceful, I had doubted myself. The questions lingered in my mind, darkening and distorting everything about my childhood: Were my eyes to be trusted? Could my own heart be deceitful?

Even Sebastian had doubted me when I told him what I had seen— because of course I told him, I worshipped my brother and kept nothing from him. He told me I was wicked for such horrible lies, and God was watching me as the evil slipped out from between my lips. Such denial from those I considered paragons of virtue and familial love damaged me, I think. Something broke in me the day I saw my mother kill for the first time. I say 'first,' because although, unlike poor dear Margarita, I did not see her hold Lavinia or Jorge or Natalia under the water of the washbasin, I knew in my heart that their deaths had not been natural, nor decreed by God. My mother went against God's will, and everyone around me did everything they could to convince me otherwise.

I never told my father what I had seen, and I am unsure if he ever knew, but as soon as I was old enough, I was sent to the Rafaelites, ostensibly for an education. Really, I think I was sent away so I would keep my secrets to myself and bother my mother no more.

I still wonder, though. Which was false—my certainty in what I had seen, or my mother's version of events? Childhood leaves no person unscathed, and I felt more scarred than most, in places no one else but God could see. God and, perhaps now, Father Bruno.

Around me, the Sisters pressed onward into the refectory, where they took their seats. With the sun fully risen, their faces were visible for the first time. The scarred Sister was there, sitting with a somewhat defiant thrust of her shoulders, and I also saw Mother Superior standing slightly stooped at the head of the long table. Most of the other Sisters were surprisingly old, perhaps even older than Mother Superior. A few younger faces peppered our group, which numbered no more than two dozen in all. The scarred Sister was one of the few younger ones, as I had expected, but she still seemed older than me. Trauma could age a person—as I knew well from my own experience.

The wind howled outside as we partook of our simple breakfast in silence. I chewed my bread thoughtfully. The almonds on my plate reminded me of the Rafaelites, of crushing fresh nuts to sprinkle on top of our confections. I did not want to eat the almonds, but, having missed the evening meal the day before, my stomach was rumbling, low and persistent. It would not do to have that bodily noise interrupt our midmorning prayer with reminders of the corporeal, so I slipped the nuts between my lips, one by one, and crunched down. Their hardness hurt my teeth, but a few sips from my mug of small beer minimized the pain.

By way of gestures, the scarred Sister made it clear that the rest of my morning duties would consist of washing up after the meal, which I set to with joy. Washing the plates felt soothing in a way that pouring the repugnant brown-green liquid into bottles simply did not. The washing water felt clean and smelled faintly of lemon, briefly banishing the abbey's ever-present fetid odor. I breathed luxuriously as I stood at the washbasin. Washing up was a task in which I could lose myself.

Despite my delight in my task at hand, I could not shake my confusion about the purpose of all that bottled liquid. I wanted to know what the Sisters were doing with it and where the liquid really came from. I knew it could not be so, but my mind kept returning to the possibility that the liquid was the drippings gleaned from their dead. Something so carnal surely could not be holy, even if it did come from a bride of Christ. Only corporeal relics from saints could be holy, as far as I knew. As I did in the chamber of divine decomposition, I fought against the gorge rising in my throat as I thought about the possible uses of such a bottle: pouring onto barren soil, sprinkling around a house, sliding down a throat. The idea of drinking fragments of another human, even a Sister, felt sacrilegious, blasphemous, a perversion of the Eucharist… but if people believed that liquid erased sin, as Mother Superior did….

I scrubbed the plates harder, trying to empty my mind, my fingers growing raw and red with each stroke, but they still did not feel clean enough.

My sinful time with the Rafaelites had shown me how incapable I was of making Godly choices on my own. I needed to have faith in Mother Superior, in the goodness of my fellow Sisters, in the guidance of God the Father. If I could just do that, then I would be at peace. I felt as if I were teetering painfully atop a thin fence line. If I fell to one side, I would be immersed in the cruel certainty of my mother's infanticide; if I fell to the other side, I would distrust my sanity as I had ever since my mother first screamed at me for lying. Was I a person who knew what she saw? Or was I a person who could not believe in the evidence of my own senses?

Another low toll of the bells signaled terce and rescued me from teetering on that agonizing fence line. Following an uneventful recitation of the psalms, I joined a few of the older Sisters in sweeping the stone path of the cloister; the fierce winds of the previous night had died down, but they had left piles of dry, crackling leaves in their wake. I tried to make eye contact with the others, but they all kept their gazes lowered, focusing on their work. I wished for even one friendly countenance, one smile to acknowledge my own existence. I felt ephemeral, untethered by human connection.

I had just swept the last tumble of leaves from the stones as the bells tolled again for midday prayer. As I filed into the church promptly so as not to offend Christ with tardiness, I meditated on the way in which my life was now—and had been for awhile, I supposed—powered by bells. Bells to wake, bells to rise, bells to eat, bells to pray. The tolling brought me comfort, always—I could hear Christ calling for me, beckoning me to the next moment of my life where I could serve Him best. Christ, speaking through the bells, knew what was right for me, and I leaned wholeheartedly into His direction. Christ rescued me from temptation, from obsession, from remembrance.

Midday prayer passed silently, except for a dry cough from one of the older Sisters. I prayed to the Lord for her comfort and peace in her time of sickness.

The tolling of the bells yet again disguised the growling of my stomach, a small mercy for which I was quite grateful. I still felt somewhat out of sorts from my long journey from the Rafaelite abbey in Barcelona—a combination of physical and mental exhaustion and a gnawing hunger that felt greedy. I wanted to extinguish that ravenous part of me as quickly as possible.

I noticed with a twinge of regret that leaves had once again gathered in disorganized piles on the stones of the cloister as I followed the Sisters to the refectory for the midday meal. With the Rafaelites, dinner had meant barley, a bit of roasted fish, stewed leeks, and almonds. I wondered what the midday meal with the Sisters of Divine Innocence would look like.

I sat on the bench next to the scarred Sister. She had been guiding me ever since my arrival, yet I still did not know her name. I hoped I would learn it that evening, when our veil of silence was lifted for a single hour.

The table before me was a gorgeous display. Good smells assailed my nostrils, a feeling that felt quite foreign after the sickly-sweet smell of corpses, which seemed to have been my constant companion since my arrival. My plate was filled with potatoes, roasted chicken, warm bread, and a sliced green vegetable I did not recognize. A perfect, ripe orange sat to the side of my plate, and I experienced a feeling akin to lust come to rest in my breast. I wanted to splash my face with cold water to rid myself of the sinful feeling, but I did not wish to cause a disruption. Instead, I prayed. *Oh God, I am heartily sorry for having offended thee.* I had become so used to uttering that particular prayer that I found my lips silently mouthing the words before my mind even issued the command.

With a creak of old joints, Mother Superior rose from her seat and walked slowly to the front of the room. On a small altar sat a book, and Mother proceeded to read from the biography of St. Joseph, a welcome and Godly interruption of the silence. I chewed slowly as Mother read, growing increasingly puzzled. St. Joseph was known as the patron of the sick and dying. The Rafaelites had always read aloud from the writings of St. Augustine or St. Gertrude instead, letting their words of faith and hope wash us clean.

As Mother continued in her authoritative voice, an ill feeling crept up my back. All of my experiences thus far with the Sisters of Divine Innocence had shown me their familiarity and comfort with the sick and dying. Their chamber of divine decomposition, their small glass bottles of brown-green liquid… without warning, the chicken turned to rubber in my mouth, and I struggled to swallow. As the bolus slid down my throat, Mother Superior concluded her reading and returned to her seat at the head of the table, plucking the bread from her plate with a firm grasp.

Somehow, I finished my meal in time with the other Sisters. As we rose to clear the plates, a bell rang—but it was not the same bell that shepherded us from one place to another, the bell that represented Christ's call. This bell sounded more like a spoon dropped upon a metal plate, tinny and hollow.

One of the Sisters ahead of me hustled through the throng and into the adjoining kitchen. I had not yet really explored the kitchen's interior, and I indulged myself in a few moments of craning my neck to look around in the bright midday light streaming through the small windows before my eyes once again fell upon the Sister who had hurried away from the table. She had set her plate down by the washbasin and was now heading for the far corner of the low-ceilinged room, where a small grate was set into the wall at about head-height from the floor. A wooden crate rested below the grate.

The Sister lifted the cover of the grate, and sunlight illuminated only her wrists, leaving her face in shadow. Without saying a word, the Sister slipped her hand into the wooden crate, withdrawing a small glass bottle filled with the green-brown liquid I had come to recognize far too well. She slid the bottle through the bottom of the grate, the glass making a harsh scraping sound across the wooden windowsill. The bottle disappeared from sight, the Sister exchanging it for a few glinting coins passed in the palm of a hand that was curiously missing every finger but the index and the thumb. Without meaning to, I gasped—thankfully, the sound was low enough in my throat that no other Sisters turned to look, and I composed my features into a look of beatific indifference once again.

The entire procedure was both hauntingly familiar, a ghost of the almond confection exchanges I had taken part in with the Rafaelites, and unnervingly foreign. I shuddered to think how that evil-smelling liquid could serve a living being. I fervently hoped its ingestion was not the answer to that riddle.

The bottles could perhaps be sold as relics—but no, I realized again, that could not be the answer. The Sisters here were engaged in holy work, but they were not saints. Their bodies decomposed in the manner of all other human flesh, so their various parts could not qualify as relics. My mind spun with uncomfortable thoughts as I rinsed my plate in the washbasin. Surely the Sisters were not being intentionally deceptive with the pilgrims about the source of the liquid.

I shrugged away my concerns as I finished cleaning my plate. After all, I did not even really know what was in the bottles. The liquid could be an organic botanical tincture, meant to cure ailments, or a fermented beverage to aid prayer, or a blessed ointment for wounds. Either way, it was not my place to judge the Sisters. There was no need to constantly struggle against my own poor judgment, which seemed to encourage me to break my vows, to break the silence, to break the order and regimentation of my religious life. Clearly, I was the broken one. I had fallen into a pit of sin with the Rafaelites by virtue of my weakness and my wild imagination. I needed to allow the Sisters to heal me.

I joined a few of the Sisters in chopping vegetables for the next day's meals, and during those few hours, the tinny bell rang several more times. On each occasion, the same Sister who had guided the transaction before hurried over to the grate, lifted it to wrist-height, pushed a bottle through the opening with a clink, and pulled coins back through. These she dropped into a large-mouthed jar on the floor which, I noticed with a kind of dull alarm, was nearly full. Amassing so much wealth could not be healthy for the soul. There must be some reason for it; they must be performing some holy service with the funds.

I continued chopping, peeling, and slicing, the sounds of my knife irregularly punctuated by the tinny bell, the screech of the grate, the clink of the bottle, the thud of the coins. The Rafaelites had, each day, given the coins earned by their confections to the Priest to be redistributed to those in need according to God's will. The weight of the coins in the Sisters' bucket, by contrast, felt as heavy as sin.

Stop, I thought. Before I could chastise myself further and throw myself upon God's mercy and forgiveness, the familiar bell, the bell I had grown accustomed to, the bell I had even come to love as an expression of God's voice on earth, rang, summoning me to midafternoon prayer. I set my work aside and joyfully answered the call.

CHAPTER SIX

Sister Rafaela

After several hours of prayer and more time spent in the foul-smelling bottlery, as I had come to know it, the bread and cheese of the evening meal slipped down my throat without my tasting it; even the scalding barley tea did not faze me. I felt both unsettled and calm at the same time, and the contrast between the two emotions left me struggling to keep my eyes downcast, as was proper for a bride of Christ. It seemed as if my entire life, ever since the first time my mother admonished me for lying, was a struggle between two opposite feelings: certainty and disbelief; understanding and bafflement; peace and grave unrest. Only God could bring me peace, and the thought gave me a modicum of solace as I finished my meal.

In just a short while, I knew I would finally be able to speak, to learn the names of my fellow Sisters, to ask questions about the liquid we were bottling and selling. The whirl of my first day in such a new and different place had engrossed me, and now my mind raced to formulate the proper questions to ask—questions that could yield forthright answers without raising ire or being seen as sinful or unseemly. Perhaps I would ask where the liquid came from, or where the money for the bottles went, or what the laypeople believed they were buying. If I was feeling bold, maybe I would even ask how one corpse could produce so much liquid.

That was foolish; of course I could not ask that. It was enormously presumptuous. None of those questions felt appropriate, and I was grateful for the enfolding silence of the refectory. I would have time to arrange the right words in the right order, praise be to God.

When the bell rang to signal the hour of our recreation and the brief end to our silence, I nearly leapt from my seat. The room came alive with the sound of Sisters' voices, hoarse from disuse. One Sister sneezed violently, as though she had been holding it in for far too long. Another coughed convulsively into her hands; for a moment, the talk suspended as we all waited to see if the coughing Sister would be able to stop it herself and draw breath. We all exhaled a sigh of relief when she finished her coughing fit with a great, shuddering inhale.

As I walked to the kitchen with my plate, the scarred Sister who had become so familiar to me fell into step at my side. "You must be Sister Rafaela," she said, a wan smile crinkling against her scars. I could not help noticing the smile failed to reach her dark eyes. "I am Sister Leonella."

"Hello," I said simply, my voice scratchy, happy to be able to finally put a name to her distinctive face.

"Mother Superior tells me you join us from the Rafaelite abbey in Barcelona?"

"Yes, that is right," I said, slipping my dish into the washbasin and rinsing away the crumbs of food that remained.

"That must have been very difficult," she said, copying my actions when I had finished.

"It was," I said, hoping Sister Leonella had no knowledge of the true horrors at the Rafaelite abbey.

I was not so fortunate. "What happened to that poor child..." Sister Leonella trailed off, but I felt heartened she had not begun that sentence as so many others had who knew of what had happened, with "What *you* did to that poor child..."

The boy had been the tipping point, the sacrifice that had gone a step too far. By that point, many of the other Rafaelites had grown restless and anxious, but I never knew who had sent the letter to Archbishop Orriva, the letter that had brought him flying to the abbey in horror. I wished it had been me, but I had failed God the Father with my trepidation. How was I to know? I had taken a vow of obedience to the abbess, and I did not understand how to act in opposition to that obligation. Then, of course, there was always the question lingering in my mind: Could my own eyes be trusted? Luckily, Archbishop Orriva had saved me from excommunication and found me a new home with the Sisters of Divine Innocence. Anyone could see I was utterly hapless, and my guilt was a colossal stone around my neck. From now on, I would strive to live a holy life, or die trying.

Lost in my thoughts as I was, Sister Leonella had to tap me on the shoulder to regain my attention. Her touch was unexpectedly heavy. "I pray to God for your salvation," she said to me, her eyes still flat and expressionless.

"Thank you," I managed, choked with painful memories.

Sister Leonella continued washing her own dish in the basin, and my chin trembled with thoughts of the orphan child the Rafaelites had lured to the abbey with promises of food and shelter, only to sacrifice the boy to appease "God the Father, the Holy Spirit, Mother Mary, and all of the earthly saints and sinners," as my Rafaelite Mother Superior had said. I should have seen she was no longer making sense, should have spoken out about the escalating abuses and perversions of God's holy commands. I should have—

A whipcrack of thunder outside shook the kitchen like a child's rattle and exiled my troublesome thoughts. The sky outside had grown dark and ominous, threatening the kind of deluge that could wash away entire villages. I thanked God the abbey was atop a hill and would be spared the destruction of any flooding. In the same breath, I prayed for the village down the hill and the safety of its people. Fleetingly, Father Bruno crossed my mind. Where did the good priest lay his head at night?

"What was that?" Sister Leonella asked from behind me, making me jump. I did not think her question was aimed at me; I did not know the answer, anyway. Something must have occurred while I was lost in my thoughts, because one of the other Sisters answered, "That was a knock at the kitchen door."

I was surprised; the way Archbishop Orriva and Mother Superior both had described this abbey to me suggested that its isolation prevented many visitors. We were cloistered, after all. As a result, the abbey atop the hill was largely left alone—except, of course, for the steady stream of villagers looking to purchase small glass bottles through the grate. Archbishop Orriva had not mentioned the liveliness of the Sisters' commerce. I wondered if he knew anything about their product—or its true provenance.

"A knock?" Sister Leonella asked. An expression finally entered her eyes—surprise, along with a hint of something darker, like a flash of anger.

At the end of the kitchen, a heavy wooden door sat squat and impenetrable next to the small grated window where the Sisters performed their transactions. The handful of us who remained in the kitchen stood motionless until another loud rap broke the silence.

Sister Leonella strode with confidence toward the door, but when she reached it, she faltered. She moved over to the small grated window and stretched her neck, trying to see who was on the other side of the heavy wooden door. What she saw there must have satisfied her, because she moved back to the door on light feet and opened it without further hesitation.

Another crack of thunder exploded in the sky, and the visitor's visage was completely obscured by the flash of lightning that ripped the darkness apart just as Sister Leonella pulled the door open completely. Behind me, I heard one of the Sisters let out a gasp that turned into a violent bout of coughing.

When the afterimage of the bright lightning faded, I was able to get a better look at the visitor. She was a woman, tall and lean, with a pale oval face and a small red mouth. Her clothing was ragged and dirty, but she appeared to be wearing a habit not unlike my own. Her veil had slipped to one side, and a tendril of crimson chin-length hair was plastered to her cheek.

An uncomfortable silence filled the room, punctuated only by the plunking melody of the rain that had just started falling. Finally, Sister Leonella spoke. "Please, do come in, Sister."

"Thank you," the visitor said. She crossed the threshold and entered the kitchen. Her words were heavily accented; I had never heard anything quite like her voice.

An older Sister next to me crossed herself and whispered a Hail Mary. An icy needle of terror traced the edges of my veins.

"Have you traveled far, Sister...?" Sister Leonella prodded, her eyes beseeching.

"Berta," the visitor answered, tucking the bright red strands back underneath her veil and righting it atop her head. "I come from England."

That explained her strange accent, the way the Spanish words were flat where they should have been full and sharp where they should have been soft.

"You have journeyed a long way, then," Sister Leonella said, still the only one willing to speak to this stranger.

"Have you not heard? The religious orders are being expelled from England." Berta paused, a harsh cough rising from her throat. Traveling so far in weather like this must have taken its toll. She swallowed loudly and continued, "I have heard from many that this abbey is a place of steadfast devotion."

"Yes, we strive to bathe in God's holy light and fulfill His requirements of us while on earth," Sister Leonella said, sounding rehearsed, a small smile raising the corners of her lips.

"Then you are exactly what I have been seeking," Berta said. I could not bring myself to think of her as a Sister, clothed so raggedly as she was, her words rough and tumbling out of her mouth like vomitus. She coughed again, bringing her closed fist to her mouth. When she drew it away, I thought I saw a bright slick of blood the same color as her hair.

Sister Leonella must have seen it, too, because she drifted closer to Berta and put a consoling hand on the tall woman's thin shoulder. "Sister, are you ill?"

Berta coughed again; this time, there was no mistaking the blood, which trailed down her wrist and pooled on the sleeve of her habit. "The journey has been long and difficult," she said. "I was not certain I would make it all the way here."

"God always provides, and never assigns us more than we can endure," Sister Leonella said, now taking a firmer grip on Berta's shoulder and steering her through the kitchen and into the refectory. "We have just finished the evening meal, but if you are hungry, we can prepare you some simple fare."

"No, thank you," Berta said, coughing again. "I have no need of food, simply a place to rest until I can regain my strength."

"Of course," Sister Leonella said. "Please, sit here at the table while I fetch Mother Superior. She can help us find the right place for you."

"Bless you, Sister," Berta said.

Sister Leonella exited the refectory in a swish of skirts, leaving the rest of us staring at the woman seated at our table. Next to me, the Sister who had crossed herself was breathing heavily.

"Are you alright, Sister?" I asked her quietly, not wanting to draw the attention of Berta.

"Yes, by God's grace," she said, but her voice was thin and unconvincing. "I just had myself a bit of a fright."

She did not offer anything more, and I did not ask. Berta's arrival had unnerved me, as well, but I could not quite explain what it was about the tall, scarlet-haired woman that seemed so… ominous. *God the Father, please forgive me for my suspicions, for my unkind thoughts. Please help me to be generous and loving, and act as your dutiful servant here on earth. Amen.*

The Sister next to me must also have felt contrite about her own fears; I could hear her whispering a similar prayer, asking for God's forgiveness. Berta was nothing more than a fellow Sister in need, and we must do everything we could to welcome her as I had been welcomed.

Finally, after a long stillness, the Sisters around me resumed their idle chatter and quotidian movements—washing dishes in the basin, sweeping the floors, clearing the rough counters of food debris. I meant to help them, but I felt a strange tug pulling me toward Berta. Perhaps God meant for me, also a newcomer to the abbey atop the hill, to make Berta feel comfortable.

I walked closer to the woman seated at the table, her hands clasped and her head bowed in prayer. When I reached her side, she opened one eye and trained that singular gaze on me. I noticed with amazement that her eye was a golden-orange hue, unlike any I had ever seen before. I reminded myself Berta was English, and I had never before seen an Englishwoman, or, for that matter, a woman with hair the same fiery red as Berta's.

"Sister," she said to me, one corner of her mouth twitching upward.

"Rafaela," I supplied, trying to arrange the features on my face into something resembling a warm smile.

"Ra-fa-el-a," she said slowly, tasting each syllable on her tongue. "I know that name."

"I was named for Saint Rafaela," I said.

"Of course you were," she said, something I thought was a rather odd response. Then again, she was English. I should not judge her for our cultural disconnect.

"And your name?" I asked.

"What about it?" That single red-gold eye was still focused on me, and I fought the urge to shiver. I wished she would open both eyes to look at me properly.

"Where does your name come from?"

"Berta means 'bright,'" she said. "It is a common enough name in England."

"Oh," I said. "And how did you come to learn Spanish?"

"I have an aptitude for languages," she said, and now she opened her other eye, finally, and turned her face toward me. Her small red mouth curled back in something that should have been a smile, but looked more like a sneer.

"That is fortunate," I said. "Did you travel on foot?"

"I did. Once I reached France, that is. I crossed the channel by boat."

"God must have blessed you on your journey."

"Oh, yes," Berta said, her eyes glinting.

"How long have you been traveling?"

"Enough questions," Berta said abruptly. "Forgive me, but I feel very weary, and I would really like to rest." She punctuated her entreaty with a hammering cough that left her gasping.

"Of course," I said, distressed. My mother had once had a cough like that when I was young. I had been so afraid she would not survive. Father had prepared us for her death, asking us to pray for her safe passage into Heaven. Miraculously, mother had recovered, but she was weaker than she had been before. There were no more babies, no more tiny coffins after her illness. I had often thought her sickness had been an act of God, meant to safeguard any more little souls that might otherwise suffer at my mother's hands. *Quiet, Rafaela*, I said to myself. *You know not of what you speak.* The voice sounded like my mother's.

A tap on my shoulder startled me, and I nearly jumped. It was Sister Leonella, with Mother Superior at her side. Sister Leonella waved me away with impatience.

"Welcome, Sister Berta," Mother Superior said, also gesturing for me to step aside.

"Thank you," Berta said, meeting Mother Superior's dark eyes with her golden ones. I thought I discerned a shadow of discomfort flicker across Mother's face, but it might simply have been a trick of the light.

"I hear you come from England," Mother said, the ghost of a smile touching her lips.

"Yes," Berta said, her nose scrunching almost imperceptibly in another sneer. If Mother Superior noticed, she did not show it.

"And you were in a religious order there?"

"Yes," Berta said. "The Sisters of Holy Light."

Mother paused, cocking her head to one side. "I am not familiar with that particular order."

Berta shrugged. "My country has expelled their religious orders. I am not surprised you are ignorant of my former order."

"Hm," Mother Superior said. "And your Spanish? It is quite good."

Berta's sneer was not subtle this time, and I saw Mother Superior flinch. "I learned from a Spanish Sister."

That explanation was very spare, and Berta knew it, but our ragged visitor was not forthcoming in details except when it suited her needs.

Mother Superior sighed, pulled her shoulders back, and endeavored to retake control. "You wish to join the Sisters of Divine Innocence?"

"In truth, I had not considered it," Berta said. "I was only seeking shelter. But now that I am here... I am struck by the beauty of your devotion. Will you have me?"

Mother looked to Sister Leonella, who nodded slightly and shrugged. If she had looked in my direction, she would have seen doubt and fear firing out of my eyes like lightning. "You may stay here as a Sister for a trial period, to see how you adjust," Mother finally said, after a long silence. "I did not receive any communication from another abbess prior to your arrival, which, as you must understand, gives me pause."

"Thank you, Mother. I certainly understand," Berta said, but her voice had a hint of insolence. She nearly spat out the word 'Mother.'

My heart began racing, but there was nothing I could say. Mother Superior had the final word on all matters. After all, I was a newcomer, and it would be inappropriate and ungrateful for me to express doubt regarding her decision in front of others. If I were going to say anything at all, I needed to seek her out separately.

Berta was still staring at Mother Superior, a small, pointed smile on her face. I noticed with alarm that her cheeks had taken on a golden color similar to her eyes, and I wondered if she was feverish. I was about to inquire about her health when Mother Superior spoke again.

"Sister Rafaela," she said, as if noticing me standing there for the first time, "you will take Sister Berta to one of the vacant cells and see she has what she needs."

At this, Berta began violently coughing, her body heaving back and forth in spasms. It seemed almost theatrical. I shivered in dread, thinking of caring for Berta. I was inexperienced and still finding my own way around the abbey, having barely been there for a single day. In no way was I the best choice for the role, but perhaps the abbess was testing me.

"And," Mother Superior added, "attend to her ailments as best you can. Sister, I hope it is nothing serious?"

Berta caught her breath far too quickly for someone gasping for air only a few moments before and said, "No, Mother. Just an aftereffect of the travel, I fear."

"Alright," Mother Superior said. She cocked her head at Sister Leonella, and they both turned in a graceful arc, their habits swishing through the air. When I recovered myself, I took a few steps to hurry after them. Berta was, in a word, unsettling, and now that I was charged with her care, I needed to tell Mother Superior of my misgivings before things went too far.

"Mother—" I began, but the tolling of the bells summoning me to night prayer stilled the words forming in my throat. Mother Superior and Sister Leonella continued walking quickly toward the church without even turning around, leaving me with Berta, alone. Alone and painfully uncertain—a condition that felt uncomfortably familiar to me, like the caress of a forbidden lover, or the harshness of my mother's gaze.

I did not know if I was expected to stay with Berta or join the other Sisters in prayer. Either way, I knew I should probably take Berta to one of the vacant cells first. Then, if she felt well enough, I would bring her with me to the church.

I turned back to take a look at the ragged woman, and I nearly screamed when I found her directly behind me. She must have stepped quietly and rapidly, and the smile she leveled at me upon hearing my gasp was almost predatory.

The golden-red hue had left her cheeks, and I figured the feverish glow had been nothing more than the reflection of the candlelight. Seeing as how she was well enough to walk so quickly, I decided to lead her to the church for prayer. Perhaps bathing in God's holy light would soothe both her soul and mine. I, for one, sorely needed it.

With the resumption of the great silence, a hush fell over the abbey, thick as a winter cloak. I walked out of the refectory, through the cloister, and to the door of the church, Berta at my heels. Her feet clopped unevenly on the stone path, and I thought how different shoes must be in England to produce such an unpleasant and ungraceful sound. When we reached the church, its many touches of gold glimmering in the candlelight, Berta followed me inside and sat next to me on a pew, her head downcast, her face ashen.

Throughout the service, Berta maintained her silence even during the spoken portion of the prayer. Perhaps she was more gravely ill than she appeared, if she could not even pray aloud to God the Father.

For my own part, I prayed for guidance, for clarity, for charity. I needed Christ to give me strength to carry out Mother Superior's assignment for me, kindness to administer to Berta in her hour of need, and courage to push my unfounded worries aside.

After prayer, I felt a newfound resolve course through my veins. I would care for Berta as a good Sister should, and I would not give space in my mind or my heart to any suspicious thoughts.

When we rose from the pews, Berta with some wheezing difficulty, I gestured for her to follow me. Once outside the church and moving through the cloister, her vigorous, clopping gait returned, and, when I glanced back, her cheeks were once again alive with healthy color. I thought the transformation strange but continued on, beckoning her.

I led Berta into the dormitory, to the empty cell next to my own. Spotting the jug of water, she grabbed at it with both hands. She lifted it to her mouth and proceeded to drain the entire vessel in a series of long, loud gulps. I had never seen anything like it—perhaps pigs and goats drank as she did, but surely no human I had encountered would allow themselves to make such sounds, especially before another person. When Berta finished, she nearly dropped the jug back onto the table and belched loudly. Were all the English uncouth like this?

She must have seen the look of disgust on my face, because she covered her mouth with one hand, affecting a demureness that felt disingenuous and flippant.

The wooden bed frame creaked as she sat down stop the straw mattress with a thud and looked at me expectantly. Unease coursed through my body yet again; although we had time before we would retire for the night, the great silence had descended and we could only engage in quiet, individual pursuits.

I had just determined to leave the room and return to my own cell to write a letter to my father when Berta seized upon the mattress quite suddenly, curling up and erupting into her most violent coughing fit yet. I thought I saw fine droplets of blood spray from her mouth, a scarlet cloud.

I rushed to her, unsure what to do, but at the very least hoping to offer comfort of some sort. I knelt at her bedside and put a hand on her quaking shoulder, but she wriggled away from my touch as if my fingers stung her.

Finally, with one shuddering, hitching inhale, she regained her composure. Her cheeks were florid, her lips pale and blue. How could she possibly have made the journey from the nearest village to our abbey, much less all the way from England to Spain, and on foot much of the way?

She closed her eyes and slumped back against the straw mattress. I stayed by her side, wringing my hands, afraid to touch her again. After a few moments, the redness drained from her cheeks, and her lips regained their normal pinkish hue. Her breathing evened out, and she appeared to have fallen asleep.

Tears of anxiety and fear pricked the backs of my eyes. *Hail Mary, full of grace.*

As quietly as possible, I rose and crept to the entrance of the cell. I paused with my fingertips brushing the door handle, listening for any change in Berta's breathing behind me. My hand felt slippery and weak, the room far too hot and close. Perhaps if—

"People are dying, Rafaela. People are dying in that village because of what you are selling. Do you think your god will save you this time?"

I wheeled around, tangling my legs in my habit and nearly falling to the floor. Berta lay on the bed, in exactly the same fashion as she had before, her hands by her sides, her eyes closed, her chest rising and falling steadily. A small snore erupted from her nostrils as I stared at her, terror turning my veins to ice. Surely she could not have just spoken? I must have imagined her strangely accented voice, because she was not delirious enough to break the great silence unknowingly, but the things she had said… those must be the ravings of a madwoman. Or so I thought.

I pressed my back to the door and watched her sleeping peacefully for a few more moments. Something was amiss, but I had nothing to take to Mother Superior, nothing I could say that would ring of truth. I only had my own misgivings, my own often mistaken perceptions, and I could never trust those. If I had imagined my own mother's acts of infanticide, then I could imagine a woman speaking while my back was turned. I was teetering on the fence line again, closer to toppling over into uncertainty than I ever had been before. The fall, I knew, would be excruciating.

Shaking, I turned back to open the door and eagerly took my leave. I half-expected to hear Berta's crackling voice again, saying more unspeakable things, but she remained silent in sleep.

Sleep! That must be it! As I entered my cell next door to Berta's, the realization came to me. I had known of others who had the habit of speaking while asleep. My own brother Sebastian had done so occasionally, crying out nonsensical things into the darkness. When mother or father had rushed to his side to help him, they always found him peacefully asleep. In the mornings, when they would ask him what he had said, he could never remember speaking at all. Thinking about it while sitting in own my cell, of course it made sense that Berta must have spoken while asleep. She was sick, and illness may have disrupted her sleep enough to fray the veil between her dreaming and waking worlds. She was not responsible for whatever words slipped from her lips as she lay unconscious. I must put the incident out of my mind. I thanked the Lord for providing an explanation that did not force me to confront whether the strange, troubling things that always seemed to follow me were the product of my own wild imaginings or cold, undeniable evidence of the truth.

Still, though, the incident lingered.

People are dying, Rafaela.

Her words echoed in my head as I changed into my nightgown and washed my face with cold water.

People are dying because of what you are selling.

That must have been nonsense. How could a stranger, newly arrived, know anything of our abbey's practices? I desperately wanted to believe her words meant absolutely nothing, but the blackness inside my own mind filled with rows upon rows of glass bottles, green-brown liquid sloshing within. I sniffed, and the sickly sweet smell filled my nostrils to near bursting.

Even though the bells had not yet rung to signal retirement, I crawled onto my mattress. The day had exhausted me, and I wanted nothing more than to slip away into a dreamless, silent sleep.

I closed my eyes and waited. Sleep was a long time coming.

A single phrase kept repeating itself in my thoughts like a threatening drumbeat.

Do you think your God will save you this time?

CHAPTER SEVEN

Sister Rafaela

When the early morning bells tolled for matins, I was relieved; the deep, rolling sounds awakened me from a nightmare the likes of which I had not had since I was a young girl. As a child, I had suffered from night terrors so severe my breath would drain from my chest and leave me gasping until my brother or father could manage to wake me. They had told me there were several times they failed to wake me before my lips turned blue, and I fell into a dark state of unconsciousness. When the doctor had arrived shortly thereafter, he had instructed my family to pray, to attempt to rid me of the mysterious malady that disrupted my sleep.

The childish nightmares were always the same. I was sitting alone in church, my legs not yet long enough for my feet to reach the floor. I was praying quietly, asking for God to protect me and my family, when a cloaked figure appeared at the end of my pew. Each time I glanced over, the figure seemed to be closer. Finally, when it could move no closer to me without forcing its body into my lap, it stopped. I looked down, and saw cloven hooves jutting from its cloak where feet should be. I looked up in alarm at the figure's face, but there was only darkness there, and it sucked my breath away.

I had thought those nightmares were as bad as anything I would ever have to experience in my life, but that expectation had already been surpassed. First, by the horrors I had witnessed at the Rafaelite abbey, then by the nightmare from which this morning's bells saved me.

I shook my head once, twice, trying to rattle the images, the sounds, the smells out of my mind—but they persisted. My eyes adjusted to the darkness of my cell, and I could hear the Caller going from room to room, waking the others. Everything looked the same as it had when I had gone to sleep, but I felt different. Even with the comfort of waking, I could still feel the grip of the nightmare clutching me close, breathing down my neck. This nightmare had begun the same way it always had, except I was now a grown woman sitting alone in the church, which was the very same sumptuously decorated one that witnessed the worship of the Sisters of Divine Innocence. My head was bowed, my eyes closed, my lips whispering the Apostle's Creed. A whipcrack sound broke the silence, and I looked up to find the familiar cloaked figure sitting in my pew. The figure moved progressively closer, as usual, finally stopping when its cloak brushed against my habit. A sour smell rose from the figure, and I tried to still my breathing. When I could endure it no longer, I let out a gasping inhale and turned, finally, to face the figure. There, as before, were the cloven hooves where feet should be, but this time, when I lifted my gaze to the figure's face, Berta's visage stared back out at me, her eyes red-golden in the light and dancing with obscene merriment. As I watched, my lips trembling and chills racing down my prickly flesh, Berta's face began to drain of color, to stretch and twist, to blacken and crack. Before my eyes, Berta rotted and reached out a beckoning palm to me. She whispered, *Do you think your God will save you this time?*

Awake now, I shook my head again, violently, rose, and splashed my face with water. The chill of the water comforted me, its texture allowing me to fully return to myself. What I saw when I slept was imaginary. The image of a cloven-hooved Berta rotting and beckoning was an impossible fantasy, unreal.

I exited my cell and joined the tide of Sisters drifting toward the church. A few were rubbing sleep from their eyes, several others were yawning. I searched each face for Berta's golden eyes, but I did not find her.

*   *   *

I searched and searched for that red-golden gaze and that errant hank of fiery hair, but Berta was not present in the church. If the other Sisters noticed, they showed no measure of unease; they simply maintained the placidity they had shown since I arrived. We proceeded as usual, but a gnawing discomfort ate away at the edges of my consciousness as I prayed. Unbidden, the Saint Michael prayer rose to the forefront of my mind, and I found myself mouthing the words out of sync with the other Sisters.

Saint Michael the Archangel, defend us in battle. Be our protection against the wickedness and snares of the devil. May God rebuke him, we humbly pray; and do thou, O Prince of the Heavenly Host, by the power of God, thrust into hell Satan and all evil spirits who wander through the world for the ruin of souls. Amen.

I clasped my sweaty palms together tightly. The last time the Saint Michael prayer had slipped through my lips was the night of Archbishop Orriva's arrival at the Rafaelite abbey; the night he had delivered me from the unspeakable evil that had infiltrated that formerly holy space.

When the bells tolled to signal the end of matins, I nearly stumbled in my haste to find Berta. If she truly had not attended matins, then there must have been something keeping her away. I had not heard her hammering cough in the night, an observation that had previously given me comfort, but now filled me with trepidation. What if her silence was not a signal of her healing, but of the opposite? What if illness had already overtaken her? That would mean I, assigned by Mother Superior to attend to her ailments, would be responsible for Berta's death—her utterly lonely death.

I shook my head with such force my neck cracked. I must not let myself think of such things as death. My mind always had the terrible habit of wandering toward the worst possible scenarios, the most horrendous outcomes. My brother Sebastian often grew exasperated with me when we played together as children; instead of congratulating him when he found an excellent hiding spot and thus evaded discovery, he would creep out to find me sobbing, so deep in my certainty that he was dead that it took hours to console me. My mother, of course, attributed my behavior to my wild imagination, which, she told me regularly, could bring harm to those I loved. In a word, I was dangerous. Me! Dangerous! Everything within me exuded meekness and vulnerability. I was a wounded animal. I was the weakest of the herd. I was no danger to anyone.

My neck cracked again as I shook my head, forcing my thoughts to change course by sheer force of will. Surely, when I entered Berta's cell, I would find her asleep on her mattress, her exhaustion so complete that the Caller had been unable to rouse her, instead leaving her to her much-needed rest. Upon rising, she would be fresh and ready to joyfully participate in the service of God the Father.

When I arrived at the door to Berta's cell, I pressed my ear against the wood worn smooth with age. The other Sisters crept into their rooms around me, paying me no mind. I could hear bed frames creak and straw rustle as the Sisters settled in for a few more hours of sleep before the bells tolled again. I listened as attentively as I could, but no sound escaped Berta's room.

Then—there it was. A sharp intake of breath and a shuddering, rattling cough.

I leaned gently against the door, hoping to peek my head in, just to reassure myself that Berta was, in fact, resting, and not in need of immediate help. At Mother Superior's direction, I was responsible for the stranger from England, even as fear of her haunted my sleep. I needed to push my fear aside, to pray to God to remove it from my soul. Mother Superior had invited Berta in, had charged me with her care. She knew better than me, and I needed to accept her judgment—it was surely better than my own.

The door opened with a soft whistling creak, the gap just wide enough for me to wedge my face through and peer inside.

Dappled predawn moonlight filled the room and fell in speckles on Berta's upturned face. Her eyes were closed, her chest rising and falling rather haltingly. *O Mary, conceived without sin, pray for Berta in her hour of sickness.*

I was about to pull my head back, close the door, and return to my own room, when Berta's jaws unhinged and she sucked in air so harshly her lungs squealed in protest. She then forced all of that air out in one forceful cough that sent her shoulders heaving forward in a violent flop. Even in the dim light, I could see the bright droplets of blood spattering her blankets. She fell back on the bed, gasping, and I wasted no time rushing to her side.

Without breaking the great silence, I knelt beside her and grasped her hand. To my surprise, her flesh was hot, almost scalding. A feverish heat radiated off her in waves, and now that I was closer, I could see her red hair was stuck to her shining face with sweat.

Berta's eyes remained closed, and after a few moments, her breathing regained its steadiness. I continued to kneel over her, praying rapidly to God the Father, to Mother Mary, to Christ, to the Holy Spirit, to Saint Michael. I prayed to Saint Joseph, the patron saint of the dying, even though his invocation pained me, even though as I prayed to Saint Joseph for a safe and gentle death for Berta if that was what God intended for her, I also prayed to God to heal her. I had already seen too much death.

I closed my eyes and bowed my head, my hands gripped so tightly I could feel my nails drawing my own blood from my palms.

I was concentrating so hard that when Berta spoke, her voice barely penetrated my thoughts. When she spoke again, however, I heard her words clearly, her voice much stronger than I anticipated, given her condition.

"People in the village are dying, Rafaela."

My eyes popped open, and I fixed my gaze on Berta.

I must have imagined her words, because her face was a mask of sleep yet again, her eyes closed and her lips relaxed. She could not have spoken.

My brow furrowed, and a sob threatened to escape from my throat. I swallowed it down and resumed my prayer.

"What the Sisters sell—you know what the villagers do with it, do you not?"

This time, when I snapped my gaze back up, I thought I saw a flicker of a smile cross Berta's features, but it could have been just a trick of the moonlight. I paused in my prayer, keeping my eyes squarely on Berta. I was so sure I had imagined her words that when she opened her eyes and returned my stare, I fell back on my heels in shock.

"Rafaela, you stupid girl. How can you not guess? How can you not know? The villagers ingest all of the liquid in those little glass bottles you fill up so carefully. They drink it, Rafaela. They drink it, and then they die."

Berta's cheeks were now almost as red as her hair, and something dark and gleeful danced behind those golden eyes. She laughed, and the sound was like sandpaper on rough wood. "You were too stupid to see what was happening with the Rafaelites, and now you are too stupid to see what is happening here. The people think it erases sin—what a laugh! You are killing people, and earning a handsome sum for the privilege."

"No," I breathed, unintentionally breaking the great silence. I crawled back until my shoulders touched the stone wall beside the door, and I could retreat no farther.

Berta laughed again. "Yes, Rafaela. God does not live here, do you not know that? Did you feel his holy light in that room of rot? I can see it in your eyes—the answer is no!" Again, the sandpaper laugh that made me feel ill.

"The chamber…" I trailed off, tears prickling in my eyes and spilling over onto my cheeks.

"What is it they call it? The 'chamber of divine decomposition?' That is a pack of lies, and you know it. There is nothing divine there. Yet, you sit here, you pray their prayers, you fill their bottles! God is not listening to you, Rafaela! God is not here!"

I pinched my eyes closed and struggled to control the wracking sobs that wanted so desperately to escape my body. I shivered against the wall, quaking, my mind so scattered I could not even think of a prayer to offer, a benediction to whisper. Darkness felt very near, encroaching.

After a few moments, I opened my clenched eyes and saw Berta sound asleep on her straw mattress, her face placid, as though she had never spoken, never uttered those awful words. Even the blood I had seen on her blankets was gone, as though it had never been there.

It was happening again—my eyes, my ears, all of my senses were deceiving me. I could not be trusted.

Without sparing another moment, I fled the room and rushed into my own cell, where I collapsed onto the mattress. I spent the rest of the long hours before dawn praying fervently, searching for the Father who must surely be there.

CHAPTER EIGHT

Sister Rafaela

The longer I prayed during that wretched time before dawn, the more certain I felt Berta was not who she appeared to be, perhaps not even a Sister at all. No Sister would speak so blasphemously; no Sister would proclaim "God is not here."

Even as I felt sure of this conclusion, a memory replayed in my mind. When my mother fell ill after delivering one of my doomed siblings, she spent nearly six days in bed. The servants brought her food and water, but nothing could douse the fire burning inside her. The doctor said it was childbed fever, and that we should prepare to say our goodbyes to our mother. He told us most women who began showing signs of the fever declined quickly without a true chance at recovery. My father refused to believe it, keeping us largely away from our mother, as if we were in danger of catching what ailed her. On the single occasion my father let Sebastian and me see her, she ranted and raved all manner of delusions, even going so far as to insist that the devil had put his mark on our family, especially on every babe she had born, and nothing we could do would change that. She said God had forsaken us, Mother Mary laughed at us in our misery, and when we prayed, we were unwittingly sending our benedictions to Lucifer.

My father ushered us out of the room, and instructed us to disregard everything mother had said. "She is not in her right mind," he said. When I asked him about Lucifer damning our family and putting his mark on all the other babes, all he said was, "Do not think of such things, Rafaela."

Of course, as a quiet, thoughtful child, I spent hours thinking of those exact things. Perhaps, in her ravings, my mother had revealed a piece of the truth, something that had puzzled me as much as it traumatized me—her motivations. I was still walking my fence line, sometimes leaning toward certainty that I had witnessed infanticide, other times becoming more sure that my own imagination was a powerful weapon I needed to keep locked away. When I heard my mother say her babes had been born marked by the devil, it almost seemed like an admission of guilt and a window into her motives all at once. Did she think killing those babes, her *own* babes, was all in service to God?

Another, darker thought chilled me even more: She said *all* her babes had been marked. Was I marked as well? Was Sebastian?

Worst of all: Had she tried to kill us, too?

As more time passed and mother grew healthy again in defiance of the doctor's prediction, I came to believe everything she had said was a symptom of her fever, an imbalance of her humors. Holding the possibility of such darkness—that my mother truly believed we were touched by the devil and had killed her own children because of it— weighed far too heavy on my soul. There was an abyss on one side of my fence line, and I was determined to keep from falling into it.

Now, considering my mother's illness while at my new abbey in light of Berta's own plight, I felt conflicted—perhaps Berta's words were nothing more than beads on a string of madness brought on by exhaustion and illness.

Then again, who was I to decide such matters? Mother Superior had welcomed Berta in, given her a bed, and instructed me to care for her. If Berta had been dishonest, surely Mother would have spotted the influence of Satan in our midst and cast her out.

Even this comforting thought failed to cool my blood; Berta's words continued to replay in my mind. Her revelations about the liquid the Sisters produced—could it possibly have even a grain of truth? I had smelled the wretched scent with my own nose; I had seen with my own eyes the transactions between Sisters and villagers. Berta had been accurate about that, at least; each glass bottle fetched a handsome sum. If the purchasers were really drinking it and then dying, I assumed a connection would have already been made, and some sort of authority would be hard at work investigating such a matter. At the very least, the fate of their fellows should discourage other villagers from ingesting the liquid themselves. Should it not? Or, if they thought it erased sin, maybe they were happy to drink it, regardless of the other consequences? Or was there more to the narrative around the liquid that I was missing?

If the liquid were really killing people, I needed to say something. I had remained silent about the Rafaelites until it was too late. I would not make that same mistake again—I could not afford to do so. My soul was in peril, and I feared God would not hold a place in Heaven for me if I failed to learn from my past sins.

Deciding to tell someone was rather painful, but identifying the right confidant was extremely tricky. There was Archbishop Orriva, but I hesitated to involve him, especially after my entanglements with the Rafaelites. If the Archbishop heard these claims of deadly draughts from me now, surely he would think the rumors of a familial darkness true. *There is Rafaela again*, he would think, *drawing darkness to her wherever she goes. She is a pox. She is a deceiver. She is dangerous.*

After all, what if I were wrong about the liquid, the Sisters, everything? By betraying Mother Superior, I would be committing a grave sin, going against my vows with impunity—and for what? Something I thought, but did not fully understand? There was much at stake; most of all, I could not lose my connection to God—I could not put my eternal soul in jeopardy on the weakness of a suspicion I had harbored for barely two days.

My mind whirled, looking for possibilities, for some sort of valve I could open to release all the pressure building within me. Perhaps I could write to my father, who had always provided rational counsel. He would know what to do; he would understand what was going on. His wisdom and worldly experience far surpassed my own, and I had always and would always defer to him.

I made a mental note to write to him after the midday meal, when I would have a short period of quiet time before midafternoon prayer.

My lungs expanded and contracted with a deep, cleansing breath. I prayed I had found some sort of solution to my thorny problem, but competing thoughts of Berta, of the potentially deadly liquid, of the charred bottlery, and of the chamber of divine decomposition filled my head. I could not trust my own thoughts, my own judgment, my own sense of direction. I saw Sister Faustina's shriveled visage when I closed my eyes. Berta had been right about the chamber, at least—God was absent in that small, hot room.

This torturous internal waffling kept me shifting from knee to knee as I knelt next to my bed, my head bowed. Even if I were to speak with Mother Superior about my concerns, I must wait until after the evening meal to break the great silence. Perhaps by then, the problem with Berta would have resolved itself.

When the bells tolled, I was already dressed and washed. I wanted to check on Berta before morning duty, to ensure she had everything she needed and would either be resting comfortably or joining us in our daily schedule. I sincerely hoped it would be the latter; seeing Berta carry out the offices of the religious life would set many of my doubts to rest. Perhaps I would not need to write a letter to my father at all. The thought of inertia, of going along with the natural order of things within this new abbey, gave me more relief than a draught of cold water after a drought.

Doors creaked open as the other Sisters rose and left for morning duty. Perhaps I lingered because I wanted to ensure Berta's safety and comfort, but, in my deepest heart, I knew I lingered because I was terrified to return to the bottlery that stank of death. If I ministered to Berta long enough, perhaps I could find another place to carry out my morning duty. If the liquid we poured was actually making people sick, I did not want to have those villagers' deaths on my hands.

When the sound of all of my fellow Sisters' footsteps died down and silence returned, I pushed open my door and shuffled over to Berta's, which, I noticed with satisfaction, was slightly ajar. I prayed that the evening's rest had cured her, and now she was following the others, engaging in some duty as best she could.

With one fingertip, I gave her door a small push. The heavy wood creaked open just enough for me to see the end of her mattress. To my dismay, the twin mounds of her feet poked up from beneath the blankets. Had no one else tried to awaken her? I listened for her breathing, but I could not make it out even in the silence.

I pressed my body through the sliver of the open door and arched my neck to get a better view of Berta's head on the pillow. Her eyes were closed, her cheeks ashen. Her flesh had a waxy quality I did not want to admit I recognized. I walked farther into the room, intent on proving to myself Berta was just sleeping.

The whoosh of the door slamming nearly sent me falling backward. I sucked in air to scream, but it only came out in a shaky breath as Berta's eyes popped open like the spring of a child's toy. Her golden-red gaze zeroed in on me, and that sharp little smile curled her lips again.

"Rafaela," she said, her voice raspy. "God is not here!" The fire returned to her face, and she coughed raggedly, once, twice, three times. Blood sprayed through the air in a gory geyser. When she could finally suck in a breath, her exhale came out as wild laughter, laughter that rolled and bucked like a stallion, laughter that sounded more dangerous and deadly than any blood-soaked cough.

"God is not here, Rafaela! He will not save you!"

Her words felt astonishingly loud, overwhelming, even though her breath was fading from that horrifying laughter to short gasps. "Renounce your god now, Rafaela! Turn away from his light—it is not holy, it is diseased, and so are you. Burn it all to the ground, Rafaela! Burn it all!"

"No!" I screamed, breaking the great silence for the second time in just a few hours. I clapped my palms against my ears and squeezed my eyes shut, but I could still see Berta and hear her hitching laughter. "No! No! No!"

I was not aware that my mouth was still screaming negatives, that my eyes were still screwed shut, that my body was still bound in a tight ball on the floor—not until a few other Sisters, who must have heard my commotion, pushed open the door with a bang and flooded into the small room. One Sister, an older one, crouched beside me. Her knees popped and crackled grotesquely. The hand she placed on my cheek was dry and papery, and it reminded me far too much of Sister Faustina and her mummified fists. I must have continued screaming, because when the other Sisters hoisted me to the washbasin and splashed me with cold water from the jug, a small flood of it entered my mouth. I only stopped screaming when the water set me to spluttering, and I spat into the basin.

When I came back to myself, I turned from the basin to find four Sisters looking down at Berta's body on the bed. The older nun who had brushed my cheek was crossing herself while another whispered a prayer aloud, an appropriate reason to break the silence, unlike my own screams.

"Our Father, may Sister Berta ascend into Heaven to serve You for eternity. May her devotion in this life secure her eternal light. Protect her passage from this world into the next. God have mercy on her soul. Amen."

I crossed myself automatically and bowed my head. After a few moments, I allowed myself to glance at Berta. Her lean body on the bed already appeared shriveled, her face hollow and gray. Surely this was not the body of a woman who had spoken to me with such force only seconds before. Of course, there was the question that troubled me: Had she really spoken at all?

Shivers crept up my spine, fighting the sweat that sheeted down in torrents, causing my habit to stick to my flesh and making me long to scratch myself violently, until my nails drew blood.

One of the Sisters pulled Berta's sheet reverently over her face. I stood, unsure what to do or where to go. Eventually, a decision appeared to have been made; the older Sister turned and glided out of the cell, and the others followed. Before long, I found myself once again alone in the room with Berta, painfully unsure.

I crossed myself again and hurried out the door. I did not know where I was going; all I knew was I needed to be away from Berta, away from the threat of her body. As I picked up speed and burst through the dormitory doors and into the drizzly dawn, I thought I heard inhuman cackles of laughter echoing down the hall.

CHAPTER NINE

Sister Rafaela

My feet carried me to the church, where the other Sisters were gathered for morning prayer. I recognized a few of the Sisters who had seen Berta's body. Their faces betrayed no alarm, no fear, barely any sorrow. Were they so accustomed to death there was no room in their hearts for grief?

Then again, why would they grieve a woman they did not know? At the same time, even when familiarity does not tinge death with sadness, the simple slip into nonexistence should at least bring tears to a few eyes. Even strangers deserved to cause a ripple of sorrow with their deaths.

I reached up and touched my face, expecting to find tears wetting my own cheeks. My flesh was flaky and bone-dry instead, and I suppressed a gasp as I drew my fingers away quickly. When was the last time I had had a deep drink of water or a reasonable rest? It must have been days.

One of the Sisters had told Mother Superior of Berta's death, because the morning prayer service featured the responsory for the dead. We chanted the call and response, and Mother Superior led the prayer for Berta as we all sat, heads bowed, in the pews. The room felt too hot, too close; the candles flickering on the altar gave the room a feverish glow instead of a holy aura.

"Lord, welcome into your presence your daughter, Berta, whom you have called from this life. Release her from all her sins, bless her with eternal light and peace, raise her up to live forever with all your saints in the glory of the resurrecti—"

The roar of flames stopped the prayer short, and a breathy scream erupted from Mother Superior's lips as she leapt back from the altar, where the candles were flaring to hideous life. What had been two small teardrops of flame were now violent conflagrations floating above the candlesticks. The heat was of an intensity I had never felt before, and sweat popped on my skin beneath my heavy habit. Around me, Sisters were whipping their heads back and forth, standing, considering an exit. The questions were pulsing in all of our heads like a frenzied heartbeat: Was this a miracle we were witnessing? An act of God's divine grace?

Or was it something else?

My fellow Sisters were dealing with the same internal struggle—their hands clasped and twisted, but their faces were calm, then the reverse— but after a few moments of indecision, wherein the flames did not grow any larger, they all appeared to settle en masse, to relax back into the pews. My cheeks were moist. The air smelled like blood.

Around me, heads bowed in prayer, as if to finish the responsory in silence. I could not bring myself to join them, terrified as I was of the twin columns of impossible flame that lit our church up so brightly I had to squint to see the altar. The golden and gilt-covered decorations pulsed with an unnatural glow. Something felt undeniably wrong. The atmosphere crackled, not unlike Berta's dying laughter, and I grimaced, shutting my eyes as tightly as I could.

God the Father, please hear my plea. Guard us against the encroachment of Satan, protect us against our own imperfection, guide us in the direction of Your holy light. Amen.

As I finished my prayer, there was a powerful, dry whooshing sound, and the intensity of the flames' strange heat left my skin. When I opened my eyes, the blazes had died down to their former flicker. Mother

Superior was beaming, her face beatific. It was clear where her thoughts about the hellish flames lay; she believed them a miracle, a small display of God's divine power bestowed upon us sinners. I sneaked a glance around the room and saw the same look of awe on the faces of the other Sisters. Sister Leonella, in particular, looked starry-eyed, glistening tracks of tears lining her cheeks, wetness catching in her scars.

My own cheeks were also wet—but the moisture was the slick of sweat, not the salty sweetness of tears.

CHAPTER TEN

Father Bruno

Despite the rising sun, the abbey seemed permanently cloaked in gloom. Ever since meeting Sister Rafaela, I had been assaulted with memories from my youth. The woods, the injury, the pain, the kind old woman, the arrest...

No, no. I would not let myself think of such things today. It was time for the Sisters' Mass, then I would take their confessions, then I would be able to return to the village, where there was no pervasive stench of decay. That being said, I would be lying to myself and to God if I did not acknowledge the small thrill of pleasure in my breast at the thought of seeing Sister Rafaela again, with her heavy, dark eyes and full lips.

Calm yourself, Bruno, I told myself. *Do not get carried away.*

When I reached the top of the hill, I pushed open the church doors resolutely. The Sisters were already assembled inside, heads bowed. The bells tolled, and Mass began.

When Sister Rafaela reached the front of the line to receive Communion, I could not help but stare. Her cheeks had a fiery pinkness to them that only made her more beautiful, like the kind of woman masterful artists rendered on canvases, permanently preserving their beauty. The chalice containing Christ's blood nearly slipped from my fingers as I brought it to her lips, so enraptured was I by her unearthly charm. I glanced quickly to Mother Superior's visage, her skin gnarled like an old tree trunk, trying to still the desire spreading, unwelcome, through my abdomen. What kind of priest was I? What kind of man?

Guilt tugged at me, my old companion, and helped to bring me back to myself.

Finally, Sister Rafaela moved back to her pew, and I expelled a shaky sigh of relief. With Mass concluded, I took my place in the confessional booth, praying Sister Rafaela would keep her time with me short today.

*   *   *

My first confessor was Mother Superior, her strong, authoritative voice sailing through the grate between us. "In the name of the Father, the Son, and the Holy Spirit."

"Hello, Mother," I said. I wracked my brain for an appropriate verse, finally landing on a short but powerful sentence from Corinthians. "'Now the sting of death is sin, and the power of sin is the law.'"

"It has been one day since my last confession. But oh, how much has happened in that single day!"

My eyebrows jumped toward my hairline; I was so taken aback by Mother Superior's breach of protocol that I was momentarily silenced. There was an uncomfortable little cough from the other side of the grate, as though Mother Superior was also realizing her mistake, and then she offered, "Forgive me Father, for I have sinned."

I regained my composure and urged her onward. "Go on, Mother."

The air in the confessional was abuzz with her excitement; Mother Superior was clearly bursting to say something. I had never felt such an atmosphere around her before, and could only wonder at what could be the cause.

She cleared her throat before beginning. "Father, I do not pray to false idols, nor do I believe the Lord's hand is at work where it is not; but something happened this morning that seems of great importance to me. A miracle, even."

A miracle? Here, in this place? The thought seemed impossible, and I stifled the urge to scoff. How could anything miraculous happen in a place so gloomy and scented with death?

Mother Superior seemed to be gathering her wits about her. "Go on, Mother," I encouraged.

"This morning, a traveler to our abbey, Sister Berta from England, died in our care," she said. She did not sound aggrieved; in fact, her voice held a measure of awe I found quite odd, under the circumstances. Death was nothing new here, but I felt affronted. Why had she not called me for last rites, especially for a fellow Catholic Sister? She continued, as if reading my mind, "I would have called for you, Father, but everything happened very quickly. We did not think Sister Berta was so gravely ill." She paused, perhaps waiting to see if I would object. When I remained silent, mulling it over, she went on, "We held the funeral service, the responsory for the dead, for her during our morning prayers. Toward the end of the service, the candles atop the altar... they..." Mother trailed off, looking for the right words. She took a deep breath and went on, her voice still holding that awestruck quality. "The flames from the altar candles exploded, as though they were knots of wood popping in a hearth. Then, the flames rose high above the candlesticks, many feet above them, and they were so bright and so hot I began sweating. When we finished the responsory for Sister Berta, there was a great rush of air, and the flames died down to their normal glow. It was... incredible." She paused, then added in a small voice I would never have associated with the domineering Mother Superior, "Miraculous."

During her confession, my fingers had found their way to my beard, where they were scratching away in confusion. Candles bursting into enormous flame, with no apparent cause? I did not have an explanation, of course, I had not witnessed the event myself, but I would not be so quick to call it a miracle. Fire was unpredictable. Mother Superior and the Sisters of Divine Innocence should know that better than most, after everything that had happened with Sister Leonella.

Mother Superior was quiet, awaiting my answer. I had little to offer. "Mother, the Lord often sends us messages. He…" I found myself grasping for words. I did not want to seem dismissive of something that had clearly had such a large effect on her, but nor did I want to feed into a delusion, if that is what it was. I was also still feeling odd about Mother Superior's equanimity about the inability of her visitor to receive the last rites. Instead of being devastated or sheepish, even, Mother Superior was unaffected. Not for the first time, I found myself shrinking away from her, even though she could not see me.

She spoke, saving me from my floundering. "Perhaps the Lord was letting us know we had done right, by taking in a weary traveler. We took care of her, until the end, short as her time with us was."

"I am certain you did," I said, relieved at finding myself on firmer rhetorical footing. "Sister—Berta, did you say her name was?—must have been very grateful to find a welcoming home here."

"Now we will give Sister Berta a proper space in our chamber of divine decomposition, as is fitting."

I hated the thought of their chamber; I had become familiar with it through other Sisters' confessions. The entire concept made my skin crawl, but it was not my place to argue against it. Theirs was an ancient custom, and who was I to deem it unholy?

Mother Superior's voice resumed its authoritative tone as she ended our confession. "Forgive me for all my sins."

She had not confessed much, and I did not know what to make of the supposed miracle or the visitor's mysterious death, so I offered her a small penance, which she accepted with a firm "Amen."

The wood of the confessional booth creaked like old joints as she exited.

Sister Rafaela, of course, was next. I—or, I suppose, my body—sensed her before she even spoke a word.

Lord, please forgive me, I thought.

* * *

"In the name of the Father, the Son, and the Holy Ghost," she breathed from across the grille. Again, I did not bother to correct her to 'Holy Spirit.' Her differences charmed me.

Involuntarily, my body leaned forward until my face was almost pressing into the grille. I pulled back with haste, trying to gather myself before I spoke—but I failed. My voice cracked like an adolescent boy's when I said, "Hello, Sister." Embarrassed, I cast about for a verse to offer her, but my mind was blank. There was silence from the other side of the grille; that silence was heavy, full of expectation. Finally, I blurted, "'Fly fornication. Every sin that a man doth, is without the body; but he that committeth fornication, sinneth against his own body.'" Realizing what I had said, my flesh ran cold. This verse was not for her; this was clearly the Lord speaking directly to me, from my own mouth.

Sister Rafaela, thankfully, moved on without any hint of surprise or shock. "It has been one day since my last confession. Forgive me Father, for I have sinned."

I tried to focus on her words, but how could I offer her penance when I myself was sinning as she spoke? I felt my arousal, painful and throbbing, and willed it to go away. *I am a priest*, I told myself. *I am a messenger of the Lord's word. Yes, I am a sinner, a grave sinner, but I must try harder to resist temptation.* The words were true, but that did not lessen the weight of my plight. As Sister Rafaela listed a few small sins, my own shame slowly shrank until I could, at last, pay sharper attention to her confession.

I wished I had not. If I had thought her last confession had been torturous—with the tale of her mother's cruelty toward her very own infants—then what she told me next was irrefutably devilish.

"Father," she said, "This past evening, a traveler appeared in our midst, professing to be an English Sister just arrived in Spain by foot. Perhaps you heard our responsory for the dead this morning… because, you see, this woman was ill when she arrived, and I was put in charge of her care, and I thought she was going to recover, I thought everything was in my head, but this morning she…" Sister Rafaela trailed off, her voice rising to a hysterical pitch. She took a few breaths, then continued in a slightly calmer tone. "She died," she finished flatly. "She did not even receive last rites. And I cannot help thinking there was more I could have done. And… and there were things she said. At the end. Evil things, unholy things. About how God was not here at this abbey, about how the tincture the Sisters sell is poisoning the villagers, about how I am now complicit in all of that evil unless I do something… Father, I do not know what to believe!" She ended in an even more hysterical pitch, and I fought the urge to cover my ears with my hands, so shrill was her voice.

I had already heard of Sister Berta's arrival and death from Mother Superior, and I was somewhat mollified by Sister Rafaela's similar account of the woman's swift and unexpected death. In other ways, however, Sister Rafaela had cast the occurrence in more sinister light. "Sister," I said as soothingly as possible, "Sister. I am sure you did everything you could to care for your charge. We are not responsible, nor should we claim responsibility, for the deaths of those around us when it is disease that claims them. That is God's territory alone. Do not sin against him by claiming his actions as your own."

That humbled her, and her breathing slowed. "Father," she said, "but what of the traveler's claims?" I noted, with interest, how Sister Rafaela refused to call the dead woman a fellow Sister.

This puzzled me. Was Sister Rafaela really so shaken by the ravings of a dying woman? Perhaps her constitution was truly as unstable as she professed. My mental image of Sister Rafaela clouded; I did not know what to think of her. I cobbled together a response as best I could. "Sister, do not give credence to the delusions of a woman on her death bed. This abbey, as you have experienced yourself, is a holy place of God. The Sisters here are all brides of Christ, as are you yourself." I said this last to remind myself as much as Sister Rafaela. "Fear not, Sister. God is here." As I made this last pronouncement, a waft of that rotting scent hit my nostrils like a nefarious blast, making me gag. I hoped Sister Rafaela could not hear me through the grille.

Sister Rafaela sighed heavily. "I fear, once again, my imagination has gotten the better of me."

A sense of dread filled me—I had unwittingly played antagonist to Sister Rafaela, as so many others in her life had been doing for years. Who was I to tell her what she had experienced with her own senses was not valid? Was I no better than her mother?

Be calm, Bruno, I thought. *You have to offer spiritual guidance. That is your job, it is the Lord's work for you here on earth. Sister Rafaela would do best to forget Sister Berta and whatever things she may or may not have said.*

Not since my youth in Albania had I felt so unsettled in my soul; my feelings of unholy lust, great unease, and mounting suspicion combined to turn my stomach—or was it just the pervasive stench making me feel ill?

Before Sister Rafaela could speak again, my mind returned to something she had said, about the tincture poisoning villagers. That could not possibly be true.

"Sister," I said as gently as possible, "about the tincture. I am certain what you have heard is untrue. The Sisters here are not poisoning the villagers. My parish is in the village, I would know. I have heard of the tincture, and it is used to heal, not to harm."

As I said this, doubt settled around me like a black cloud. Now that I thought about it, I had noticed a slight increase in parishioner deaths, but then again, plague had recently swept through the region. I had heard from other priests of periodic outbreaks cropping up among their parishioners, and we all remembered the devastation in Seville, where over half a million souls had perished of disease. Death was inevitable and common; hastening its arrival with poison hardly seemed necessary.

On the other side of the grille, Sister Rafaela sighed before speaking once again. "I am sure you are correct, Father." She sighed again, then changed the subject. "I told you before that there were sins far greater at my Rafaelite abbey than simple pride in our confections." She paused, gathering herself. "I wish to confess to the other sins, the graver ones."

"Go on, Sister," I squeaked, still feeling weak from my own internal battle against the powers of lust and everything else that was making me feel helpless. I steeled myself for what Sister Rafaela was about to say. I knew it would not be good.

"At first, everything was normal," she said. "Or, I suppose, what I took to be normal. Besides my father's house, the Rafaelite abbey was the only home I had ever known. I trusted them completely; I followed all of their rites and chanted their prayers. I attended all of their services. I received an education. I did what they told me to do. I know… I know that cannot excuse what came next, but I need you to understand. I had been with the Rafaelites since I was a child of twelve. To me, they were doing the Lord's work, and who was I to question it? Of course you know I was also, and still am, afflicted with a wild imagination, to the effect that I cannot always trust my own senses."

She paused, giving me a chance to think back to her previous confession. She had spoken with such certainty about the infanticides. Was all of it, possibly, false? Had she concocted the events in her mind, or had her mother succeeded in making her doubt herself? I did not know what to believe, so I urged her on. "Please continue, Sister."

"The rites and daily schedules of the Rafaelites were very similar to what the Sisters of Divine Innocence follow here," she said. "We, too, took a vow of silence; we, too, sold a product; we, too, attended matins and lauds, Mass and confession, and everything else in between. We had our hour of recreation in the evenings. We were wedded to the Lord."

I was listening intently, and all traces of my arousal had vanished, thank the Lord. In my mind's eye, I saw a young Sister Rafaela, unsure and frightened, in the Rafaelites' den of iniquity, and my heart broke for her.

A loud gulp came from across the grille before she went on, her voice shaky. "At first… at first, we performed our services and prayers just as the Sisters of Divine Innocence do. Then… then, one day, something changed. I do not know what happened, all I know is that one evening, our vespers service was different. There was… there was an animal."

My abdomen cramped, fearing the horror Sister Rafaela was about to relay.

"Mother Superior was praying over the animal—I believe it was a goat—and it was quiet, calm. Then, Mother raised a silver dagger; it had a jeweled hilt, and the rubies caught the glow of the candles and flashed in my eyes, momentarily blinding me. I thank God every day for not having to see the kill stroke Mother delivered. I wish God had sealed my ears, too, because I heard the nanny goat's dying screams. When my eyes adjusted again, the animal was dead, and blood was pooling on the altar, dripping down onto the floor. It was so gruesome. Mother was giving thanks to the Lord and offering up the goat as a sacrifice. The other Sisters around me were unaffected by the slaughter, as though it was expected, natural. They did not look horrified, so I hid my terror. There were others, too… the milk cow was awful, the way it lowed when Mother Superior cut into it… but I thought it was all normal, even then…"

She trailed off, letting out a single, choking sob. I did not want to hear the rest, but I knew she needed to tell it. "When did you realize it was not normal?" I asked.

"When I saw the boy," she said.

A jolt went through my body, as if my flesh could sense the oncoming horror more viscerally than my mind. As I had during her first confession, I clenched my fingers around my rosary, trying to find some sort of solace in the discomfort.

"I cannot be sure how it all happened," she said in a small voice, so quietly I had to lean close to the grille to hear her. "Some of what I know was told to me by Archbishop Orriva in a series of letters; some of it is just a guess based on what I experienced. It had been awhile since the last sacrifice of the cow, and we had resumed our normal cadence and rhythm. Things made sense again. Until, of course, the boy appeared. I was sitting in my pew, waiting for vespers to begin, and a small boy of no more than five years walked past me down the aisle. I remember… I remember how he smelled, of boiled vegetables and unwashed skin. He looked like an orphan, and I later learned from Archbishop Orriva that my guess was correct. He was being led down the aisle by Mother Superior, and his eyes… they were so bright and innocent, so eager. I could hear his stomach rumbling as he passed by me. God forgive me, I thought he was being taken in as a ward. I thought we were going to help him. I am sure he thought so as well."

She was silent a moment, and a small sob came through the grille. "What happened, Sister?" I prodded, even though I did not want to know. With every fiber of my being, I wished to remain ignorant of what had happened to that boy—because I knew it must be horrific.

"Mother Superior led him up to the altar," she said, her voice barely above a whisper. "He turned to face us, and he was smiling. I—I smiled back at him. He reminded me of my brother at that age; even though he was alone in the world, he looked fearless. I thank the Lord every day that the poor boy did not see the blade coming."

I could not help myself—I gasped. I tried to disguise my shock by coughing lightly into my hand, but Sister Rafaela was not fooled.

"I know, I know!" she said, her words rising to a wail. "It was horrendous! It was devilish! Mother Superior slit his throat like an animal and left him there on the altar to bleed, and all the while she claimed it was a worthy sacrifice to the Lord, that this was a holy thing God had commanded of her, of all of us! She made us all complicit, but I promise I had no knowledge of what was going to happen to that poor boy! None at all! I even tried to save him, I ran up to the altar after the others had left and tried to staunch the wound, but it was no use... he was gone and there was blood everywhere, and the next thing I remember is Archbishop Orriva guiding me out of the church."

Sister Rafaela dissolved into tears, great wracking sobs exploding through the grille.

"Sister," I said, trying to calm her as best I could. "Sister. What happened at the Rafaelite abbey was horrific, but those who were responsible will be punished, and those, like yourself, who ask for forgiveness will receive it." I quoted the book of John, "'If we confess our sins, He is faithful and just, to forgive us our sins, and to cleanse us from all iniquity.'"

Sister Rafaela's sobs had dwindled to wet sniffles. She hiccuped out one last sob, then said, "Thank you, Father."

Her story was so sensational, so diabolical, that I was stunned I had not learned of the profane events that had transpired at the Rafaelite abbey before. Perhaps, with Archbishop Orriva's involvement, the matter had been handled quietly. Such an act of grisly murder would be a stain on the Catholic church, and the Archbishop would not have wanted word to spread far. At the same time, there were bound to be laypeople who knew what happened, surely? A crime of that magnitude....

On the other side of the grille, Sister Rafaela was speaking, but I only heard the end: "These are my sins, and I am heartily sorry."

I offered her absolution and penance just as the bells tolled, but I could not focus on my task. Sister Rafaela herself admitted to having a wild imagination, and so far her confessions, though few, had been uniquely traumatic. Could one person really be witness to so much sin?

I could not ask Sister Rafaela herself, of course—but there was one person who could add validity to the Sister's story. I needed to correspond with Archbishop Orriva.

* * *

I was not unfamiliar with Archbishop Orriva. It was he who had offered me my position in the village and here at the abbey. He was a good man, taking a chance on a young Albanian just returned to Europe from the New World.

After everything that had happened in my home village—the memories still painful to the touch, like a fading bruise—I had been sent away by my local parish priest, who took pity on me. With my parents' blessing, he had sent me to a monastic school in Tirana, farther from my village than I had ever been before. There, I received an education from the monks—reading, writing, languages, and theology, of course. The monks were strict and kept me at a distance, as though they were afraid of offering any sort of paternal affection. I wondered what they had heard about me, if they knew why I had been sent away from my home. I suspected they did, because they treated me as though I were tainted. In exchange for my education, room, and board, I performed all the duties of a servant. Cooking, cleaning, washing—no forms of labor around the monastery were spared me. My hands grew rough and callused from hauling buckets of water and chapped from emptying chamber pots in the dead of winter.

Throughout my loveless adolescence, I learned to turn to God for comfort and succor, to find all the affection that was denied me by the monks. Time passed, and I grew into manhood—but I was still haunted by memories from my past. In my nightmares, I heard the creak of the gallows.

When a priest visiting from Rome came to our monastery, he spoke of the New World with such awe that I could not help but feel a ravenous interest grow in my breast. I asked the man every question I could think of—what were the people like? What did the earth feel like? How did the air smell? Finally, with a laugh, the man told me I could find out for myself. Shock overwhelmed me—could I really leave Albania? A sense of stagnancy had crept under my flesh during my years at the monastery, and, without meaning to, I had resigned myself to living the rest of my life with the monks in Tirana. By speaking to the Roman priest, hopes of an entirely new future blossomed in front of me like the most beautiful of flowers.

Once I had resolved to leave, the arrangements were quickly handled. The Roman priest helped secure me passage on a merchant ship, and many months later, I found myself in the New World, spreading God's word to the savages.

My time in the New World, despite its hardships, brought me more joy than I had ever before known in life. My world expanded, and God filled it with His wonders. Seeing so many new things brought life and color to all of the religious teachings I had absorbed from the monks in Tirana. I felt reborn.

I would have stayed in the New World until my death if not for God's direction. After many years of ministering to the savages, God called me back to Europe, simply and sincerely. A merchant ship conveyed me to Spain, where I found shelter at a monastery in Barcelona. The warmth reminded me of the New World, and, perceiving no contrary direction from God, I stayed. I learned Spanish among the monks, and I was content.

Nearly a year after my arrival in Spain, it was in that Barcelona monastery where Archbishop Orriva found me. Perhaps he had been called by God as mysteriously as I had been; without preamble, he offered me my current position. Missing contact with others outside of the monastery, I accepted.

That was the path to my current situation, performing Mass for the Sisters of Divine Innocence, hearing their confessions, and ministering to the nearby villagers. I was not as happy as I had been in the New World or even in Barcelona, but I did not hear God calling me elsewhere.

I was needed here, and I would serve.

I walked back to the village and my austere rectory, where I sat at my table and prepared to write. The parchment lay before me, the quill in my hand, but doubt overcame me. The seal of confession prevented me from sharing anything Sister Rafaela had said to me, but that did not prevent me from asking the Archbishop for some sort of corroboration of her story. I did not need to provide any details; I could let him provide them.

My hand shook as I wrote.

> *Archbishop Orriva,*
>
> *A newcomer has joined the Sisters of Divine Innocence. Her name is Rafaela, and she comes from the Rafaelite abbey in Barcelona. I know she is acquainted with you, and I was sincerely hoping to avail myself of your knowledge of this Sister, so that I may best minister to her. Any guidance or wisdom you could provide would be most welcome and appreciated.*
>
> *Yours in God,*
> *Father Bruno Prifti*

I folded the parchment and sealed the letter with wax, hoping Archbishop Orriva's words could offer much-needed insight into a woman who so baffled and intrigued me, who so clouded my vision and my thoughts, and in whose presence I had great difficulty controlling my own body.

* * *

Sister Rafaela was the strongest temptation the Lord had placed before me since I entered the monastic school in Tirana. She was beautiful, she was vulnerable, she was, I thought, an innocent soul. I was not so naive as to think men of the cloth never sinned; in fact, I knew of several priests who had quenched their carnal desires in secret, even fathering children. These men, despite their sins, continued to minister to their flocks. This duplicity always puzzled me; did they think confessing their sins completely absolved them, even when they continued to indulge in the same lustful acts?

Even if I found the opportunity to alleviate my own sexual urges, I knew I would be unable to bring myself to actually complete the act. The stains already present on my soul were too dark; I needed to do everything in my power to lighten them.

I still had not forgiven myself for what happened to the old woman who saved me when I fell in the forest.

After spending the night in the old woman's home, I woke in the morning with a warm, affectionate feeling enveloping me. I was disoriented, but even though I knew I was not home with my family, I felt safe and comforted. My arm itched and ached beneath the bandages, which were stained with dried blood. The fire was still roaring in the hearth, and the old woman was, once again, stirring something delicious in the bubbling pot.

"Aye, you are awake, little one," she said, smiling at me. "Let us have ourselves a little breakfast and then it will be back to your mamma, who I am sure is worried about you."

These words should have made me happy, but all I felt was a sort of dull disappointment. Here, with the old woman, I was showered with sumptuous food, loving attention, and warmth. At home, I was seen as a boy who needed to finish growing up already, or as an extra caretaker for my siblings. I supposed I was not quite ready to leave the embrace of childhood behind after all.

Regardless of my reluctance, I knew my mother would indeed be worried, and I needed to return home to her as quickly as possible. I was strong enough to sit up on my own, and the old woman ladled a warm, fragrant porridge into a bowl for me. It was thick and hearty, and this time, I was not shy about asking for a second helping, which she happily supplied.

"It is lovely to have a man in the house again," she said, and while her comment gratified me, I found I missed being called 'little one.'

She was silent as I finished the rest of my porridge. After handing her back the bowl, which I had licked clean, she helped me with my shoes, then pulled me to my feet. My legs were slightly shaky, but after a few stretches and calm breaths, I felt steady enough to walk.

"Take this with you," she said, handing me a small cloth-covered bundle. "It is just a bit of dried meat, but you need all the nourishment you can get so you can heal properly."

"Thank you," I said, genuinely touched.

She walked with me through the forest until we reached the path I recognized, the one that would lead me back home. When we got to the trail, she stopped. "This is goodbye, then, little one," she said. Tears shone in her eyes, and, against my will, in mine, too.

"Thank you," I said, my voice cracking.

"Perhaps you could come back and visit me sometime," she said.

"Yes," I said eagerly. "I would like that."

She smiled sadly, then patted my head. "You are a good boy. You will grow up to be a good man, I have no doubt."

With that, she turned on her heels and headed back in the direction of her house. Within seconds, the thick forest enveloped her, and I could neither see nor hear her. With her departure, I felt more alone than I had ever felt before, and I fought the urge to cry like a small child.

When I walked back into my home, my mother was sitting in front of the fire with the twins. "Bruno!" she squealed, sounding equally angry and relieved. "Where have you been? Your father and sisters have been looking for you all night! How could you leave us like that?"

Her anger cooled when she saw the bandage on my arm, stained dark red. "Dear Lord," she breathed, setting the babies down on the floor to play. "Bruno, my son, what happened to you?"

"All is well, mother," I said. "I fell in the forest, but a woman found me and took care of my wounds. I am alright."

Her gaze sharpened. "What woman? What did she do to you?" Her entire countenance changed, from fear and relief to suspicion, and the anger was creeping back in, too. My mother was clearly demonstrating why the old woman lived alone in the forest—even good people like my mother were prone to suspicion. My heart ached, with pain both mental and physical.

My arm was pulsating with dull pain, too. It was far too warm with the fire blazing, and I tugged on my collar. Sweat beaded on my upper lip, where a fuzz of mustache was just beginning to show.

"I am fine, mother," I said.

Then I fell to the floor, and darkness claimed me once again.

CHAPTER ELEVEN

Sister Rafaela

Time must have passed, but I felt as though everything had slowed to a turtle's pace, seconds dripping into minutes into hours like melting wax. Before long, I was back in the refectory for breakfast, but I had no interest in the plate before me. I could not bring myself to lift the heel of bread to my lips, nor the plump almonds. Crunching their hardness would feel like chewing on bone, splinters breaking off to pierce my gums. My thoughts were still scrambled by the painful memories I had divulged in the confessional. Surely Father Bruno's handsome face would smile down on me no longer, not after what he had learned about me and the secrets I had kept, the horrors that had enveloped me like a poisonous fog. With a thirst that felt unquenchable, I downed my ration of small beer, dimly wondering if the Sisters made the brew onsite, or if it came from the village. The latter seemed more likely, given how I had not seen any fields or evidence of beer production, but I had not yet seen the whole abbey, either. Still, something about the idea of the Sisters themselves sorting barley and malt and fermenting the brew was distasteful, as though the liquid they bottled and sold tainted any other product they might make. It was a silly thought, I knew, but I also knew I was prone to fanciful imaginings despite my best efforts to stifle them.

I drifted through the midmorning and midday prayers like a sleepwalker, becoming aware of myself once again as I sat before my midday meal plate. I felt nauseated by the scent of roasted fish. Although thoughts of the young boy bleeding on the Rafaelite altar had faded, I could not dismiss Berta from of my mind. The awful things she had said at the end, commanding me to burn the abbey down, that God was not here. These were not the words of a religious. They were the words of the Great Deceiver.

If that were true, why could none of the other Sisters see it? Nobody else looked distracted, or ill, or even particularly troubled. Each face I saw echoed Mother Superior's beatific gaze from morning prayer, each countenance reflecting the grace of a miracle.

What had happened in the church with the hellfire candles did not feel miraculous. I felt even more like an outsider, unable to feel what all the other Sisters were feeling. That sensation was sadly familiar to me, but I had sincerely hoped joining the Sisters of Divine Innocence and having a fresh start would cure me of my otherness. I was beginning to think I was wrong.

These thoughts and others like them tormented me as I carried my still-full plate back into the kitchen, silently asking God to forgive my wastefulness. I chopped vegetables for the evening meal with the other Sisters, again witnessing no small number of transactions through the grate. Each clink of a coin sounded like the click of a cloven hoof on cobblestone.

Joy filled my heart when I finally had a moment to retire to my cell. I wanted to write to my father, to express my misgivings, to ask for his counsel and guidance. Father had always supported me when I floundered, built me up when my ingrained weakness led me toward collapse, soothed me when my imagination embarrassed me with its vividness. I yearned for his firm hand to push me in the right direction, to remind me what was real and what was false.

I composed a letter to my father in my head as I walked to my cell. I pushed open the heavy door and hurried inside, shutting it behind me. I did not realize I had been holding my breath until I fell back against the door, my chest heaving.

My gaze fell to the stone floor, where a crisp envelope lay. I recognized my father's ornate wax seal holding it shut, and a welcome warmth flooded my veins. My breathing relaxed, and I stooped to pick up the letter. I broke the seal and withdrew the stiff parchment, settling in at my table to read.

Dear Daughter,

My heart is broken as I write this. Your dear brother, my only son, has departed this life. He fell ill so quickly. I would have written to you sooner, but the physician assured us Sebastian would recover.

Your mother is inconsolable. I fear a new darkness will overtake her if she cannot find some form of peace.

Dear Rafaela, please pray for your brother, for his safe passage into Heaven. Pray for your mother, for her to find comfort in God's holy light. Finally, pray for me, for God to give me the strength to ask you what I must.

With Sebastian departed, you, dear daughter, are our only child, our only blood. What I am asking you is not easy, and I know it is not fair, either.

Our family line will end if you do not bear children to carry on our legacy. I beseech you to leave the religious life and return to us, to marry, to bear children, to shepherd our family into the next generation. Without you, the work of our ancestors has just ended with Sebastian's death.

Think, daughter. Think and then come home.

Your loving father,

Alejandro de Fuentes Piedra

A black sense of dread bloomed explosively behind my eyes, and my fingers trembled so severely I was unable to hold the letter steady enough to read it through another time. Sebastian, dead? The idea made no sense to me; it was as though father's letter had been written in another language. Sebastian had always been so full of life, so energetic, so strong. To think of him still, cold, and in the grip of death was unfathomable. How had this happened so quickly? I must have become an only child as I traveled from the Rafaelites to this abbey atop the hill. Which of my footfalls had coincided with Sebastian's last breath? Most of all, why had I not felt him depart this world?

As if Sebastian's death were not enough of a shock on its own, I also had my father's outrageous entreaty to consider. With Sebastian dead, what did it mean for me to leave the religious life, to remove my habit and step back into my role as dutiful daughter, the only remaining child of the de Fuentes Piedra family? My father was asking so much. I would have to leave my home, new as it was, divorce Christ, break all of my vows. I did not think my eternal soul could survive such irreversible actions, or that God would forgive me for turning away. I was not strong enough.

Then again, I must consider what would happen if I rejected my father's plea and remained with the Sisters of Divine Innocence. I would likely lose the love of my father, my mother would descend into an impenetrable darkness, our family line would die, and distant relatives would war over our land and our wealth. The nagging, excruciating question remained: Could I do violence to my eternal soul to prevent violence from befalling my earthly family?

Abandoning the abbey and returning to my father would also mean marrying a man whom I did not know, birthing children I could not fathom. Wifehood to a corporeal man and motherhood to squalling babies seemed so inconceivable, but I had a duty to my family. I also had an unbreakable duty to God.

The choice was impossible, yet I had to make it.

The tolling of the bells wrenched me from my thoughts, a phenomenon for which I was becoming increasingly grateful. Even as a child, thoughts of what I should or should not do seesawed in my mind, leaving me trembling and paralyzed with indecision. Father had been right to thrust me into the regimentation of the religious life so young; yet now, he wanted to rip me from it.

I shook my head and exited my cell, hoping midafternoon prayer and the rest of my daily duties would give me the clarity I so desperately needed. God said to obey my father, but what was I supposed to do when my responsibilities to my father and to the Almighty Father were at odds?

After midafternoon prayer, I lost myself in work, sweeping the stones of the cloister path yet again. I felt safer with the stiff broom in my hand, as though I could physically keep my burbling and boiling thoughts at bay. Perhaps my soul was not meant to know peace.

I was sweeping the path by the church door when the clomp of heavy footsteps nearby made me pause. I looked up and saw several Sisters carrying Berta's mattress; the tented sheet atop it confirmed Berta still lay there, still dead. One of her pale hands fell from the mattress to dangle in the air, a grotesque wave of farewell. The smell of sickness on her flesh wafted out to greet me. *Hail Mary, full of grace.*

I stepped aside, and the Sisters conveyed Berta into the church. I peered around the open door and saw them marching her body between the velvet pews, past the opulent altar, and through the small door that led, I knew all too well, into the chamber of divine decomposition beyond.

A wracking shiver coursed through my body at the thought of Berta rotting in the chamber. She should not have been here at all, and now we would all have to pray over her body, to hold her dry, withered hand, to contemplate the divine while staring into her sunken eye sockets. The air around me felt charged with an electric darkness, like the sky before a lightning storm. I felt we were at the precipice of something enormous, something dangerous. Something that could destroy us all.

*   *   *

Rivers of discomfort and confusion flowed through my mind from the moment I saw Berta's body being hefted into the chamber of divine decomposition. It was only during the evening meal that I finally came back to myself. Being fully present in my own body again felt like wearing a set of clothing that was too small, and I shifted uncomfortably in my seat. One thought kept beating in my brain like a chant: *Berta's body does not belong in the chamber.* So far as I knew, her status as a religious was unconfirmed. I knew we must not be quick to judge, but perhaps my fellow Sisters were too quick to trust. I knew from experience how such a quality could lead one grievously astray. Either way, her body's presence in a place that was supposed to be holy felt sacrilegious, and I worried God would punish us for this transgression.

I was also concerned about the liquid in the glass bottles. I was growing more and more certain of its source; although, each time I sought to fully commit to believing one thing over another, I was pulled back to that fence line I constantly walked upon, where indecision was my sole companion.

I did not want to believe what Berta had said in her final moments, but with lives—not to mention eternal souls—hanging in the balance, I could not afford to ignore her claims completely. God told us to learn from our mistakes, and when I had stayed silent about the Rafaelites' descent into damnation, we had all paid the price. My inability to act still haunted me; I could have written to Archbishop Orriva the first time fresh blood was spilled on the Rafaelite altar, but I had not.

Before acting now, there were things I must ascertain. First, I needed to fully understand the liquid's provenance and its purported holy purpose. Just as staying silent would be damaging, voicing such shocking and shameful suspicions would destroy my reputation, and possibly that of the entire order of the Sisters of Divine Innocence. I had to tread carefully.

Then there was my home in Barcelona, my family. My father and mother needed me more now than ever before. I could be a comfort to them in their grief, and they to me in mine. Perhaps the trauma of losing the child she had wanted had softened my mother's hard shell enough that she would be able to embrace me. Plus, I could serve the family in a more corporeal capacity, ensuring the birth of a new generation of de Fuentes Piedras. This notion made sense to me, but at the same time, there were my vows to consider.

These thoughts consumed me so completely that I could not taste the bread or hard cheese on my supper plate. Even though my tongue was numb to flavor, my mind continued to work as I chewed. My hour of recreation was fast approaching, the one hour of the day I would be able to converse with the other Sisters. Perhaps I could speak with Mother Superior, or even Sister Leonella, to share my reservations about Berta and pose my questions regarding the liquid in the glass bottles. Perhaps everything was a misunderstanding on my part, a confusion caused by silence.

I wanted desperately to believe three things: Mother Superior had somehow confirmed Berta's status as a religious; the liquid in the glass bottles was nothing more than an herbal tincture meant to cure aches and pains, and the 'holy essence' from the chamber that erased sin was entirely separate from the bottling operation; the coins earned from the sale of the liquid served to spread God's love and light, not to line the pockets or ornament the church of those who had taken vows of poverty.

The bells signaling our hour of recreation tolled, and with trembling hands and my blood beating in my veins at a rapid clip, I decided to approach Mother Superior and Sister Leonella. I walked more quickly than usual as I carried my supper plate to the kitchen washbasin, hoping to sidle closer to Mother Superior, who was currently speaking in a low voice to Sister Leonella. I could not hear everything they said, but I caught something that sounded like "…bring the bucket for her."

I washed my plate quickly and nearly stumbled over my habit in my hurry. I reached Mother Superior and Sister Leonella just as they emerged from the kitchen back into the refectory.

"Mother," I said, but my voice was so creaky and quiet from disuse and anxiety that she could not hear me. I tried again, this time more loudly. "Mother Superior," I said.

She came to a swift halt and turned around, her right eyebrow raised. "Yes, Sister Rafaela?" Sister Leonella also turned to face me, and I would have found her matching expression almost comical if I was not so deeply terrified.

I paused, struggling to find the right words, the right questions to ask.

"Well, Sister?" Mother Superior said, her left eyebrow now rising to meet its sister. The expression made her seem both surprised and exasperated. I cringed, and my collar felt all at once too constraining.

"Well, Mother," I said. My questions competed for first in the birth order on my tongue. At last, I said, "Has Berta been moved to the chamber of divine decomposition?" I already knew the answer, but I endeavored to begin the conversation as innocuously as possible.

"Yes, she has," Mother Superior answered, her tone neutral, her face regaining its placidity. "Is that all?"

"No," I said. "I was wondering if, um, you have confirmation that Berta was a religious? Or that you will soon seek it?"

Mother Superior scowled, and I stepped back as if slapped. "Confirmation from whom, exactly? God gives me all the confirmation I need, Sister."

"Yes, of course," I said, rushing to rectify my mistake. "But—Berta said some strange things to me before she passed on, and they were, um, rather shocking and sinful."

"Many people say strange and even sinful things when in the ravages of death," Sister Leonella said.

"Sister Leonella is correct," Mother Superior said. "Besides, these matters do not concern you."

Mother Superior and Sister Leonella began to turn away, but I knew if I failed to ask my remaining questions, I would have to wait another twenty-four hours in silence before I would even get the opportunity to speak to them again. As I had discovered, much could happen in twenty-four hours. It would not do to wait.

"Um, Mother," I said. Turning back toward me, the scowl reappeared on her face, and I took a short, shuddering breath. "I was working in the bottling room the other day, and I wanted to ask—what are we bottling?"

Mother Superior sighed, as if she were getting ready to explain something simple to a small child. "Have you not already discerned that for yourself?" At my blank look, she sighed, irritated and somewhat disgusted. "I have told you before—it is a holy essence. We collect it, on the instructions of our Lord God Himself." She leveled a steely gaze at me then spat, "Is that all, Sister?"

"And what is it for?" I blurted indecorously, pushing for further explanation, trying to hide my shock at having Mother Superior seem to confirm my fears: at least a portion of the liquid ladled into the bottles did indeed come from the corpses in the chamber of divine decomposition. Or was I misunderstanding yet again?

Mother Superior waved a hand dismissively in the air. "For saving souls and reserving places in Heaven, of course. As I told you before, Sister—it erases sin."

Sister Leonella added, "You will not be involved in preparing the holy essence, so you need not worry about it, Sister."

Holy essence? For 'saving souls?' For 'erasing sin?' I was still mystified. Mother Superior's words neither confirmed nor refuted what Berta had told me in her death throes. I could not be satisfied with such an answer, but pressing any harder could be dangerous. Cautiously, I tried a more innocent angle. "Of course," I said. "I only asked because I hope to learn more about botany and herbal medicines."

Mother Superior narrowed her eyes at me, and I took an involuntary step back. "Take care, Sister," she said. "You would not want anybody thinking you engage in witchcraft."

I gasped and crossed myself. "No," I breathed. I had heard of the witch-burning, mostly in the Basque country. For Mother Superior to invoke such a threat meant I must have overstepped egregiously. I needed to be even more circumspect. "Forgive me, Mother. I was only curious."

A smirk flickered across Mother Superior's face, and she rolled her shoulders back. "Curiosity was the cause of original sin, might I remind you. You would do well to channel your curiosity into learning more about God, Mother Mary, and Christ, Sister Rafaela."

"Or perhaps the lives of the saints," Sister Leonella added, affecting the same posture as Mother Superior.

I nodded almost imperceptibly. "Yes, thank you, Mother, I will do that," I said, the smile on my face more of a grimace.

"If that is all…?" Mother Superior said, as if daring me to ask her another question, as if she relished the consequences she could bestow upon me for my impertinence.

"Yes, Mother, that is all," I replied, my voice so quiet I could barely hear it myself.

"Very well. Come, Sister Leonella, we have business to attend to."

Mother Superior whipped around and began walking toward the door. Sister Leonella winked at me before turning on her heel and following the abbess out of the refectory.

I wanted to let the matter rest, but Mother Superior's dismissive explanation of the liquid in the glass bottles was far from satisfying. Perhaps another Sister would be more forthcoming. I hoped so, but at the same time, I feared word getting back to Mother Superior and Sister Leonella that I had not been content with the information they had given me. That would surely mark me as malcontented, which was untenable. The Sisters of Divine Innocence had already taken a chance by accepting me, given my past, and I could not afford to alienate myself further. Once again, I was teetering on the fence line, and I was starting to lose my balance.

I again thought of father; perhaps writing him a letter would settle some of my doubts and quiet the turmoil in my heart. Surely he would either see what I could not, understand what slipped through my fingers, or, at the very least, offer me the advice I needed to find some measure of peace.

I resolved to write to my father after compline, the night prayer, hoping that in the meantime, I would find the right words. I knew I must not sound too alarmed; given how desperately father wanted me to return, he would use any hesitation or misgivings on my part as evidence for why I should abandon the religious life. I still could not believe he was asking something so imprudent of me, something so irreversible. I was not certain father's good relationship with Archbishop Orriva would save our family from disapprobation if I broke my vows to God and the church. My parents must be unquestionably desperate to put our reputations, if not our eternal souls, at risk.

I stood so long in the refectory, lost in thought, that the bells tolled to signal compline before I had a chance to question another Sister. Agitation crept through me, but it was clear God did not intend for me to extend myself further that night. The dust needed to settle.

Later, when the bells tolled to release us to our free time, the other Sisters rose and filed toward the back of the church instead of out the door into the cloister. Confused, I fell in line with them. It quickly became clear we were trudging toward the chamber of divine decomposition.

Toward Berta's body.

The small door next to the altar opened with a creak, and I felt the hot breath of air coming from within, even though I was at the back of the line. The Sisters moved steadily into the close space. There was nothing I could do but follow.

Somehow, we packed into the small room, and the warmth was oppressive. We were all facing Berta's body, which had been placed upright in one of the stone chairs, just as Sister Faustina's had been. I noticed that Sister Faustina was now absent—perhaps she had finally been moved to a more comfortable resting place. The graveyard?

With so many Sisters standing in front of me, I had to stand on the points of my toes to see Berta's head. I almost fell backward when I looked into her face, which was so lifelike I was sure she would begin speaking at any moment. Her golden-red eyes were open, her cheeks were pink, her lips were curled back in the tiniest of smiles. I had seen dead bodies, but none had ever looked as undead as Berta. I had heard tales of people who had fallen into unresponsive states, and, having given them up for dead, their relatives buried them. Only when they heard muffled yelling and screaming coming from the graveyards did they realize their mistakes. In some cases, it was already too late, and the inner lids of the coffins they exhumed were rough with scratches and bloody pieces of fingernails. Perhaps Berta was in such a state? If so, at least she would not suffocate in the chamber of divine decomposition.

I heard a few sharp inhales from the other Sisters in the group, who must have shared my surprise at the state of Berta's body.

Mother Superior stood at the front of the crowd next to Berta, her head bowed. She led us in prayer, but my lips did not want to shape the words I knew so well. Speaking to God on Berta's behalf felt disingenuous, even insidious, given everything she had said to me.

After an interminable bout of prayer, during which the heat grew so intense that my habit again stuck like a second skin to the sweat pouring off my body, Mother Superior lapsed back into silence. I assumed we would be able to leave, having prayed for Berta's safe passage into Heaven.

I was not so fortunate. The ritual must have been familiar to the other Sisters, because they wasted no time in lining up as best they could in the small space. I fell somewhere in the middle, and I watched with growing horror as each Sister knelt before Berta's body, grasped her fleshy hand, kissed her bright cheek, and smoothed the fresh habit she now wore, which, I could barely see in the dim candlelight, was hiked up in the back, pooling around her pale thighs. Clearly it was insufficient to simply pray for her; we also had to pay our respects quite physically. My stomach lurched at the thought.

The line moved rapidly. I sniffed the air, trying to detect even the smallest hint of fresh decay, but the only thing I could smell beyond the ever-present scent of old rot was the growing strength of body odor as the other Sisters fanned themselves, trying to circulate the still air. Before long, I reached the front of the line, face to face with Berta. Even though it was impossible, I was certain I saw her eyes narrow and her lips curl back even farther when I approached, as though she had been waiting for me, only me.

The other Sisters were watching; there was no escape. I knelt and put a tentative hand on Berta's habit-covered wrist. I could not bear to touch her actual flesh—that felt far too intimate, even though I had performed that exact action with Sister Faustina not two days earlier. I supposed the difference was that Sister Faustina was clearly dead, irrevocably passed on to Heaven. Nothing was clear about Berta.

I could not bring myself to pray, so I counted down from fifteen as I knelt. When I rose, another Sister took my place, and I filed out of the room. The blast of fresher air that hit me as I passed through the small doorway was a revelation, and I thanked God. I crossed myself as I reentered the church.

The church was empty, the others having dispersed to enjoy their remaining free time before the bells tolled for us to retire. I sat in one of the plush pews and bowed my head.

The Saint Michael prayer slipped into my mind, and I found myself mouthing the words before I was fully aware of what I was doing. *Saint Michael the Archangel, defend us in battle. Be our protection against the wickedness and snares of the devil. May God rebuke him, we humbly pray; and do thou, O Prince of the Heavenly Host, by the power of God, thrust into hell Satan and all evil spirits who wander through the world for the ruin of souls. Amen.*

The Saint Michael prayer had always cast a measure of fear into my heart, but tonight I was glad for it, glad to reach for strength to face the misgivings I could not shake.

CHAPTER TWELVE

Sister Rafaela

My feet were heavy as I trudged back to my cell. I still needed to write a letter to father, both to seek his guidance and somehow respond to his impossible request. A rebellious part of me wanted to pretend I had never received the letter; perhaps, if I just ignored it, I could pretend everything could continue on as usual, with Sebastian still alive and my eternal soul safe with the Sisters of Divine Innocence. Of course, such a course of action was not really actionable at all, and I knew it. Things could not become real simply because I wished with all my might.

So, with a heavy heart, I sat at my small table, a piece of parchment before me. I could not ignore my father. There was nothing to do but respond.

I began:

Dear father,

My quill stalled, and I stared down at the mostly blank page, which seemed to mock me and my indecision. I dipped my quill again into the ink, hoping the action would fill the tip with words, words that would flow beautifully across the page and convey everything I needed to say without disappointing my father or breaking my vows.

Dear Father,

My heart is heavy with the news of Sebastian's death. I will pray for his safe passage into Heaven, and for a soothing spiritual balm for your grief and mother's. Lean toward God during this difficult time, father, and He will comfort you and mother.

I must give serious consideration to your request. I of course wish to obey you, my father, but I feel I cannot break my holy vows to God the Father. Surely you can understand my predicament, you who started me in this religious life and have always guided me fairly?

Would my leaving the Sisters of Divine Innocence warrant serious consequences for our family? If so, I do not think that is an action we would be able to survive. Is a chance at extending our family line here on earth worth the sacrifice of our eternal souls?

I eagerly await your response, dear father.

I felt rather clever, deferring a firm 'yes' or 'no' by asking my father further questions; at the very least, I would allow myself more time to think. Before I could sign the letter and seal it, I remembered my other purpose for writing to father.

I also hoped to ask your advice on a difficult matter that has arisen here. I have become concerned that a certain substance the Sisters prepare, which Mother Superior calls a 'holy essence' used to erase sin, may in fact be a source of great illness. I have heard that the tincture is sickening those who purchase it, but I cannot be sure this is the truth. After the horror of the Rafaelites, you can understand my apprehension—I cannot stay silent if someone is being harmed, but I feel so unsure of myself. Please, father, help guide me to the right actions, the actions that will preserve my eternal soul and strengthen my relationship with God.

Your loving daughter,

Rafaela

I put down my quill, feeling somewhat dissatisfied with the letter I had managed to pen. The words to describe the small, potentially lethal bottles of liquid only came with great difficulty, and I feared I had not adequately communicated my serious concerns. I was not sure father would understand my predicaments—neither the one he had placed me in with his request, nor the one involving the tincture. Even if he did, it was quite possible his own desire to bring me home to continue the de Fuentes Piedra legacy would take precedence over dispensing any sage or practical guidance.

The bells tolled for bedtime just as I was sealing my letter with the abbey's red wax. I quickly addressed the letter before washing my face in the basin and changing into my nightgown.

The mattress rustled as I laid down. A comfortable position eluded me. When I closed my eyes, images of Berta filled my mind, as silent and deadly as poison. I wondered if the other Sisters felt as haunted as I did, if golden-red eyes peered out from their dreams, too.

To alleviate my angst, I tried to regulate my breathing and focus on God. The turmoil in my mind of late had distracted me from my duty to the Father, and a warm but not entirely unwelcome shame flowed through me. God the Father towered above all else in my small life, and my worries about Berta, about my family's legacy, were minuscule in comparison.

With my thoughts firmly entangled in God, I finally drifted off to sleep.

The coughing awoke me shortly thereafter.

*　*　*

Pulled from a deep sleep, it took several moments for me to understand that the harsh hammering assaulting my ears was coming not from my own throat, but from one of the cells nearby. Tears of terror filled my eyes as I realized the cough sounded painfully similar to Berta's. Another

Sister must have fallen ill.

I listened attentively, but when the cough did not repeat, the exhaustion of the previous two days overwhelmed me and dragged me back into sleep.

However, before too long, the cough came again, yanking me back to consciousness like a fishhook, and a small scream escaped my lips. The cough now sounded closer, as though it were coming from the cell directly next to me—from Berta's vacated room.

I knew that was impossible, but the conviction that Berta remained in that bed, coughing and dying, would not leave me. I did not want to slip back into sleep, for fear of finding myself mired in dreams of Berta. Quietly, I swept my feet from beneath the blanket, rose, and treaded lightly across the floor to the doorway. I needed to see Berta's cell for myself if I was to find any measure of peace.

My door creaked, but Berta's opened with unexpected ease, as if it had been greased at the hinges. With one cold and shaking hand, I pressed the rough wood of the door, which swung inward like an invitation.

My eyes landed on the table, the small chair, the jug of water— nothing out of the ordinary. The bed frame came into view, the mattress, the twin mountains beneath the blanket—

No. No, there could not be feet under that blanket—this cell was empty, no one could possibly be sleeping here…

My eyes drifted up from the mounds of blanket, lingered on the outline of a body, and stopped as they locked gazes with a pair of flame-colored irises burning in the middle of eyes that glowed red where they should have been white.

"No!" I screeched, a violently vocal reaction I could not suppress. I bowed my head, gripped the rosary that hung around my neck, and prayed to Mother Mary. *O Mary, conceived without sin, pray for us who have recourse to thee…*

A small *pop* pierced my prayerful concentration and I looked up.

Where there had been a body in the bed, now there was nothing but rumpled blankets. Berta was not there.

I was alone.

CHAPTER THIRTEEN

Sister Rafaela

I lay awake for hours before the Caller knocked on my door for matins. Each time I tried to close my eyes and drift away, I saw those golden-red eyes burning like hot coals, and my blood raced through my body, drenching my nightgown and blanket in sweat.

The knock startled me, even though it was not unexpected. I arose quickly, splashed cold water on my face, and rushed from my cell. As I joined the tide of Sisters heading to the church, I heard a small chorus of coughs, almost dainty. Nothing like Berta's wracking wheeze that threatened to break her ribs with its force.

Even though the moon shone brightly in the cold predawn sky, I felt a dark, insidiously warm miasma pervading our abbey atop the hill. I eagerly hoped for a strong breeze to blow the bad air away, to pull the incipient coughs from the Sister's chests, to purify Berta's body of whatever sinful thing possessed her and used her mouth to say such horrible things.

I tried, with difficulty, to concentrate on God, Christ, and the Holy Mother during matins. I had come to the Sisters of Divine Innocence to grow in Christ, to enhance my devotion, to be a better person, to atone for my sins. So far, I had succeeded only in irritating Mother Superior, nurturing suspicions, and harboring ill thoughts in my heart and mind.

O dear Lord, please forgive me my sins, my distractions, my incompetence, and help me to grow in my love and praise of Your eternal holiness.

By the end of matins, I had managed to partially refocus on worship, but that concentration quickly evaporated when, yet again, the Sisters lined up not to leave the church, but to reenter the chamber of divine decomposition—to pray over Berta's body.

I had no choice but to fall in with them, to carry out what they viewed as a divine duty, even as resentment and discomfort bubbled in my throat like bile.

When I pressed myself into the chamber with the others, I risked a short glance at Berta. Nearly an entire day had passed since her death, but her body still appeared lifelike, as though she could easily stand up and walk out with the rest of us. Several other Sisters threw flitting glances around the room, obviously as surprised as I was by the pristine condition of Berta's body. Even her eyes, which remained wide open, retained their luster. I fancied I saw light dancing behind them.

One of the older Sisters took Berta's hand as Mother Superior prayed; the dead woman's fingers looked just as pliable as they had been in life, even appearing to grasp the Sister's hand in response. I was not the only one who saw that impossibility; a few Sisters gasped, earning a sharp glance from Mother Superior. Dread bloomed in the pit of my stomach.

How long would it take for this body that looked so alive to resemble Sister Faustina? Her body had been dry and withered, completely drained of life. Berta, in contrast, looked hale, healthy, full of vigor. Although my experience with corpses was not vast, even I knew her condition was abnormal. In fact, nothing about Berta was normal.

Finally, Mother Superior ended the prayer with a soft "Amen," and we left the hot chamber.

Would we repeat this ritual after every service? The thought seemed too horrifying to entertain. Being in Berta's presence displaced God from my mind; she demanded all of my attention. Were the other

Sisters feeling as I was?

I would have to wait to find out.

As we walked out of the church and back through the cloister, there was a new urgency in the chorus of coughs, a harshness that had not been present before matins. Hot gusts of air slapped against my cheeks as several other Sisters hacked away, some even bending over to catch their breath. One Sister's head struck my shoulder, and I turned to offer assistance. When I looked into her upturned face, I saw a blank mask of terror that left me feeling far more unsettled than even Berta's body had. I offered a fevered prayer of healing and protection to the Lord as my feet clicked on the cobblestones.

Back in my cell, I lay on my straw mattress and prayed for forgiveness, for clarity, for strength, for courage. I entreated God to fill me with all that I lacked, all the resolve and character and certainty that had faltered and died inside of me. I wanted to be an empty vessel for the Lord, His to fill as He saw fit.

I prayed and prayed, and eventually fell back into a thin sleep. When I awoke to the sound of the bells tolling for morning duty, I still felt hollow.

*　　*　　*

After dressing and preparing for morning duty, I stood in my cell for a moment, fingering the stiff parchment of my letter. How was one to dispatch a letter in this place? My letter from father had appeared without preamble in my cell, so I had no idea where to go to send my missive to my family. Outside my door, I could hear Sisters scurrying to their duties and realized I could idle no more. I left my letter for father on my small table, hoping, through the course of the day, to find some answer to my question. With luck, my letter could be dispatched today.

I desperately needed a kind word from home, something to anchor me more definitively to my identity and my purpose. I felt unmoored with the Sisters of Divine Innocence; because of our vow of silence, broken only for one hour in the evenings, I still did not know many of their names. Mother Superior Maria Innocentia and Sister Leonella were the only living Sisters known to me, and I did not consider them allies.

While I waited for father's response, I needed to come to a decision about my continued life as a religious. Father would expect an answer with my next letter, and I feared the disappointment, even disavowal, that would follow a refusal to acquiesce to his demand. A father disowning his daughter was a terrible tragedy, but a Sister abandoning her vows to God and leaving the religious life seemed far more heinous to me.

Perhaps a better understanding of the mystery of the holy tincture would help me both distract myself and find the answers I craved. Were I to stay with the Sisters of Divine Innocence, I needed to know they still bathed in God's holy light, that they had not strayed and become hostage to the Great Deceiver by participating in sinful acts. If I were to defy my father, my eternal soul must be safeguarded. I also wanted to disprove Berta's claims once and for all, so I could close my eyes without seeing her golden-red stare boring into the depths of my soul.

After wiping anxious sweat from my brow, I joined the trickle of Sisters in the cloister and hurried to the bottlery, gripping my arms for warmth. A breeze had arisen in the predawn darkness, but it did nothing to banish the forbidding, malodorous miasma that engulfed the abbey.

Entering the noxious warmth of the bottlery did not dispel the chill in my bones, and I continued rubbing my arms as I took my seat at one of the long benches. The buckets lined against the wall were far fewer in number than the last time I had labored here. The transactions through the kitchen grate continued steadily, and I was shocked to contemplate the sheer volume of bottles the Sisters were really selling.

Sister Leonella was not present among the bottlers that morning, and I exhaled slowly in relief. If I were to do what I planned to do, I needed courage—and my courage invariably faltered in the presence of Sister

Leonella. It was something about the dark amusement in her eyes, the ghost of a sneer that lived permanently on her face next to her scars.

A few of the older Sisters also seated on the benches looked up as I began my work, but then returned their gazes to their own tasks. I heard a few coughs, which grated on me with their roughness.

I filled a few of the small bottles from the bucket at my side, stoppered them, and placed them in a wooden box set out to collect the filled vessels. After a few minutes of normal work had passed, I glanced around surreptitiously and, finding no direct gazes trained on my hands, I filled one bottle halfway, quickly pushed the cork in, and, with numb fingers, slipped it into the interior pocket of my habit. Perhaps by examining the tincture in private, I would be able to draw some sort of conclusion.

O my God, I am heartily sorry for having offended thee. I said the prayer with sincerity, asking for forgiveness for my sin of theft as the bottle pressed against my flesh. With creeping dread, I noted how familiar the Act of Contrition was becoming to me.

I prayed that examining the tincture close up, without prying eyes or ears around me, would resolve some of my questions, if not all. I was unsure how I would test the liquid inside, but I prayed to God to help me find the clarity I needed, even if that meant ingesting the tincture myself. I recoiled at the thought of drinking the drippings from a corpse—but, perhaps I had misunderstood Mother Superior. It was very possible the tincture was nothing more than an herbal remedy, and I was simply confused. After all, the villagers sought the tincture eagerly and were presumably consuming it, so it could not be grievously dangerous, could it?

The bells tolled for lauds not too long after, and I rose with haste, eager to be out of that dark den that smelled of ashes and decay, especially now that I had set my private investigation in motion.

Mass came and went, and the Eucharist tasted sweet on my tongue where Father Bruno placed it. Standing in the glow of the altar, his face lit from both behind and below by flickering candlelight, he looked Christlike, rapturous. When my eyes met his, he smiled warily, then flicked his gaze away, as if he sought to be rid of me quickly. To my embarrassment, my stomach growled loudly as I returned to my pew, and I hung my head to avoid meeting any other wandering eyes.

After the final 'Amen' of Mass, I once again rose to head for the confessional booth along with the other Sisters. Despite my hunger-related peccadillo, I felt joyful. We were not headed toward the back of the church, toward the chamber of divine decomposition. My life had been a delicate dance of following orders, of following others, but never had I felt that regimentation so strongly as I did with the Sisters of Divine Innocence. Perhaps it was due to the advanced age of the other Sisters, how their actions were so practiced they were almost automatic.

To my pained dismay, when I reached the confessional, Mother Superior was staring at me. Although she was shorter than I was, she still gave the impression of looking down on me. She shook her head as I began to step into the booth, and gestured for me to move out of the line. When I complied, she said nothing, only pointed at the back of the church—toward the hot little chamber.

My face must have paled, because Sister Leonella, who had appeared at my side, put a hand on my shoulder that felt more oppressive than supportive. With a firm grip, she turned me around and walked me back. The temperature increased incrementally as I neared the chamber, or was that just my imagination? Sweat slicked down my spine, making my habit feel itchy and tight. With all my heart, I longed for the confines of the confessional booth, for the smooth salve of Father Bruno's voice, the comfort of his listening ear. Why was I the only Sister singled out for the chamber? Was I being punished, or was this Mother Superior's idea of a reward? There was little chance this was a reward; nothing in either Mother Superior's or Sister Leonella's demeanor indicated even the slightest hint of kindness.

Sister Leonella released me near the altar with a little push before retreating quickly to join Mother Superior and the other Sisters in line for confession. I turned back to find them both glaring at me, clearly waiting until I entered the chamber before they turned their attentions elsewhere. Sister Leonella's eyes were dancing with cruelty, and there was no imagining the smirk that distorted her formidable features.

There was no choice, a predicament that was familiar to me—like a hated food that nevertheless makes a constant appearance on the supper table, as if demanding to be eaten. Refusing to enter the chamber would violate my vow of obedience, something I was not yet ready to do—at least not so openly. I also did not want to raise the ire of Mother Superior against me any more than it already was. By asking questions of her the previous night, I had placed a target on my back—a target of irritation, of suspicion, of barely restrained vengeance. I must enter the chamber and pray for protection, for strength, for the grace of salvation.

With a melancholy heart, I pulled open the heavy door and crept into the chamber of divine decomposition, where Berta waited for me in the hot darkness.

*　　*　　*

A single lone candle burned in a niche on the wall opposite Berta, casting her face in a flickering glow that made her seem even more alive. Her body was still uncomfortably vivacious, those golden-red eyes dancing beneath a raised brow.

The room felt oppressively hot, and the streams of sweat on my skin turned to rivers. Thirst crept like a predator onto my tongue, and I prayed to God for my sojourn in the chamber to be a short one.

When I was a child, my father had taken me with him to visit his cousin, a very wealthy man who lived in a large stone house on the edge of the city. While my father spoke with his cousin, I had had free rein to explore the house, an unexpected source of delight. I had run off, thrilled to be given a modicum of freedom, but I had quickly grown bored of the bedrooms, kitchens, and parlors. We had had all of those rooms at my house, too—they were not novel or wondrous.

Then I had come upon a large set of glassed double doors at the end of a hallway, with light spilling through the panes and onto the floor like melted gold. I had rushed through those doors, eager to find something different, something interesting. I had found myself in the middle of a room full of plants and greenery, a room whose ceiling was made entirely of panes of glass, the opulence of which was breathtaking. Moisture had beaded up on the panes and dripped off the tip of my nose. The plants had had an earthy, loamy smell that reminded me of the fresh potatoes the servants brought from the market. I had been ready to explore, about to hop off on a journey around the incredible indoor forest, when the sun had emerged from behind a veil of clouds and unleashed the full force of its light into my small newfound kingdom.

The result had been immediate—the room had transformed from a sort of balmy, pleasant warmth to a searing heat that had left me gasping and running for those glassed double doors. When I reached the exit out to the hallway, the doors had refused to open under my weight. I was unsure whether they had locked instantly behind me, or if I had twisted a knob the wrong way or rattled a key unknowingly to lock myself in. Either way, I had been trapped in a room that seemed intent on frying my flesh like fish in a hot pan.

I had banged on the doors with my fists as sweat dripped into my eyes, clouding my vision. I had screamed until my throat was raw, and then I had screamed some more. My strength had left me rapidly, and just as I had felt ready to collapse, I had heard footsteps pounding down the hallway to the hot glass room. When my father had finally opened the doors and I fell through into the dark coolness of the hallway, I had lost consciousness. I had awoken hours later, in my own bed, moonlight streaming through my window. My mother had been sitting in a chair at the end of my bed, but when we locked eyes, she hadn't looked relieved or happy to see me awake. There had been nothing in her gaze—no love, no happiness, no light. Just dark, hollow emptiness. After she had seen to her satisfaction that I was not in danger of imminent death, she had whispered with the force of a cannon, "You will not embarrass our family like that ever again." I had been sent to the Rafaelites the very next day.

This particular memory was not comforting as I stood above Berta's body in the chamber of divine decomposition, sweat running down my legs and pooling in my thin shoes. That hellish greenhouse felt far too close, my mother's disgust and disapproval far too near, and I fought against the panic that wanted to strangle me where I stood.

I bowed my head to pray, but instead of communion with the Lord, all I could feel was Berta's golden-red gaze boring a hole through my furrowed brow. For a corpse, she emanated so much energy, so much presence. She was difficult, if not impossible, to ignore.

I turned away from her, facing the flickering candle instead. Prayer came more easily when I could not see Berta's rigid stare. *O Mary, conceived without sin, pray for us who have recourse to thee, and for those who do not have recourse to thee, especially the enemies of the Church and those recommended to thee. Amen.*

A familiar voice broke the silence.

"Mother Mary won't save you now, Rafaela."

My gorge rose in my gullet, and breath refused to fill my chest. My head shook on my neck like a flower bud in a harsh wind, and my vision began to fade at the edges. Surely that voice, Berta's voice, had been my imagination. She was dead. The power of speech was beyond her now.

I bowed my head again, fighting against fainting and against the tricks of my own mind. *Angel of God, my Guardian dear, to whom God's love commits me here, ever this day be at my side, to light and guard, to rule and guide. Amen.*

I let out my breath in the blessed quiet that followed, letting my shoulders relax. The heat of the room had unnerved me, that was all, and perhaps the voice I heard had even been the beginning of a waking dream brought on by exhaustion. That was all. I would—

"I know what you have in your pocket. You dirty little thief."

I wheeled around, nearly slipping in my sweaty shoes. Berta's body sat just as it always had, its expression unchanged. No, wait—was there a new redness to the lips, or had I simply not noticed that before?

"Dear God, please protect me from the temptations of the Great Deceiver, please give me strength and courage to resist the pull of sin, and please help me to grow in my love for You. Amen," I spoke aloud, hoping to imbue my prayer with more power. I blinked, surprised at myself. I had broken my vow of silence yet again because of Berta.

Berta's face did not change, but was that a shift in her eyes, a new tempo to the dance behind all that golden-red color?

My fear and frustration grew as I stared at her body, the body that was conspicuously not rotting, the body that still looked pristine and smelled fresh. I entertained the possibility that perhaps Berta was not dead after all, that maybe we had all been mistaken in thinking her so, and in fact she was simply unable to move. Was it possible she was as terrified as I was, being immobile and sequestered in this awful space?

"Say something!" I finally pleaded, hoping to settle the matter once and for all.

Her lips did not move, but those golden-red eyes danced even faster. As I studied her features, I felt my own body drain of energy.

"What do you want?" I said again, quietly, hoping that no Sisters in line for confession out in the church were capable of hearing my spoken transgression.

Berta remained silent.

Tears coursed down my cheeks, but they were not tears of sadness. Rage simmered in my belly, ignited by terror and exhaustion. Something strange was happening here at this abbey, and everything was conspiring to keep it from me. Perhaps whatever was speaking through or inside of Berta, even if it was my own imagination, was trying to save me from falling from grace with the rest of the Sisters of Divine Innocence. Maybe my best course of action was to leave this life once and for all to be the daughter my family needed, even though it meant spending more time with my mother. At least she was not nearly so terrifying as Berta.

I turned away once again, wiping my wet cheeks with my veil.

"She told you it was a holy essence! How ridiculous!"

Yet again, I wheeled around. Yet again, Berta's body remained still.

I tried a new tactic. With my back to her, I spoke quietly. In a trembling voice, I said, "What do you mean?"

A choking laughter that chilled me to my core echoed from behind me. "You know what those bottles hold, Rafaela. Mother Superior told you as much. Believe it: You know its source. You know that is why they brought me to this room. They want that essence from me, so they can bottle it and fill their coffers."

"No," I breathed, hoping my negation would render all of her claims untrue, even though I suspected that very same thing. I stared into the flickering candlelight, looking for answers.

"Mother Superior and that lackey of hers do not care about my identity, Rafaela. They care only about my body. And only then if it is dead."

The thought was so horrible I squeezed my eyes shut against it, but that did nothing to prevent my ears from hearing Berta's words.

"Just watch, Rafaela. Watch and listen, because they are watching and listening to you. Be very, very careful." That choking laughter bounced around the room again, and I shivered in spite of the oppressive warmth.

My attention must have unleashed a torrent, because Berta did not stop speaking after issuing her warning. She sought to hammer her point deeply into my mind, as if it were a nail and I a piece of dense wood. "They will come for you, too, Rafaela. Why do you think they accepted you here, after knowing what happened with the Rafaelites?

Knowing about your complicity?"

"No," I breathed, but Berta continued.

"They will collect something from you, too, Rafaela," she said. "Have you noticed you are one of the only young ones here? Mother Superior was quite purposeful in her choices. The older ones die to supply their foul tincture, and the young ones, like you, will supply an addition that will fetch a considerably larger amount of coin. They will take whatever they can get!"

"I do not understand," I said.

"Oh, but you will. Keep a close eye on your rags, Rafaela. Your blood may come from your body, but it will no longer belong to you. They will sell it as the blood of a saint, can you believe it?" Again, the harsh caw of laughter rang around the room, making my head spin.

"They will steal my blood?"

"And so much more than that, Rafaela!"

My mind raced; I could not hold a coherent thought long enough to understand anything. "What do I do?"

There was an unexpected silence behind me, and when it stretched longer than I could bear, I turned around. Berta's body was unchanged, and as the silence continued, I felt sure I had imagined the entire conversation, that the heat was putting strange notions in my head.

I turned back around, intent on praying away my sinful thoughts, when Berta spoke again.

"You must—"

A knock on the door sent me pitching forward in shock, nearly burning my face on the candle flame. The door to the chamber swung open, letting in blessed light and cool air. Standing in the doorway was an older Sister whom I did not recognize. Her gnarled hand beckoned to me, and I hurried out of the chamber, but not before I stole another glance at Berta's body.

One of her eyelids had closed in a horrid, leering wink.

A familiar twist of pain low in my abdomen struck with ferocity, annihilating any lingering feelings of hunger. I had not expected to feel that ache for several more days, at least. I still felt like an outsider among the Sisters of Divine Innocence, and, for some reason I could not completely understand, the irrepressible corporeality of my body embarrassed me. The rumblings of my greedy stomach, the tears leaking from my eyes, the blood of my womb—it was all so loud, so messy. As I followed the Sister into the church and out the doors into the cloister, something worse than my womanly pains tormented me: I had not heard Berta say how I could save myself.

CHAPTER FOURTEEN

Father Bruno

Ever since I had first seen Sister Rafaela, I had been tormented by thoughts of my past, the childhood cut short by tragedy. For years, I had avoided immersing myself in that pain, instead focusing on healing the suffering of others. Something about Sister Rafaela, and her troubled girlhood, unlocked my vault of memories, letting all the vitriol pour through.

Worse, my body reacted physically to her presence in a way not befitting of a priest, especially one with as much to atone for as I had. At Mass, she accepted the Eucharist with such eagerness I could not help but smile. She held my gaze too long, setting things to stirring below my vestments. Quickly, I looked away, but the damage was done. How would I ever be able to properly minister to this woman when she made me lose control of myself?

I concluded Mass in a dark mood. Maybe it was time for me to move once again. I had not seen my mother, father, or siblings since I had been sent off to the monastery after everything that had happened. The twins would be young women by now, maybe even with children of their own. I could take a post near my old village, perhaps even have a chance to interact with my family again.

The thought should have brought me joy, but all I felt was weariness.

It was nothing more than a fantasy; in my heart, I knew my family would not welcome me back with open arms. Too much anguish lay between us, so many things left unsaid. It was too late now.

My steps were heavy as I walked to the confessional booth, and my thoughts continued to race. Where else could I go? Another posting in Spain? I had learned the language, after all, and I liked the generally mild climate. The people, on the whole, were kind and devout. Perhaps, when I received a response from Archbishop Orriva, I could include a request for a new posting in my reply.

I was barely settled into the booth when a crusty voice said, "In the name of the Father, the Son, and the Holy Spirit." Mother Superior, of course.

"Hello, Mother. 'And the just man shall hold on his way, and he that hath clean hands shall be stronger and stronger.'" The quote from the book of Job leaped like a young frog from my lips, and I felt the verse deep in my bones. It was more for me than for Mother Superior, but it seemed to resonate with her as well.

"Aptly said, Father. It has been one day since my last confession." She paused, emitting a delicate cough. Mechanically she added, "Forgive me Father, for I have sinned." She did not sound repentant, but then again, Mother Superior rarely did. Privately, I thought the power of being in charge had begun to corrupt her, as air and moisture corrode metal over time. Her soul was becoming rusty, but there was nothing much I could do to help her beyond my usual ministrations. She did not seem bothered.

"Continue," I said, fighting the urge to yawn. I had been having trouble sleeping the past few nights, ever since I had met Sister Rafaela and the old memories had come flooding back. I felt like Noah, but I was alone on a small boat instead of a crowded ark. I prayed God would save me.

"God forgive me if I am wrong, but I believe we may have a case for canonization developing here on our premises with Sister Berta," she said, her crackly voice proud.

Canonization? Could she be serious? Sainthood for a woman who had not received last rites, no less? I choked in surprise. "Sainthood—but Mother, that is extremely rare."

"I know it is, Father. But I have also witnessed enough in my many years to recognize the signs. We cannot ignore the miracle of the candle flames, for one. And of course, Sister Berta is dead, there can be no denying that, but her body is still full of life." Mother paused to cough again, then continued in small, breathy bursts. "Father, what I am telling you is that Sister Berta's body is not decomposing. She may very well be incorruptible."

I was aghast. Scarcely an entire day had passed since Sister Berta's death. It was far too early to label her body incorruptible. Mother Superior was being excitable—she knew better than that. "Mother," I said carefully. "This is a very serious claim. We cannot act hastily." Mother Superior knew as well as I did that a recognized saint would bring incalculable acclaim and fame to the Sisters of Divine Innocence, and even though such things should not influence Mother Superior one way or another, it was clear that the rusting of her soul had made it weak.

"Father," she said, with a sneer in her voice, "I have been around many, many bodies. I have seen decomposition in every stage. I have held the hands of the dying and the dead. I can tell you with certainty that Sister Berta's body is different."

I could not deny that Mother Superior had vast experience with corpses given the Sisters' practices involving the chamber of divine decomposition, but I still found the idea of Sister Berta's sainthood preposterous. That the potential saint in question was also a traveler from England cast greater doubt on the entire idea. Mother Superior knew almost nothing of Sister Berta; she did not know if the woman had led a life of virtue, or performed any heroic or selfless deeds. All she had was a purported 'miracle'—the odd behavior of the candle flames—and a body slow to rot.

"I do not doubt that your long experience with the matters of death is greater than mine, Mother, but—"

She cut me off, a shockingly uncouth behavior, especially during a confession. Her voice was breathy and enthusiastic again, and it made me itch with discomfort. "Father, you must document these occurrences to send to Archbishop Orriva. Just think, a true saint in our midst! You have already heard my testimony of the miracle of the candles, so you can include that in your biography. There is no time to waste, Father!"

The confession had gotten away from me, and I was unsure how to return everything to a sense of normalcy. "Mother," I said, attempting to calm her. "A few more days to observe the body cannot hurt. Let us wait and see before we alert Archbishop Orriva."

She was silent a moment, but when she answered, her voice was petulant. "Well, Father, I suppose that is for the best. In the event that I am wrong in my assessment, please forgive me for praying over a false idol." Almost as an afterthought, she added, "I am sorry for all of my sins."

When she finally left the confessional booth with a sigh of exasperation, I felt my body relax. Mother Superior always made me feel tense and vulnerable, as though I were a young boy again, having my knuckles rapped by the monks for some small transgression or another. I longed for the days I had spent in the New World, engaging with new Catholics and basking under the blue skies that stretched as far as I could see. Surely God would not put my best, happiest days in my past.

My next penitent was so feather light she barely made a noise as she took her seat.

"In the name of the Father, the Son, and the Holy Spirit," she said, and I recognized her voice instantly as Sister Cecelia, one of the oldest members of the Sisters of Divine Innocence. Despite her advanced age, the woman had an eager youthfulness about her, as though she drew all of her energy from the Lord's light. In truth, I thought she was an exemplar of what a Sister could be, and I always looked forward to her confessions—mostly because her sins were insignificant, but also because she took such joy in the act of penance that it was infectious.

"Hello, Sister," I responded. "'Even to your old age I am the same, and to your grey hairs I will carry you: I have made you, and I will bear: I will carry and will save.'" Sister Cecelia had previously expressed anxiety about aging, even though she had lived, as far as I could tell, an extremely pious and admirable life. I always tried to comfort her with verses about longevity; today, it seemed I had achieved my goal.

"What happiness that verse brings me, Father," she said. "I am a child of God, a bride of Christ, and I know the Lord will keep me safe."

A smile spread across my face, lifting a few hairs from my mustache into my nostrils and tickling me. I barely managed to avoid sneezing. "Indeed, Sister."

"It has been two days since my last confession. Forgive me for not coming yesterday, Father—I was feeling unwell." As if to add veracity to her statement, a rattling cough erupted through the grille.

"Sister," I said, concerned, "are you quite well now?"

She coughed again, and I could hear phlegm rattling in the back of her throat. "I am fine, thank you," she finally managed, even though she sounded far from well. "Father, I know it is not my place to judge another human being, but many of us are starting to believe that Sister Berta, who died very shortly after arriving here, may require consideration for canonization."

Oh no, not this again. I tried to keep the skepticism from my voice—poor Sister Cecelia deserved respect. "And why do you think that, Sister?"

"You see, Father, her body still remains fresh in our chamber, even though all others like her after this same period of time start to look… well, different. They start to fall apart, to enter the normal process of decomposition—but not Sister Berta. Then, too, there was a mighty display with the candle flames during her responsory, and…" Sister

Cecelia trailed off, then launched into another coughing fit.

When she had quieted after an alarmingly long time, I said, "Sister, you know as well as I that saints, true saints, are rare."

"Oh Father, I know!" she said, but there was no anger in her voice, only a sort of childlike enthusiasm. "I have wished so heartily to see a miracle before I die, and I know my time is coming soon, I can feel it. To be in the presence of a saint while I still live… it is a great gift from God."

"'Beware of false prophets, who come to you in the clothing of sheep, but inwardly they are ravening wolves,'" I quoted from the book of Matthew.

When she responded after another long pause, Sister Cecelia's voice sounded old for the first time since I had known her. "Of course you are right, Father," she said. "Then this is my sin to confess: that I have wished for things I have no right to desire, and I have placed belief in what may very well be a false prophet. These are my sins, and I am heart—heartil— heartily—" She erupted into another series of harsh coughs before she could finish her 'sorry' that lasted for so long, I considered stepping out of the confessional booth to seek aid. When she finally regained control of herself, she finished weakly, "Sorry."

"Take heart, Sister," I said. "You are a virtuous woman." I offered her absolution and penance, and she thanked me in a rasping whisper. I could not help thinking I might soon be called for Sister Cecelia's last rites, if that cough did not improve.

After Sister Cecelia, a few other Sisters came to offer their confessions; each listed a few venial sins, and several mentioned Sister Berta, whom they all seemed to believe had the glimmerings of sainthood. Their collective certainty gave me pause; perhaps I was the one being too hasty in my assumptions. I had not yet seen the body, of course; maybe everything they were saying was irrefutably true. As I exited the booth, then the church, then the abbey grounds, to head back to my parish in the village, I decided to put my disbelief aside.

After all, I had seen many strange things in my life. Encountering a true candidate for sainthood in a place that seemed uniquely unlikely to hold such a miracle did not seem so impossible.

*　　*　　*

Back in my rooms, a letter was waiting for me, bearing the seal of the Archbishop. I was both surprised and pleased at the speed of his communication. Every day, the world became a smaller place. The thought made me smile. Perhaps one day, we would be able to communicate with even more speed, sending messages to distant friends and relatives as instantly as our prayers reached God's ears.

I shook my head to clear it of fantastical thoughts and turned my attention back to the letter. No matter the Archbishop's response, my own letter in return should probably contain some mention of the possible incipient saint at the abbey of the Sisters of Divine Innocence. If such a miracle were, in fact, true, Archbishop Orriva should be made aware of it as soon as possible.

With my little knife, I slit the letter's seal and unfolded the stiff parchment. I was standing as I began to read, but the contents of the letter quickly unsteadied my knees, forcing me to sit. When I finished, my mouth was open wide with shock, and a light sweat dampened my underarms and the backs of my knees.

> *My dear Father Bruno,*
>
> *I am quite familiar with Sister Rafaela, as I have been a close confidant of her family since before her birth. The poor girl has suffered devastating tragedy, and I assume from the tone of your letter that you have gathered as much. I will be frank with you, Bruno, because you deserve to hear the unvarnished truth. Sister Rafaela must be handled very delicately, and I apologize that I did not have the foresight to write to you sooner without your prompting. You*

see, I helped place Sister Rafaela with the Rafaelites when she was a young girl. Her father believed she would receive the best education, and I always sensed her mother was not overly fond of her. For many years, Rafaela did well in the abbey, and we maintained an occasional and genial correspondence. It was nearly a year ago when her letters became strange; she wrote of shadows following her, of her fellow Sisters plotting against her, of nightmares of blood and death. I was, as you can imagine, alarmed, and I wrote to the Rafaelite abbess with my concerns. Shortly after that, Sister Rafaela's letters ceased altogether, and the abbess assured me that all was well. Something felt wrong to me, and after praying on the matter, I felt the Lord leading me to the abbey, to ensure everything was indeed alright.

Bruno, what I found there would make even the stoniest man weep. When I arrived at the abbey shortly after dark, I heard wailing coming from the church. I rushed in, fearing someone had been injured, and there before the altar, I found Sister Rafaela—bathed in blood, writhing on the stone. Next to her, a small boy lay unmoving. Sister Rafaela began screaming hysterically, and I surmised she had found the dead boy and lost herself in horror and grief.

I did not know what else to do besides take Rafaela away from there. I of course questioned the abbess, but she could not provide a satisfactory answer as to how Rafaela came to be before the altar next to a dead child, and Rafaela herself was in no state to speak coherently. Of course there was a discreet investigation, but all I could determine for certain was that the child was an orphan. No one could tell me how he had come to be on the altar, or under what circumstances he had died. I still do not know what happened, and, to be honest, I do not wish to know. In the wake of the tragedy, I closed down the abbey and sent the Sisters elsewhere. I thought the Sisters of Divine Innocence, one of the only abbeys with space for her, would be a place for Rafaela to recover.

In answer to your question about how best to minister to her, I would urge patience. The poor girl is no doubt still reeling from the shock. Now more than ever, she must cleave to the Lord and bask in His eternal light. I can think of no priest more suitable than yourself to return Rafaela to spiritual health.

Please do not hesitate to write to me again should any further problems arise. I promised Rafaela's father I would watch out for her.

Yours in God,

Archbishop Juan Leonardo Orriva

When I finished reading the letter for the first time, I read it through again, then a third time. Archbishop Orriva's account did not exactly corroborate all that Sister Rafaela had confessed to me, but neither did it directly contradict any of her statements. I supposed it was possible Archbishop Orriva had found Rafaela at the altar with the dead boy after the abbess had killed him, but the whole thing seemed so fantastic in the light of the Archbishop's calm recollection. Yes, a tragedy had clearly occurred, but if the Rafaelite abbess had really killed that boy, I couldn't help but think the truth would have come out. Whereas Rafaela's story was sensational and horrific, Archbishop Orriva's was sad and strange.

At least I had confirmation of one thing: Sister Rafaela had indeed encountered a dead child in the Rafaelite abbey. I should have been comforted to know she had not confessed a litany of lies, but something still did not fit. My mind kept coming back to two questions: How had the boy really died?

Then, even more chilling: Who had really killed him?

*   *   *

Suspicion was never something I felt comfortable harboring. After what happened to the kind old woman who saved me as a child in the forest in Albania, any feeling of suspicion was as painful as a freshly closed wound—one hard jab, and the blood would ooze again.

Following my misadventure in the dark woods, my last few weeks with my family in my home village were traumatic. I lost consciousness following my return to my family's home; this was a fact, I knew, but it felt as though it was from someone else's memory. I knew I was beginning to feel feverish as soon as I crossed the threshold and saw my mother and the twins, but I have no memory of any sort of sense of foreboding or doom. In hindsight, I cannot help but feel as though I should have known what was coming.

I was lost in the darkness of unconsciousness for several days. Afterwards, at the lowest points of my life, I wished that I had stayed in that darkness and never emerged, never had to see what happened to the kind old woman who was simply trying to minister to an injured child.

At first when I awoke, my skin clammy, my back wet with sweat, I thought I was safe and cared for, mostly because the first face I saw when I opened my eyes was that of the old woman. I soon realized something was horribly wrong, however. Instead of a warm smile, her face was a mask of terror, and her eyes darted wildly around the room. I followed her gaze, and was stupefied to see we were in the main room of my little home, and it was filled with men and a few women from the village. My mother and father were not in my field of vision, and I could not understand what was happening.

"*Gjyshja?*" I questioned the old woman, using the Albanian word for 'grandmother.' I did not actually know her name. Even after all these years, I still did not.

"It is alright, little one," she said, but there was no confidence in her words, and her voice trembled. Her eyes were still moving from here to there like a caged animal.

"What is happening?" I asked, trying to sit up but quickly falling back to the pillows in my weakened state.

"*Shtriga!*" one of the village men yelled, and several others joined in the chorus. Some chanted "Witch! Witch!" with such hatred, it made my ears burn. Were they really condemning this kind old woman as a blood-draining killer of children?

"No!" I said, using all the meager strength I could muster. It was futile; no one but the old woman heard me over the yelling of the villagers.

"Do not be afraid, little one," she whispered to me. Tears leaked from the corners of her eyes, tracing the grooved wrinkles in her cheeks as if they were dry riverbeds.

I tried to respond, but only a small squeak came out of my throat.

"Cure the boy!" a man I recognized as the village butcher called out. "Cure him now, *shtriga!*"

Cure me? I did not understand. I was still recovering from my injury, that was all. The old woman had already done everything she could— she had saved my life and gotten me safely back home.

"Cure him!" the other villagers joined in. By the hearth, I could see several women touching their pinched fingers to their eyes, lips, hearts, and stomachs before throwing something into the fire. It was at that point I finally understood the full extent of what was happening. The women were performing the traditional ritual to ward off a *shtriga*, using pinches of salt to protect themselves. My eyes flicked over to our doorway, where a large cross sat propped against the wooden frame. If the ritual were being followed properly, then it was made of pig bone.

I knew the old woman would be unlikely to leave my house unharmed.

"Cure him now!" the butcher yelled again, punctuating his command with a harsh shove to the old woman's back. She squealed and stepped forward, nearly falling on top of me. "Waste no more time, *shtriga!*" the butcher screamed, his face contorted in a gruesome mask of hatred. I saw evil in that moment, and it was not in the old woman. It was in the face of every villager gathered in that room to punish an innocent woman for simply trying to care for a sick child.

"I am so sorry, little one," she breathed. "Just close your eyes and open your mouth. It will all be over soon."

I knew as well as every other Albanian that the way to reverse a *shtriga*'s curse was to have the supposed witch spit in the afflicted child's mouth.

I also knew that the villagers would not leave the old woman alone until she had performed to their satisfaction. If I could just withstand the ritual and show them I was better, I hoped they would let her go, that they would see the error of their ways.

I opened my mouth.

A villager pushed the old woman roughly toward my bed again, and she brought her wrinkled, tear-stained face very close to mine. "Please know, little one, I would never hurt a child. I am not what they say I am."

Tears formed in my own eyes, too, and I did not care who saw me, a boy nearly grown to manhood, crying. There was no way for me to stop the tears, even if I wanted to. "I know," I said. Then, "I am sorry."

"Now!" the butcher yelled, and there was nothing else left to do but finish the ritual.

With a grimace, the old woman pursed her lips, then spit weakly into my mouth. Her saliva was too thick, and it tasted of old potatoes. I gagged, and another villager, this one a woman, forced a cup of water to my lips and poured it onto my tongue, to wash down the curative spit of the *shtriga*.

The water wasn't enough. Without much warning, I pitched forward, nearly knocking my forehead against the old woman's, and vomited onto the floor. Several more waves of retching followed, until I felt hollowed out and aching with the force of it. I fell back against the pillows, exhausted.

"Illness still plagues him!" one of the villagers yelled. "It did not work!"

"Kill the *shtriga*!" another yelled.

"She must pay for her crimes!"

"Douse her with holy water!"

Someone stepped forward holding a cup, then threw it unceremoniously onto the old woman, who was cowering by the foot of my bed.

"Die, *shtriga*!" the thrower screamed. "Die for what you have done!"

She finally spoke in her defense. "I have done nothing wrong!" Her face and hair were dripping with holy water, and she was the most pathetic creature I had ever seen. My heart broke for her even as the rest of my body ached with fever and sickness.

"The witch lies!"

"Kill her!"

"To the gallows!"

Everything I was witnessing felt like a feverish dream; the screaming, the heat of so many bodies pressed into one small space, the white-hot fire of their anger and hatred, burning me to a crisp. I looked into each face, but I could find no trace of the neighbors and friends I had known since birth. I saw only animals—animals who had cornered their prey and were readying it for the slaughter.

Dear God, I tried to call out, tried to protest against what was being set in motion, the evil that was about to be perpetrated, but I was so weak from fever I could barely speak, much less move. The mob had worked itself into such a frenzy, it was unlikely they would have heeded my word anyway. They had fixated upon a horrible falsehood, and they were not going to stop until the woman they saw as a *shtriga* hung by her neck until she was dead.

As I watched, horrified and nauseated, the mob of villagers descended on the trembling old woman, pulled her forcefully to her feet, and dragged her out of my house. All the while, they were hurling insults at her, calling her witch, *shtriga*, devil, vampire. They said she deserved to die, and that God would think them righteous for ridding the world of such evil.

Everybody emptied from my house, but I could still hear the roar of the villagers as they took the old woman down the road to the town square not far away, where the gallows stood proudly, a symbol of justice. Not once did I hear the old woman scream; if she did, it was lost in the clamor of the villagers as they yelled, then heckled, then jeered, then cheered when the last breath left her throat. There was no way this could be true, but I was certain I had heard the *pop* of her neck snapping.

For weeks, I existed in a liminal space between nightmare and waking. Over and over in my delirium, I heard the sharp *crack* of her snapping neck, tasted the sourness of her saliva, felt the intense heat coming off the villagers as they crowded into my home. I thought I would never escape that hell, but eventually, little by little, I emerged from my terrible illness.

It was not long after that I was sent away to the monastery near Tirana. In truth, I was happy to go. I could not stand looking into the faces of my neighbors anymore; I saw only evil there—evil and a lack of repentance, which was worse. I was living in a village full of souls bound for hell, and I could not stay there without slipping into the fire with them.

Suspicion had been the seed that germinated into the evil I had seen in each and every face that day, and I vowed, from then on, to never let suspicion take root in my own heart for as long as I lived.

*   *   *

My mouth was dry and I felt sick and shaky as I composed my response to Archbishop Orriva. His information about Sister Rafaela had been illuminating, but it had not answered my most pressing questions. What was Rafaela's role in everything that had happened? Who had really hurt that poor orphan boy?

Worst of all, I was extremely uncomfortable with my own questions. They smacked of suspicion, and suspicion was anathema to my soul. The last thing I wanted was another witch hunt. I would not be able to bear even more death laid at my door.

I puzzled over what to say to the Archbishop about Sister Rafaela. I had never been very skilled with the political aspects of my calling; diplomatic language, especially in Spanish, eluded me. It was no secret that I would never become a bishop or archbishop myself; I lacked the mettle for it. I was content with my own shortcomings, unless, as was the current case, my lack of skill at navigating difficult situations rendered me useless.

The Archbishop was clearly very close to Sister Rafaela's family, so treading carefully was essential. If he knew more than he was disclosing, he obviously did not want to tell me. I could not obtain any more information from him, I felt, without putting myself in an adversarial position, which I in no way wanted. As a foreigner, it was necessary to have friends in high places, and I did not want to cast doubt on Sister Rafaela, or present myself as questioning or flouting authority.

My response to Archbishop Orriva was, as a result, an anodyne, bland version of what I really wanted to communicate.

Archbishop Orriva,

Thank you for your illuminating letter. I appreciate your candor and your faith in my abilities. I am saddened to hear of Sister Rafaela's experiences with the Rafaelites. Thank you for your advice. I will do my best to help her heal her spiritual wounds.

I also must apprise you of an unusual situation here with the Sisters of Divine Innocence. It seems as though they took in a traveler, a woman who presented herself as an English member of a religious order, calling herself Sister Berta. The poor woman arrived ill, and shortly thereafter perished. Her death was so swift and unexpected that she was unable to receive last rites. The Sisters have placed her in their chamber of divine decomposition, and now they report to me that Sister Berta's body has remained vital since her death. There was also the suggestion of a miracle, but I did not witness it. I have also not seen the body in question. You know as well as I how rare true saints are, but I wanted to ensure you were aware of the suggestion that one is here in our midst.

Yours in God,

Father Bruno Prifti

I put down my quill, folded and sealed the parchment, and set it aside.

My mind was reeling, and when I raised my hand to my face, I was surprised to find my fingers wet with tears.

I had not felt so alone since I heard the old woman's neck snap on the gallows.

CHAPTER FIFTEEN

Sister Rafaela

I had no idea how long I had been alone in the chamber with Berta, but when I followed the older Sister into the refectory, hoping I would have at least a small breakfast to distract me from the growing pain in my abdomen, the other Sisters were clearing their plates and shambling into the kitchen. Another meal missed, it seemed. At least my hunger was mostly a memory by then.

With no chance of sustenance, I followed the Sisters into the kitchen, hoping to be able to chop vegetables or fruits or prepare meat during the work period, something productive but banal. More importantly, I wanted to be able to observe the transactions through the grate in the corner more closely. Suspicion enwrapped me like an itchy blanket.

I sighed, upset with myself. Instead of trusting in Mother Superior and the other Sisters, in my father's and Archbishop Orriva's judgment, I was now looking everywhere to prove Berta's claims true instead of to unmask them as false. What sort of Sister was I?

God felt curiously silent in that abbey atop the hill. I prayed constantly, but I felt as though I were praying to empty space, something I had not felt even at the Rafaelite abbey during its time of horrors. Something felt very, very wrong, and the only person I believed I could lean upon in any capacity was Father Bruno, but he was only available for a small period of time each morning. Things were happening too quickly for him to keep up, I feared.

Perhaps this was a sign from God that I should obey my earthly father and return to my family after all. I could picture my father's warm smile, my mother's teary-eyed tolerance at my presence. My father would find a suitable match for me, a man with wealth and status, probably quite a bit older; perhaps he had found one already. We would marry, I would become a mother, as naturally as every other woman of my station. I would carry on the de Fuentes Piedra legacy.

I did not find this progression of events completely distasteful, but it lacked the sense of fulfillment that I had grown used to as a member of a religious order. Would attending Mass only on Sundays and holidays fill the spiritual cavity within me? I thought not, because that cavity was deep, dark, and prone to infection when denied regular attention. My mood turned dark as I chopped potatoes one by one, pulling them from a woven basket and sliding my knife into their flesh.

Then, of course, there was the problem of the 'holy essence.' The small half-filled bottle was still in the deep pocket of my habit; it bounced and sloshed against my thigh with each step, like some sort of irregular self-flagellation. In the cold, rational light of day among my other Sisters engaged in work, my plan to test the liquid myself seemed hopelessly foolish. If the tincture was indeed making people sick, it was possible I could accidentally kill myself trying to demonstrate the liquid was safe, which would be a grave sin. That raised the question: Why would villagers continue to buy the tincture in droves if it harmed them? Did they not realize it was harming them? Or, and the possibility was almost too horrible to consider, did they buy and ingest the tincture because of its power to harm them? Was it some sort of self-righteous path to martyrdom, or a bleak, terrible path to suicide? Mother Superior had said it was for erasing sin, saving souls, and reserving places in Heaven—did the villagers believe this, to their own spiritual and corporeal detriment? I could make no sense of it, and the madness of the entire situation was causing my head to ache.

I also had to consider what it would mean if Mother Superior was telling the truth. If, in fact, the liquid was a holy, healing essence, as Mother Superior had indicated, then I had stolen something valuable from God, the abbey, and all the pilgrims who might have benefitted from ingesting it, which was a grave crime.

Maybe I would just smell the tincture, observe it at a closer range. The dimness of the bottlery and the scrutiny of the other Sisters prevented closer examination of the tincture as I poured during morning duty. In the privacy of my own cell, perhaps I would be able to find things in the bottle that would put my mind and soul at ease, once and for all. Then, of course, I could replace the bottle in the bottlery as a way to atone for my theft and repair the damage done. I would lay out the entire situation to Father Bruno at my next confession.

I shook my head, feeling exhausted. I must attempt to solve the mystery of the tincture, at the very least. That much was clear. I could not continue in such a state of moral and spiritual uncertainty; it was wreaking havoc on my eternal soul, spoiling my relationship with God and with the other Sisters. Something must change.

As if in answer to my thoughts, a horribly strong cramp rolled through my abdomen, and I resisted the urge to cry out, instead doubling over and taking a few deep breaths. Something had indeed changed; I had experienced monthly pains before, but never anything like this. Compared to this nauseating stabbing, my previous pains had been like insect bites, irritating but inconsequential.

In times of great pain, of which there had been but few in my life, thank the Lord, I had always tried to focus on the plight of those less fortunate. I wanted to meditate on and pray for relief from their agony, so that my own would recede in importance. I searched my mind for something meek, something pitiful, something I could use to center myself.

In a flash, the image of the poor man missing all of his fingers except his index and his thumb, the man who had come to purchase the tincture the previous day, popped into my mind. He had barely been able to grasp the bottle and pull it back through the grate. I wondered what accident had befallen him; perhaps a farming mishap, or a bloody fight over land or love. I thought about this man, prayed for him to find peace, prayed for—

The harsh ding of the bell by the grate interrupted my prayers. My head snapped up, and I saw the same older Sister who had retrieved me from the chamber standing near the jar full of coins. She was staring at the wooden windowsill when a hand that was hauntingly familiar, as though summoned by my very thoughts, slid through the grate. An empty glass bottle rolled across the wood. The disfigured hand pulled back, then reappeared with coins clutched between the only two fingers that remained—his index and thumb.

As I looked on, my hands hovering over my potatoes, the Sister righted the bottle, punched a funnel into its top, picked up a ladle, and filled the bottle with liquid from a bucket I only just noticed at her feet, the same sort of bucket I saw in abundance in the bottlery.

I shivered—this was the same man, back for another dose, even with the same bottle to refill. Surely, then, if he was well enough to travel all this way and purchase more, the tincture could not be harmful. The climb up the hilltop was not exactly treacherous, but it required a decent amount of strength and stamina, a feat that would be impossible for a severely ill person. Perhaps I would not need to investigate further after all; this man's presence seemed to answer all of my most pressing questions.

My blood slowed its rush through my veins and calm settled over me. The presence of this man felt like the sign I had been waiting for—now, I would not have to conduct my own haphazard investigation, I could disregard everything Berta had said, I could reevaluate my continued life at this abbey free from worries of evil or Godlessness.

I regretted my letter to my father, which had mentioned Berta's lies. My words would only add support to his argument that I should abandon this abbey. I had not sent it yet; maybe there was time yet to retract and revise it. Everything would be as it should.

My attention returned to my potatoes, my spirit calm for the first time since I had joined the Sisters of Divine Innocence.

I was reengaging with my work when, without warning, a commotion at the grate interrupted my gentle rhythm of grasping, handling, and chopping the potatoes. The older Sister screamed; the bottle of half-filled tincture slipped from her hand and shattered on the floor, sending liquid flying in all directions and choking the room with that sickly-sweet smell. At first, I was confused as to why she had reacted so violently, but then I glanced to the grate and the answer was clear. I could only see his body from fingertip to elbow, but it was obvious that the man on the other side, the repeat customer, had collapsed. Both of his arms now thrust through the grate at an odd angle, as though he had fallen in the act of reaching through to grasp the bottle, and now he was wedged against the metal lattice. There was also a new smell, a bilious scent that drifted into the room, twisting and combining with the odor of the tincture. Now I could see it—the man had vomited, and his excretion was dripping over the wood beneath the grate and spilling onto the floor in our kitchen. The vomit looked black and evil.

The older Sister screamed again; I think she had taken a step forward and cut her foot on a piece of the bottle glass, which pierced through her thin shoe. She fell backward, her foot in the air. I wanted to rush to her side, but I was rooted to the floor with fear, the chopping knife still in my hand.

What did this mean—this man who had purchased the tincture before, this man whom I had assumed was healthy, who would be the answer to all my painful questions, had just collapsed on our doorstep.

Was he dead? The possibility returned the chill-bumps to my flesh, and I crossed myself. *Hail Mary, full of grace.*

In the space created by the indecision that held me motionless, three other Sisters who had been chopping in the kitchen with me rushed to the grate. Two helped the fallen Sister up from the floor, half-leading, half-carrying her to a low chair against the wall. The third Sister peered tentatively at the man whose arms were still thrust through the grate. As I watched, black vomit dripped onto the Sister's shoe. She must not have noticed, but I was sure the smell would haunt her later. It would take several scrubbings before a scent like that would leave, if it would ever leave at all.

I expected the Sister attending to the man to tap his arms, snap her fingers, do anything to return him to consciousness and assess his wellbeing. Incredibly, the Sister did none of these things. Instead, she simply grasped both of the man's hands in hers and pushed roughly, sending him back through the grate. I heard a loud *thump* as his body hit the earth outside. Perhaps he really was dead. The callousness of the act appalled me.

The Sister at the grate grabbed a rag and a wash bucket and proceeded to clean the vomitus from the wood and floor, as though the cleaning duty she was performing was perfectly normal, perfectly routine—as though she were not cleaning up after a dead man.

With that thought, I finally lost the battle with my own body. I turned as swiftly as I could, trying to make it to the washbasin against the wall, but my body betrayed me. I vomited onto the floor, the contents of my stomach mostly thick strings of mucus, seeing as how I had eaten very little since my arrival at the abbey.

All four Sisters in the room looked up at me, crouched as I was, still heaving. The Sister at the grate rolled her eyes, and I intuited the thought that flitted through her mind—*No doubt I will have to clean that one up, too.* The others simply glared at me before returning to their business of administering to the Sister with the bleeding foot.

I stood up, beset yet again not by nausea, but by a painful, shuddering cramp. What was happening to me? I had barely been ill a day in my life, and now I felt nearly rotten to my core. Something was not normal here, and my body was trying to force that realization upon me.

Once again, the tolling of the bells saved me from further embarrassment. Before the other Sisters could move, I hustled out of the kitchen, hoping midmorning prayer would reset my mind and my body.

* * *

The chorus of coughs in the church during midmorning prayer was stronger than I had ever heard before. Although I was surprised at the speed of the coughing Sisters' deterioration, I was unsurprised by their bodily reactions to breathing in the dark miasma permeating this abbey atop the hill. Perhaps coughing and illness were constant companions for the Sisters here; they all had handkerchiefs at the ready, as though their ragged breathing was a seasonal ailment, as regular as the sun rising and setting.

I took a deep inhale myself, curious to see if there was a hitch in my breath or a tickle in my throat, anything to indicate an oncoming illness. Why should I be spared when everyone around me was succumbing? I had not been at the abbey long, and I was, as far as I could tell, far younger than most of the other Sisters. Perhaps my youth and my short exposure to the abbey air protected me. Whatever the reason for my continued health, I thanked God. Then, as a cramp hit me hard and fast yet again, I prayed for deliverance from my woman's pain. I would have rather had the cough.

After midmorning prayer, during which I repeated the Saint Michael prayer silently, in spite of Mother Superior's alternate recitation—*Saint Michael, the Archangel, defend us in battle*—two groups of Sisters formed as we all rose from the pews. One group headed for the open doorway into the cloister, where weak sunlight streamed through the arch and onto the stone floor. The other group clustered around the altar. I was confused, but only for a second; the group around the altar funneled through the small door and into the chamber of divine decomposition. I noticed, not without concern, that most, if not all, of the Sisters with serious coughs comprised that group, as though they expected prayer to Berta's body to heal them.

Standing as I was between one group and the other, I quickly made up my mind and headed for the sunlight, which grew dimmer even as I emerged into the open air of the cloister. Mother Superior led this group, and I half-expected her to shake her head and point me back into the church as she had done before with barely concealed relish, but she only nodded and began walking through the cloister, the rest of us at her heels. Maybe I had been spared the chamber because I was free of coughing. Of course, now I was more than willing to take my woman's pain over the cough.

My skin was just beginning to warm beneath my habit when God tested me with the fiercest cramp I had ever felt. It ripped a hole through my abdomen and sent me sprawling on the stone walkway, writhing in pain. I must have cried out, because the other Sisters turned abruptly, falling upon me with a mixture of concern and annoyance on their faces. Mother Superior stayed erect, staring down at me with an almost pleased expression.

Nobody spoke, but the Sisters seemed to know what to do. They lifted me up, none too gently, and walked me back to my cell, moving quicker than I would have expected of older women. They laid me atop my straw mattress and drained from the room like rainwater from a roof, leaving me alone and in pain. Despite their caretaking actions, I felt no comfort whatsoever. Once again, I felt irrevocably alone.

Wetness bloomed between my legs shortly thereafter, finally bringing me some relief. The rush of my blood usually had the effect of silencing the cramps, or at least reducing their intensity. With fierce concentration, I prayed to God that the pattern would continue, and my pain would diminish to a more manageable level. As I spoke to God, I rose to grab my rags, which I tucked in place to catch my blood. It would not do to stain my habit with such grave uncleanliness.

While hovering near my washbasin, I glanced at my table. It was bare, my letter nowhere to be found. A Sister must have dispatched it for me. Unexpected relief overwhelmed me, and I realized a small part of me had, in sinister partnership with my wild imagination, thought I might never be able to speak to my father again. Deep within my heart, I had feared my ability to communicate with him would be obstructed. With the letter most likely safely with the courier now, I felt my body unclench muscles I had not even realized I was tightening.

With my mind closer to ease and my rags secure, I lay back down, resolving to enjoy the short respite I had been granted. My body felt exhausted, but my mind would not disengage. As seemed to be the new way of things for me at this abbey, thoughts swirled and fought within my mind—thoughts of my father, thoughts of Berta, thoughts of the tincture. The tincture!

I remembered with a start that the small bottle was still in my pocket. I thrust a hand deep into my habit, my fingers grasping for the glass. I felt nothing. Panic rose up the back of my throat, and I stuffed my hand deeper into my pocket, into every nook in the coarse fabric. It must be there somewhere. I had not heard it drop to the ground. Could someone have taken it?

The Sisters' rough handling of me when I fell to the cloister stone suddenly made a horrible sort of sense. Dark suspicion crept into my mind; somehow, one or even all of them knew my secret, and in the commotion, someone had slipped a hand into my pocket, removing my only clue, my only evidence, the foundation of my investigation. They knew about me, they distrusted me, and soon they would come for me. Archbishop Orriva would soon return to spirit me away to yet another abbey, or worse, take me back to my father and out of the religious life altogether. I was a failure; I had failed myself, my family, my Sisters, and, worst of all, God. There would be no turning back.

Stop! I finally screamed inside my head. *Stop this tide of darkness immediately!* I was losing control of myself, letting my suspicions and fears take charge. It had to stop now. A verse from the book of James came to me then: 'Detract not one another, my brethren. He that detracteth his brother, or he that judgeth his brother, detracteth the law, and judgeth the law. But if thou judge the law, thou art not a doer of the law, but a judge. There is one lawgiver, and judge, that is able to destroy and to deliver. But who art thou that judgest thy neighbor?' It was true. Who was I to judge the other Sisters, Mother Superior, even Berta? Humility mingled with shame and crept over me like a fog.

I sighed and stilled my searching hands. Rational thought would help me, of course. I had probably simply lost the bottle. Even now, it was likely lying to the side of the cloistered stone path, wedged in a tuft of grass. Or, if somebody had indeed taken the bottle from my pocket, then they must have had a good reason. After all, no one had come forth to accuse me of wrongdoing, so it was possible whoever took the stolen bottle was looking out for me, helping me to turn the other cheek away from sin.

Or, a voice in my head whispered conspiratorially, *I am being watched—just as Berta said.*

I shook my head, trying to clear it. Whatever had happened to the bottle, I needed to tread very, very cautiously—both to avoid sin and to avoid raising the ire of my fellow Sisters. I had promised Archbishop Orriva I would be pious and obedient here, that I would recover. It was time to start keeping my promises.

I rolled onto my side in the bed. Despite the chill of my cell, sweat broke on my brow, and a spiky but less painful cramp skittered through my belly. I could feel the flow of blood as it exited my body, and I wondered with a sort of detached disgust if this was what it would feel like to sit in one of those stone chairs in that small, hot room and feel your essence drain out of you into a bucket.

* * *

The bells tolled for midday prayer just as a knock came at my cell door, awakening me from a light doze. I wanted to stay within sleep's realm forever.

Nevertheless, I must answer God's call. Fresh blood gushed from me as I stood up slowly from the bed. The rags between my legs felt saturated and sticky; I would need to change them before I could reenter the church for prayer. Unlike the Jews, Catholics had no reservations about menstruating women entering holy spaces, and I considered myself lucky. I had been told Jewish women went into seclusion for several days until the flow of their blood ceased, and that everything they touched while bleeding was considered unclean. I could not deny that uncontrolled bleeding certainly made me feel unclean, but there was an important difference between cleanliness of the body and cleanliness of the spirit. Some of the most holy people, including saints, were wreathed in filth.

Reaching my basin, with a swiftly practiced hand, I swapped the soiled rags for clean ones. The used rags dripped scarlet onto the floor, and I tossed them into my small basin, intending to clean them properly when I had the opportunity.

Later, when the Sisters rose to exit the church after midday prayer, the same two groups formed once again. This time, however, the members of each group were swapped, as though they were visiting Berta's body in turn, which I supposed was exactly what was happening. Without looking at Mother Superior's scowl, I knew which way she intended for me to go. With mounting dread, I shuffled to join the group poised near the altar.

The chamber of divine decomposition felt smaller than it had previously, even though there were half the number of Sisters crushed into the close space. Despite my misgivings, I was curious to see if Berta's body had finally succumbed to decomposition. Since I was again at the back of the group, I had to raise myself up on my toes to get a better look over the other Sisters' veils.

One thing struck me immediately, before even noticing the condition of Berta's body; shockingly, Berta was no longer alone in the chamber. In the stone chair next to Berta, with her still-bright golden-red eyes and her impossibly rosy pink flesh, sat a figure dressed in only a rough jacket, naked from the waist down. As my gazed trailed downward, it did not take long for me to realize this was a man. I could not help but gasp—a man? In one of the holiest places in this abbey? Likely a villager, no less, which was even more puzzling. My eyes drifted again, and then I saw his hands, resting inert at his sides.

One of them was missing all fingers except for the index and the thumb.

A breathy gasp of horror rushed up my throat, but I choked it back down, disguising it as a cough. I recognized that man, the man who had bought a bottle of tincture, had come back for more, and had ended up collapsing on the other side of the grate. I had not fully realized he had died, even though I had strongly suspected it. I had been so engrossed in my own interior dramas that all thoughts of the man's possible death had been pushed from my mind. *Dear Lord, please deliver me from my wicked vanity!*

I could deny it no longer; death had taken this man. He had been, without a doubt, the man who had drunk the tincture, the man who had perished in front of me. Was that evidence enough to support Berta's claims that the tincture was killing innocent people? Was it possible my suspicions, sinful as they seemed at first, were actually correct?

Whether the answers to those questions were yes or no, a more urgent one arose in my mind—why was this man's body here, of all places? He was not a religious, he was not an aristocrat—that much was clear by his clothing. There was nothing singular about him. Then, of course, there was the fact of his masculinity. Having his corpse seated so close to Berta felt wrong; it felt like a violation.

Heat flushed my cheeks as another cramp sent blood coursing into my rags, which were quickly becoming saturated yet again. The Sisters in front of me had all bowed their heads, and the silence was deafening, broken only a few times by small coughs. With their heads lowered, I could see the man's body a bit better. To my astonishment, and in stark contrast to Berta, his flesh appeared to already be decomposing, and at an unexpectedly rapid pace—his fingers, at least those which remained, had turned black at the tips, and his eyes were closed and sunken in his pale, withered face. A delicate *drip-drop* broke the silence.

It was not coming from Berta.

A verse from Philippians sprang into my mind unbidden: 'Beware of the dogs: beware of evil works: beware of those who mutilate the flesh.' I swallowed hard and bowed my head to pray.

O Mary, conceived without sin, pray for us who have recourse to thee, and for those who do not have recourse to thee, especially the enemies of the Church and those recommended to thee. Amen.

If this man was in the chamber, and the Sisters were collecting his bodily fluids as if he were a fellow religious, what did that mean? Had there been other corpses like this man's here in this room? Were the Sisters profiting off of death in such a gruesome and unnatural way?

I did not want to believe it, but all the evidence led to that simple conclusion with an even simpler motivation: greed. On my first day at the abbey, Mother Superior had told me this chamber served as a place to honor our fellow Sisters in death. She must have been lying or, at the very least, not telling the entire truth.

Stop, stop! Going down this path yet again would surely lead to breaking a vow. There was some innocent explanation, there had to be. Perhaps this man's family had paid for a special burial, or the Sisters were honoring him, given that his death had happened at our door? This evening, when we had the chance to speak, I would ask someone. Perhaps not Mother Superior, but one of the older Sisters. I would hear the explanation, and I would be satisfied.

The *drip-drop* invaded my thoughts again, and more of Mother Superior's words returned to me: "We collect this holy essence." When I had asked her why, she had only said, "It erases sin." In light of everything I had experienced since, that conversation seemed to be a further confirmation of Berta's claims. For what other purpose could they be collecting the bodily fluids, if not to supply the 'holy essence' that filled those bottles, which they could then turn around and sell as panaceas for the mortal soul?

A new avenue of thought opened itself to me, a dark alley that chilled me to my core. If the Sisters worked each day to fill the small bottles, then they must have a steady supply of those bodily fluids. Yet, until now, I had only seen Sister Faustina and Berta in the chamber—and Berta was not the source of any bodily fluids, that much was clear from her perpetually rosy complexion. The man sitting beside her with his missing fingers was not a religious, had not devoted his life to God in that way. Was his essence still considered holy? I could not imagine that was the case.

So, where—or, more accurately, who—were all of the fluids coming from?

CHAPTER SIXTEEN

Sister Rafaela

My belly felt like a hard little stone by the time we flowed out of the chamber and into the musty air of the church. Sisters were coughing harshly around me, their breath hitching and pounding almost rhythmically. I still felt no tickling in my chest, but the pain in my abdomen was enough to keep me mired in discomfort.

The more I pondered how full bucket after full bucket entered that bottlery, the more certain I became that the Sisters did not quibble over the source of their tincture. How could they, when the demand to erase sin was so high, and their supply had to match it? Could it be that in their lust for coin, they had ceased to make any distinction between the 'holy essence' of a religious and the drippings of a layperson's corpse?

These dark musings seemed to lay the lies bare, extinguishing my appetite as I sat down in the refectory for the noon meal. When I saw my food, my stomach fluttered with distaste. The plate in front of me, much to my surprise, held a generous cut of red meat, cooked so lightly it was almost raw. The blood pooled on my plate, tinting my potatoes a nauseating pink. Even my mug of small beer had a reddish sheen.

I looked up, searching for a different, less offensive place to rest my gaze, and found every other Sister's plate bereft of meat. Instead, they dined delicately on small filets of roasted fish, nibbling around the bones.

What was the meaning of this? Why had I been singled out? Perhaps the Sisters were welcoming me with a special meal seeing as I was still new to the abbey, still in need of a welcome—but, given how the meal had been served without ceremony, without any sort of pomp, that explanation felt hollow. Had they simply run out of portions of fish, and I happened to be the lucky one to receive a cut of red meat? Where had they even procured it?

The aroma rising from my plate made my stomach growl despite my misgivings, and I picked up my fork. Wasting food was a sin, one I had already been guilty of committing, and I could not risk offending the Sisters or God the Father yet again by refusing this perfectly good, if not sumptuous, meal. My cramps had abated, so I tucked into the meat with only slight hesitation.

The meat was indeed nearly raw, but I found I had missed that fleshy, primal taste. When I was a child, my family's dinner table had often sported expensive cuts of meat, imported fruits, green vegetables, even chocolate and coffee. I was no stranger to fine food, but I had not had the taste of such things on my tongue since entering the Rafaelite abbey all those years ago.

My knife cut through the meat as if it were freshly churned butter, and before long, the only remnant of the roast was the cooling pool of blood. My appetite ignited, I fell upon the scarlet-stained potatoes with vigor. When my plate was clean, I reached for my mug. After one sip, I realized it wasn't red-tinted small beer in my cup, but rich red wine. The alcohol slid down my throat like a snake. With my mug drained, I sat back, stifling a belch.

A cramp rolled through me then, but its intensity had lessened considerably. I thanked God the Father for my meal and for the gradual lessening of my pain. I supposed I also had the Sisters to thank, even though no one had displayed even a modicum of friendliness toward me.

With a newfound vivacity, I stood with the other Sisters to clean my plate. I stepped into the kitchen shyly, the morning's violent episode still very clear in my mind. Where there had been broken glass and black vomitus at the grate, now there was only freshly swept stone and scrubbed wood. My own sick had been mopped up as well, and I felt my cheeks blushing at the thought of a put-upon Sister cleaning up after one of her own.

I busied myself sweeping the cloister in the fresh air until our period of quiet time. The day was overcast, but the thin sunlight that did peek through the clouds partially dispelled the dark miasma hovering perpetually over the abbey like a fine mist. I tried to steer my focus toward tranquil meditation as I swept stray leaves and dirt clear of the cloister stones, but my mind veered back to the dead man in the chamber. With nourishing food and drink filling my belly and minimizing my woman's pain, my suspicions were less urgent, less damning. Yet, I could not help but wonder: Was the man's presence in the chamber a proper part of the abbey's religious rite or a sinful transgression?

As I swept, I felt my blood rushing, saturating my rags, and when the bells tolled to signal quiet time, I hurried to my cell. I planned to clean and exchange my rags and possibly pen another letter to my father. I believed I now understood more, or, more accurately, had now been exposed to more, and I felt my letter of the previous day required further explanation, or at least greater detail. I did not want any guidance father offered to be colored by sentiments and observations of mine that no longer reflected my true concerns.

As I entered my cell, I became aware of two things simultaneously. First, my soiled rags from earlier in the day were not in my washbasin where I had left them. Second, there was a small piece of parchment with a ragged edge resting on the floor just in front of my open door.

I turned first to the parchment—had someone left me a note? I sighed in relief at the thought of a fellow Sister offering words of encouragement, or sympathy, or explanation—anything, really. I felt starved for companionship in this lonely abbey where I still did not know most of the Sisters' names. The only person with whom I felt kinship was Father Bruno, and such a relationship was, due to custom and necessity, quite limited. I could speak to him only during my confession; any other contact would be improper for a bride of Christ.

I knelt down and scooped up the rough parchment. I could see scribbles of writing as I unfolded it, and I sat down at my table to read.

A dim horror grew steadily in my breast as I read words that were all too familiar:

I also hoped to ask your advice on a difficult matter that has arisen here…

My heart seized—it was, without a doubt, my letter to father. The letter I assumed a thoughtful Sister had posted for me. Instead of putting it in the hands of a trusted courier, someone had stolen my letter from my table, slit open the envelope, read my missive, and ripped from it the most important portion, the part where I revealed my suspicions about the Sisters' 'holy essence.' Then, that person had shoved the torn, offending piece of parchment under my door.

To my dismay, I had been right to be suspicious and fearful, after all.

What did this disturbing violation mean? Was it a reprimand? A warning? A threat? All three? My skin felt suddenly itchy, and a cramp, strong yet again, sent me doubling over in my chair. Someone was watching me, that much was certain. My private correspondence had been compromised. I could not even summon the optimism to hope the remainder of my letter had been sent to father; the other half of my parchment was probably ashes by now. What would my father think of my lack of response, and how could I reopen that channel of communication? I did not want him to believe his only daughter was ignoring his request, disregarding his grief through callous silence.

What to do? Write another letter? If someone was incensed by my very circumspect disclosure of the 'holy essence,' surely talk of the dead man and the possible body of lies the Sisters perpetuated was unthinkable. If I were to get a private message to my father without interception, I needed to either watch the letter travel from my hand to the courier's or write in some sort of code. I slumped in my chair, overwhelmed. Neither option seemed feasible.

Wait—there was a third option. It was clear I could not trust the Sisters, and I still did not yet know how to dispatch a letter of my own. Asking another Sister for assistance was an invitation to have another letter of mine stolen. However, there was one person I could trust. One person who would be able to evade the Sisters: Father Bruno. If I could slip my letter to him, there was a good chance I could reach my father after all. I resolved to have a new letter ready to give to Father Bruno at my next confession.

Warmth trickled down my leg, snapping me away from my plotting. What was happening? Never before had my woman's curse been so severe. I stood to retrieve fresh rags and exchange them for my soiled ones, when the absence of my previous rags in the washbasin returned to the forefront of my thoughts.

I quickly cleaned myself and exchanged my rags, rinsing the dirty one in the basin and hanging it to dry. I was certain I had not cleaned the previous one; in my haste, I had tossed it in the basin, resolving to clean it later. Had someone taken it to clean it for me?

A derisive snort erupted from my nose before I could stop it. Was I a fool? Surely so; only a fool could think the same Sisters who would steal and destroy private correspondence would also perform laundry service. I wanted to think well of my fellow Sisters, to assume the best of others, I truly did, but those sentiments felt weak and insubstantial, and above all, foolish. I could not afford to be foolish anymore, not when I was being so closely watched. Someone had stolen my rags, and I did not know why. Given my experience, the reason could hardly be good. Sharp shivers jabbed at my spine as I stood, staring at my basin.

In my short experience with the Sisters of Divine Innocence, unspoken answers to my internal questions were usually tinged with darkness. What had happened to the man who collapsed at the grate? He died, and the Sisters placed his body in the chamber next to Berta. Where did the liquid come from? It was the 'holy essence' collected from decomposing bodies. Where did the Sisters obtain the bodies? The answer to that question, I was quickly coming to believe, was anywhere they could get them. Why did someone steal my bloody rags? I was not sure I wanted to know the answer.

When the bells tolled for midafternoon prayer, I crossed myself, feeling weary and exhausted. I was not sure I could endure another spell in the chamber of divine decomposition, watching the dead man rot as Berta stayed vital, those golden-red eyes dancing and laughing. Perhaps I would be lucky this time.

I hustled to the church, hoping the time between now and our hour of recreation would pass quickly. As I walked, I cast a suspicious eye on every Sister. Was she the one who tore apart my letter? Or was it her? Did that older Sister steal my rags? Without meaning to, I locked eyes with a middle-aged Sister, her forehead creased with wrinkles. She offered me a hesitant, wan smile, dousing the fire kindled by my doubts, fears, and suspicions. Was my mind running away with things, yet again? I feared I could not trust my fellow Sisters, but maybe it was myself I could not trust.

I felt the desperate need to speak to someone, anyone—except for maybe Mother Superior and Sister Leonella—who could offer even the tiniest bit of clarity to the picture forming in my brain of this abbey atop the hill and its strange customs. The feeling of being an outsider, an unwanted one at that, had only intensified, and, much to my dismay, the thought of exiting the religious life and returning to the comfort and protection of my father's home began to feel devastatingly attractive.

O God, please shine your holy light on my life, help me to make the right choices, help me to obey my vows, to be a good and gracious servant to You, and a helpful fellow to the other Sisters. Please take the fear and suspicion from my heart and replace it with strength and peace. Amen.

When midafternoon prayer ended and we all rose, I nearly sobbed with relief when Mother Superior ignored me. I emerged from the church, refreshed with God, into the dim light filtering through gray clouds. I still felt confused, but some of the weight had been lifted.

Behind me, the coughs of the Sisters remaining in the church were now so loud, I could hear them clearly even as I walked away. Some sickness was descending on our abbey, and it was moving at a rapid pace. Even as I prayed to God for salvation and protection, health and peace, I wondered if the illness was a punishment for sinful acts. The thought chilled me to my core, explosively rekindling my fears. If the growing chorus of coughs was indeed a punishment, then I thought I knew what actions comprised our sins—and, terribly, they were numerous. Raising up dead bodies as holy, capturing, selling, and having others consume a tincture of drippings from the corpses… and those were just the beginning of the sins I suspected.

A verse from Micah crept into my brain. 'The holy man is perished out of the earth, and there is none upright among men: they all lie in wait for blood, every one hunteth his brother to death.' I could not speak for the other Sisters, but I certainly felt the breath of the hunter at my back.

My stomach churned and churned, but I continued walking with the others toward the refectory. I hoped to perform a menial task during work period, something that would be repetitive enough to distract me but simple enough to avoid aggravating my angry body, which felt poised to revolt.

Before I could pass through the doors into the kitchen, Sister Leonella stepped in front of me, her eyes slightly frantic, her scars standing out in stark relief against her pale face. Without saying a word, she produced a broom and thrust it into my hand. I would be sweeping the cloister yet again—a task I really did not mind much, since the dark miasma was a bit lighter out of doors.

I made to turn away when an older Sister poked her head through the doorway, a question in her eyes. Sister Leonella turned, and in the shoulder-width crack of light left open, I could see into the kitchen.

Oh, what I saw. My view gave a perfect frame of the kitchen washbasin. A Sister was standing before it, a bucket at her feet. In her hands was a bloody set of rags, rags that looked far too familiar, even though there was nothing particularly distinctive about them. I heard the dribble as the Sister wrung out the rags into the bucket, wrung out my woman's blood, I was certain of it. Sister Leonella did not see my horrified expression, for I turned and fled just as she disappeared into the kitchen herself.

I made it barely outside the refectory before I bent over and vomited for the second time that day. The acrid smell clung to my nostrils, and I stood up with great difficulty, leaning on my broom handle. What I had just seen—

Breathe, Rafaela, breathe. I took one heaving inhale, then let everything out in a rush that felt like a half-sob. Losing my composure would serve no purpose. What had I really seen, anyway? I had seen one of the Sisters wringing out dirty rags. Any number of explanations could apply to that scenario—the Sister was washing rags dirtied by cleaning the counters, or perhaps she was even graciously cleaning my woman's rags for me, as I had hoped when I found the rags missing from my washbasin. I needed to stop being so quick to assume the worst of my fellow Sisters, even when I thought I had reason to do so. Was that the right action to take? Or were my instincts trying to protect me from making the same ghastly mistake I had made by ignoring my concerns regarding the Rafaelites until it was too late? Was now the time to speak up, or to stay silent?

I bowed my head, desperate for clarity. *Our Father, Who art in heaven, hallowed be Thy name; Thy kingdom come; Thy will be done on earth as it is in heaven. Give us this day our daily bread; and forgive us our trespasses as we forgive those who trespass against us; and lead us not into temptation, but deliver us from evil. Amen.*

'Deliver us from evil.' Even at the Rafaelite abbey at its worst time, I never felt those words of the Lord's prayer so acutely. *Please, God, deliver me from evil.*

I dismissed my worries about the rags and tried to focus on sweeping the leaves from the cloister. Deep breaths rolled into and out of my chest. The rags did not matter, not really, anyway. Why should I care if someone had taken them? My hands shook slightly, and I gripped the broom more tightly. The sun passed from behind a cloud, but its rays offered no warmth, only a searing, cold light that pained my eyes.

I lost myself in the rhythm of the sweeping—left, right, left, right, step forward—until the door to the refectory opened, and the Sister I had seen with the rags trudged out. A bucket swung from one of her clenched fists. *Oh God.*

I had swept my way back to within a few paces of the refectory door, so the Sister walked close to me. When she passed me without glancing up or acknowledging my presence in any way, I caught a whiff of scent from the bucket that almost made me dizzy. It was the unmistakable coppery smell of blood.

No, no, no. Something was wrong with my mind, that couldn't be possible. It was probably just soiled wash water, tinted with the blood of animals. I had not bled enough to fill a bucket even a few inches, and even if it was my blood inside the vessel, that was no reason for hysteria. I knew my thoughts were reasonable, but they did not lessen my alarm. All I could think about was a bucket full of blood, full of *my* blood, impossible though it was. I gagged, then swallowed hard to keep myself from vomiting again. If I did vomit, would they collect that, too?

I stopped sweeping, the broom now motionless in my hands. I stared after the Sister, her bucket sloshing with each step. *Stop, Rafaela,* I told myself. *It is nothing. Stop this before you do something you cannot take back!*

I yearned to stop my whirling thoughts, but everything felt out of my control. Despair and an aching, growing horror blossomed in my breast when the Sister turned on the cloistered path and headed for the bottlery.

I knew what happened to liquids in buckets within that charred, dark place.

*   *   *

Work period transitioned into vespers, and numbness crept through my limbs like a not entirely unwelcome intruder. Around me, more Sisters coughed, but their faces held an almost lustful excitement. Whatever had given them such joy eluded me. Nothing on this abbey atop the hill was as it seemed, and I was starting to wonder if God was trying to steer me back to my father's house.

Before supper began, all of the Sisters crowded around the small door to the chamber of divine decomposition. A few Sisters were nearly bouncing on their toes like children. Dread filled me, and I hung my head as I followed. There was nothing else to do but go with the others.

The chamber was much the same as I had last seen it, with one exception: the dead man had withered considerably. His remaining fingers, from what I could see, were black and curled inward. His eyelids were sunken, his face white, his stomach bloated. A constant *drip-drop* echoed around the room.

The Sisters, however, were not focused on the dead man. All of their attention was fixed on Berta.

With a sudden, nauseating clarity I understood what filled them with such elation. Berta's body, in stark contrast to her companion's, was even yet still pink and fresh. Her golden-red eyes were fire-bright, her face full. Her body had not swollen under her habit, nor had her fingers blackened or curled. She looked as though she were simply holding her breath, waiting for the right moment to inhale and speak.

There was now no doubt. Berta's body was still not decomposing as it should.

I, and every Sister in that room, understood what that suggested. Could Berta really be incorruptible? The thought of Berta as a saint repelled me in a very visceral way—a new cramp rolled through my abdomen, and I felt another gush of fresh blood. She had said such horrible things to me, and the way the light danced behind her eyes set my body to trembling.

Mother Superior led us in prayer, one of her hands placed on Berta's shoulder. A beatific smile now graced Berta's features, and the incongruity of the whole tableaux stung my eyes. Madness crept toward me on insectile legs, and, not for the first time in my life, I felt untethered from reality.

Stop, stop, Rafaela. It is only a lack of sleep and your woman's curse that make you think this way. I tried to reassure myself—because, truthfully, it had been several days since I had slept peacefully, and my woman's pain was as bad as it had ever been. My mind was primed to see conspiracy where there was none... was it not?

I began to question everything, and my suspicions about the tincture, my woman's rags, and all else I thought I knew began to flicker and fade. I was certain about nothing. I teetered on my fence line, the wood starting to cut into my feet.

Dear God, please give me the clarity to see what is true, the strength to carry out Your will, and the courage to bear it all.

Finally, after what felt like an eternity, Mother Superior finished her prayer, and we all filed out of the hot chamber. The thought of supper felt impossible, but, as with entering the chamber, there was nothing else to do but follow the others. I calmed myself with the knowledge that after I had choked down my food, I would have an hour wherein I could speak to the others. I could gather information, I could ask questions, I could finally have a chance to understand what was happening at this abbey. I could put the torments in my head to rest, once and for all. I would find a way to be content here, to serve God here. That was all that mattered.

Even cloaked in silence, the refectory buzzed with excitement, reminding me of the hive of bees I had once found in a tree on my father's property. I had been a young child, unsure of the world, and I had poked the hive with a stick. The bees had come rushing out, and I had run so fast my legs lost feeling. Even then, I had been stung.

The Sisters tore into their food with an almost greedy gusto that seemed inappropriate, and I picked up my fork to face yet another hunk of very rare red meat. The scent of iron drifted from my plate, too similar to the bucket of blood I thought I had seen that Sister carrying to the bottlery. My stomach recoiled, but I ate the meat anyway, slowly and steadily, interspersing my bites with sips of scarlet wine, as fine as any I had tasted at my father's table.

I distracted myself as I chewed by formulating questions in my head. I had to start with something concrete, something inarguable. The dead man in the chamber came to mind—his presence was a certainty. Forgetting to chew, I swallowed a large chunk of meat, nearly choking on the mass. Spluttering, I earned disapproving looks from the other Sisters as I chased the lump with more wine. When I was finally calm, determination filled me, far preferable to the writhing uncertainty that had been my near constant companion.

I needed to know why the dead man had been placed in the chamber of divine decomposition. With that question answered, perhaps I could gain a new perspective on the Sisters and the abbey. Perhaps there would be no need for more questions.

But, if not, I must ask about the tincture and its source—but I would have to do this very gingerly, as I did not want to raise the ire of Mother Superior and Sister Leonella yet again. Finally, I wanted to ask about my rags, to better understand where they had gone, what I had seen… and, potentially, what was being done with my blood.

* * *

When the bells tolled to signal our hour of recreation, the refectory erupted in talking, gasping, and giggling, all punctuated by rough coughing. The shock of the noise after so much silence startled me as I rose to clear my plate with the others. I listened hard, trying to decipher the meaning from all the overlapping voices.

The source of the Sisters' giddiness became clear very quickly—only one thing was on everyone's mind: Berta's body. Many of the Sisters were already declaring her incorruptible. For my own part, nothing I had observed of Berta, besides her body's curious resistance to decomposition, had marked her as saintly. She was more of a devil, in my opinion.

Of course, I had been wrong before—but still. I felt unsure of most things in this abbey, and in my life in general, but my one unwavering certainty was that Berta was no saint, and to think and speak as if she were felt like blasphemy. Spain was already full of saints—Saint Casilda of Toledo, Saint Ignatius of Loyola, Saint Laura of Córdoba, Saint Teresa of Ávila, and of course, Saint James in Santiago de Compostela— and those were just a handful. Those were real saints--people with good works and miracles to their names, who never cursed God nor laughed at his servants.

"Did you see her eyes?" one Sister walking near me asked another, her voice too loud. "With Sister Faustina and Sister Juana, their eyes were one of the first things to leave their bodies. Sister Berta's eyes are remarkably intact."

"I must say, standing in front of that golden gaze feels holy," her companion replied, a little smile on her wizened face. She coughed once, hard, into her fist. It sounded wet. "I pray extra time with Sister Berta will banish this cough of mine."

I turned away from their conversation, feeling ill. Were they blind to what was happening? That 'golden gaze' was far from holy; staring into

Berta's eyes felt like looking through a doorway to hell.

Then again, if all the others could feel something, and I was the only one who could not, what did that say about me? If I was the outsider, was I in the right or in the wrong?

I washed my dish in the kitchen basin, catching wind of another, similar conversation.

"Her hands are still so perfect!" one Sister said. "With the man, regardless of his deformity, his remaining fingers are already blackened and twisted, and his time in the chamber has been far shorter than Sister Berta's!"

I was struck by the callous way she referred to 'the man,' as though his death could not be laid at our door, as though he was nothing but rotting meat.

"I never thought I would live to see an incorruptible body," another Sister replied, her breathing fast and shallow with excitement.

"Let us not be hasty, Sisters," Mother Superior's voice rose above the din, but she sounded indulgent instead of reproachful. "It has not been very long. Please suppress your enthusiasm, carry out your duties with reverence, and remember to direct your prayers to the holy Father, not to an earthbound spirit. Nothing has been confirmed."

"Yes, Mother," a few Sisters responded, their voices tight, as if holding in squeals of joy.

Mother Superior nodded once, then swept out of the kitchen, Sister Leonella at her heels like a dog, as always. When the door swung shut behind them, the room once again exploded with talk of Berta's miraculous body.

I crept toward a small cluster of older Sisters who were speaking in lower tones, whether due to some sensitive subject matter or their age, I could not be sure.

"This will require verification," one Sister said, the oldest I had seen so far.

"Well, of course," another responded. "Did you not hear of the Italian woman, Zita? The Church exhumed her body a few years ago and found it incorrupt, but they have yet to declare her a saint."

"What could be taking so long?"

"You know the inspection of the relics requires a bishop, and that can happen only after the relics are sealed in wax and sent to Rome. It is a very involved process."

"That makes sense, I suppose. The Church could not declare every body with abnormal decomposition a saint."

"Of course not. There is also the question of miracles."

I chimed in at this point. "Miracles?"

A Sister who had not yet spoken said, "What Sister Cecelia means is Sister Berta must perform miracles to even be considered for sainthood."

The oldest one, Sister Cecelia, spoke again. "Miracles after death, that is. Which is why it is especially important for us to visit Sister Berta and pray, to give her the chance to plead with God on our behalf."

Sister Cecelia's words made sense, but their meaning frightened me. The Sisters intended to spend even more time with Berta's body? I wondered if Berta would speak, or perhaps had already spoken, to other Sisters in death the way she had spoken to me.

If she had spoken at all, that was.

One of her companions asked, "But, Sister Cecelia, what of the candles? Surely that was miraculous, how they burst into brighter flame before our very eyes during the responsory?"

Sister Cecelia shrugged one bony shoulder. "That was an impressive display, to be sure, but I do not think we can say it was miraculous."

The other Sisters murmured in reluctant agreement. They wore their hope baldly on their faces; we all knew what it would mean for the abbey if we could claim a true saint. Pilgrimages, honors, royal visits, and, of course, mountains of coin.

"And if she is not a saint?" I asked, earning irritated looks from the other Sisters.

"Then our prayers will shepherd her to heaven anyway," Sister Cecelia said. "We must—"

The rest of her words were swallowed up in an abrupt fit of coughing, which bent her over in pain with its force. One of the other Sisters held her shoulders to keep her from toppling over.

"Perhaps you should spend time praying in the chamber now," she said, releasing Sister Cecelia as the coughing passed and she was able to catch her breath.

"I think that would be wise," Sister Cecelia said, her voice thin and fluttery.

"Shall I accompany you?"

"No, no, it is best I pray alone," Sister Cecelia said, waving her away. "Peace be with you, Sisters."

We mumbled our responses as Sister Cecelia shuffled away.

The other Sisters dispersed in pairs, except for the one who had held Sister Cecelia's shoulders as she convulsed. I remained standing there with her, studying her. She was also older, but not as old as many of the others. Now was my opportunity, and I did not want to waste it.

"I am Sister Rafaela," I said, by way of introduction.

She looked up at me warily. "I know who you are. I am Sister Catherine."

I plunged forward, albeit carefully, determined to receive some sort of answers to my questions. "I must ask you something, Sister. I have been working in the bottlery these last few days during morning duty, and I was wondering something."

Sister Catherine lifted one eyebrow. "And what is that, Sister?"

My body wanted to curl inward, wanted to avoid the Sister's stony gaze, but I had to ask my question. There might not be another opportunity. "I was just wondering… what is it we are bottling?"

Sister Catherine's blue eyes hardened so quickly I took a small step back, as if pushed. "A holy essence," she said through gritted teeth.

Impressed by my own fortitude, I pushed again, even though fear tickled the back of my throat. "Yes, Mother Superior said as much, but... how is it made?" I wanted—no, I needed—to hear someone say the truth, plainly and frankly.

Sister Catherine coughed lightly into her palm, then frowned. Her eyes bored into mine, sizing me up before answering carefully, "It is not my place to say."

I stifled a sigh and tried a different strategy; after all, I was fairly certain of the liquid's source. "Today, at the grate, that man who passed on—I recognized him from before. Do you think he could have had a reaction to... to the tincture?" My voice raised almost an octave at the end, and I felt lightheaded. I had not phrased the question as delicately as I could have, but I had at least gotten it out of my mouth.

Sister Catherine coughed lightly again, not bothering to cover her mouth this time. "I will say it again: that tincture is a holy essence. It erases earthly sin. He would only have had a reaction to it if there were darkness in his heart."

I took a greedy gulp of air and posed my most inflammatory question yet. "If that were the case, would he still be placed in the chamber of divine decomposition?"

Sister Catherine narrowed her eyes until they were snake-like slits. I felt like Eve, approaching the Tree of Knowledge knowing she would succumb to the enticing fruit. "Sister Rafaela, a good body must never go to waste." She turned on her heel as if to leave, but thought better of it and swiveled to speak to me once more. "'For which cause we faint not; but though our outward man is corrupted, yet the inward man is renewed day by day.' From Corinthians. You would do well to remember that, Sister."

With her commanding words spoken, she turned away with an air of finality and walked toward the door into the refectory. When she left, I found myself suddenly alone in the kitchen, wrestling with the riddle of her words. A life well lived meant no body was ever wasted, surely?

Except for those of the wicked? I shook my head, trying to reconcile these contradictions. I could not do so.

While I had been speaking with Sister Catherine, the other Sisters had filed out without my notice. Even though the kitchen should have been a cheery place, it felt oppressive and dark. The sun had set in the cold winter air, and no light filtered through the high windows. Only the light from a few lamps kept me from being plunged into total darkness. There would be no more opportunities to speak to other Sisters tonight, that much was clear.

I plucked a candlestick, its flame flickering, from the counter and left the kitchen, too, ruminating on everything I had heard. The idea of the Sisters spending even more time in Berta's company made me shiver, but I was still clearly an outsider, not yet privy to the deeper secrets of the abbey. Could the other Sisters have an inkling of my history, of what had happened with the Rafaelites? Of course they might have suspicions, but that also meant everything I said, every question I raised, every opinion I voiced, would be met with double, if not triple, scrutiny. Word of my insatiable curiosity would make it back to Mother Superior, there was no doubt. Once again, I had put myself in what might prove to be a dangerous position, playing the hapless fool.

If I had to confront the forces of evil here in this abbey, I would have to do it alone.

Or would I? Father Bruno's face floated into my consciousness, his thick, dark beard, those piercing eyes. Against my better judgment, I yearned for him in a way that felt anything but proper. He was a shining beacon of hope in this dark abbey, the one person I felt would truly have my best interests at heart, the one person who would believe me, the one person who might be able to act if he learned something horribly wrong was happening. Even in the woman's world of the abbey, it was the man who had the power.

I would go to confession again the next morning and have my chance to speak with Father Bruno. What would I tell him? Would I tell him my suspicions about the source of the tincture? About the man who died? About Berta's pristine body, about my intercepted letter, about the blood of mine I thought was taken from my cell? Even I could hear the incredible nature of my thoughts, how silly and impossible my suspicions sounded. Then again, Father Bruno had listened when I had told him of my childhood, of my time with the Rafaelites. He had listened, and, more importantly, he had believed me. That was more than most were willing to do. Maybe I could trust him with all of my suspicions, after all. With a desperate pang of loneliness, I realized I had nothing to lose by confessing everything to Father Bruno. Either he would help me, or he would not, but at least the burden would be off of my heart.

The only thing I was reticent to share with Father Bruno was the suspicion about my rags. What man, even a man of the cloth, wanted to hear about a woman's pain, a woman's blood? Worst of all, what if he connected my misgivings to my woman's pain, surmising that all of my wild imaginings could be tied to my blood? He could easily dismiss my fears as nothing more than simple hysteria. He would have a legitimate reason for doubting me.

Then again, what of the rags? They were still a mystery. I had not had the opportunity to ask Sister Catherine or Sister Cecelia about what I had seen—the wringing of rags into a bucket, the iron-copper scent of the sloshing blood. I did not think I would ever get an answer to that particular question, seeing as how everyone was so tight-lipped about the tincture's source. Their secrecy confused me; Mother Superior herself had told me the corpse drippings were a holy essence meant to erase sin, and that the tincture was also a holy essence with the same purpose. Obviously, the two were one and the same, so why would no Sister say so, in simple terms? Why would Mother Superior leave me so many breadcrumbs to follow without confirming what lay at the end of the path? Would Father Bruno be able to follow the breadcrumb trail to its end, if I laid it out carefully enough for him?

Then there was the letter I had written to my father, the way the portion about the tincture had been ripped from the parchment and left in my room. The Sisters must also know I had a family of good standing and powerful connections. Archbishop Orriva had interceded with the Sisters on my behalf in the beginning, after all. I was sure they wanted no questions raised about their service to God, their customs, their duties. I could understand that, even if I found their methods of concealment and their secrecy unnerving at best, terrifying at worst.

I exited the refectory into the icy darkness, pulling my habit tighter around my body. The chill was a welcome distraction from my roiling thoughts. My cramps had abated for the time being, and strolling in the fresher air felt freeing, despite the cold.

The door of the church opened farther down the cloister path, and I saw Sister Cecelia emerge. In the light of her candle, I could see the beatific smile on her face, which was marred only by her increasingly violent fits of coughing. I hurried over to her to offer my assistance.

"Sister Cecelia, are you quite well?" I asked, reaching out to steady her as she regained her composure. I could use a friend in this dark place, and Sister Cecelia was one of the few who had not already sneered at me.

"Quite," she said. At this close distance, I could see the red shine on her lips, could smell the blood on her breath. Something was very wrong.

"Sister, I think it would be best if you lie down for awhile," I urged, trying to steer her toward the dormitory.

"No, no, nonsense. The bells will ring for compline soon. There is no sense in traveling so far, only to turn back around again. I am an old woman, after all."

"Sister—"

Another coughing fit interrupted me; this time, Sister Cecelia sprayed a fine spatter of blood on the stem of her candle, tinting the pale wax with red. It looked like a severed bone.

"Sister Cecelia, you are bleeding," I said, pointing to the candlestick.

"'For I will close up thy scar, and will heal thee of thy wounds, saith the Lord,'" Sister Cecelia quoted Jeremiah, that smile returning to her features.

I felt helpless, caught yet again in a space of indecision. I could not force Sister Cecelia to rest, nor did I want to upset her further with questions or directives. She looked so tired. I did what I could; I simply stood with her by the church doors, my own pool of candlelight intermingling with hers.

We were still standing there, our shoulders hunched against the chill, when the bells tolled yet again, summoning us to prayer.

I opened my mouth to say something, but then closed it again, the great silence descending over us all. Frustration made my palms sweat; I had wasted my one hour of recreation. I had spoken to several Sisters, but I had learned nothing that fully answered my questions; worse, I had likely raised their ire and suspicion, and all of it would soon be known to Mother Superior. I would have to wait an entire day before I could speak to anyone else—besides Father Bruno, of course. Perhaps that was just as well. Resigned, I joined the throng of Sisters streaming from various parts of the abbey into the church. There I was again, the inveterate follower.

CHAPTER SEVENTEEN

Sister Rafaela

I had always enjoyed compline, the way the candles glowed on the altar, illuminating the upturned faces shiny and rapturous with worship. Night prayer brought me especially close to God, and I usually left the church feeling lighter, peaceful, cleansed.

Not so that evening. I still felt fractious as I sat in a pew, and blood was rushing from my body with renewed vigor. I jumped lightly in my seat every time a Sister coughed, which was often. In fact, I could barely hear the prayer over the sound of coughing. Things were definitely getting worse.

I still could not understand why coughs were not erupting from my own throat when so many of the other Sisters were afflicted. I did not want to think too much about it, about anything, really. Ever since I had arrived at the abbey, I had been thinking too much—about sin, about transgression, about right and wrong, about imagination, about perception. It was all too much for one person to hold inside herself. My skin felt too tight, and I was bone-weary.

When the service concluded, I could hardly wait to leave the church, and I was one of the first Sisters out into the cold air after the last prayer ended with a sputtering "Amen." Behind me, a knot of Sisters crowded into the chamber of divine decomposition, no doubt to pray further over Berta. Sister Cecelia's words came back to me, about how important it was for us all to visit Berta and pray, to increase her opportunity to perform miracles. I shuddered; I wanted nothing to do with Berta's 'miracles.' Some might claim hearing Berta speak from the dead was a miracle, but it felt more like devilish trickery to me.

I resolved not to be alone in the chamber with Berta again, as much as it was in my power to do so. After everything I had seen, everything I had observed, I was terrified at the thought of what Berta—or, more accurately, her corpse—might say to me in the cloak of privacy. Would she tell me again what was really happening with my rags, with my woman's blood? Would she leave me questioning everything and everyone around me? Would she tell me how the man next to her had really died?

I was fairly certain I knew the answers to those questions already, but the thought of hearing them from a corpse made the edges of my sanity ripple and shake, and I grabbed great fistfuls of my habit and squeezed, trying to return to myself.

I was in my cell for the rest of the evening before bed, trying to read a biography of Saint Gertrude, but the words swam before my eyes in the flickering candlelight and my mind popped and sparked with unwelcome images: a Sister wringing out my rags into a bucket; the dead man's curled, blackened fingers; Sister Cecelia's bloodstained lips. Something was wrong at the abbey, had perhaps been wrong for quite some time. For whatever reason, darkness had tightened its grip on the Sisters of Divine Innocence, and I could not help but wonder if opening the door to my own arrival had left a crack wide enough for the devil to slip through.

Feeling very heavy, I splashed cold water on my face, changed and rinsed my rags, and slipped into my nightgown. I had heard of other women being particularly sensitive during their monthly bleeds, and it was possible that all of my fear, all of my dread and indecision and suspicion, might well be the result of an especially difficult woman's time.

How wonderful that would be, if everything that frightened me only looked frightening as blood left my body, and that the end of my bleed would bring an end to my fears. I prayed to God for it to be so, even as I cringed at the idea of Father Bruno thinking my revelations during my confession were the products of hysteria.

I laid down on my straw mattress and pulled the blanket up to my chin. My cell was cold, and the walls were thin. Other Sisters were coughing in their own beds, and each hammering thud sent my shoulders hunching closer to my ears. The sound made me anxious, and I prayed for sleep to release me from consciousness, if only for a few hours. I coveted the sweet and empty respite of dreamlessness.

Somehow, I slept. My slumber was not dreamless, but the images that did drift through my mind were fuzzy at the edges, indistinct. A young girl playing in a field, a boy trailing behind. Sebastian… in the midst of all the upheaval and strangeness I had felt at the abbey, I had forgotten Sebastian. Even in my sleep, I felt a great wave of grief wash over me, and my face warmed from the river of tears coursing from my eyes. Perhaps Sebastian's death felt so unreal simply because it had been many years since I had seen my brother in person, or any other member of my family, for that matter. We had communicated through letters, but our correspondence had reduced from a boil to a simmer during my time with the Rafaelites. Since Archbishop Orriva had taken me away from Barcelona, I had heard nothing from my brother at all—and I now understood why. I would never hear from my brother again.

As a cloistered Sister, it was easy to feel detached from the wider world and from the people living within it. I lived wholly in the world within these walls, and sometimes I forgot there was anything beyond my own small orbit. Often the feeling was comforting, as though I were huddled snugly within a cozy pool of God's light; other times, such as now, it felt isolated, cold, distant. If I reached out to touch something, someone, I would grasp only dead air.

When I finally woke, it was not to the sound of the Caller knocking at my door for matins—it was to the bellow of a coughing so violent it seemed to shake the walls.

I leapt from my bed, finding the collar of my nightgown soaked with salty sorrow. Outside my door, other Sisters noisily wrestled with pulling on shawls and slipping feet into shoes before exiting into the hallway.

Hurriedly, I pulled on the door handle and poked my head around the corner into the dormitory hallway. The Sisters were not streaming toward the church; instead, they were clustered around one cell in particular. From within came that horrible hacking cough again; it sounded violent enough to break bones.

Without a sound, I drifted to the edge of the group and stood on my toes, trying to see within the cell. In a pool of flickering candlelight, Sister Cecelia was lying on her straw mattress, her blanket in a twisted bunch at her feet. Even in the dimness, I could see the sheen of sweat on her face and the scarlet glow of blood on her lips and chin. The old woman coughed again, the force of it sending her convulsing up from the bed, her body a horrible V-shape as she hacked. When the cough finally released her, she collapsed back onto the mattress, her breath coming out of her mouth in a maddening rattle.

As I stared at Sister Cecelia, I could not help but think of Berta. Her death had looked so similar—violent coughing, fine blood spraying from deep within, the feverish face, the wild eyes. I hated myself for thinking so, but I doubted Sister Cecelia would survive the night.

At the bedside, Sister Leonella crouched, dabbing Sister Cecelia's face with a damp cloth. Mother Superior was nowhere to be seen.

Around me, the Sisters bowed their heads in prayer, clasping their rosaries in their hands, no doubt beseeching God to heal Sister Cecelia, to keep us all healthy and free of illness. I wanted to join them, I wanted to believe it would make a difference, but in my heart I felt God was not listening—we were all drifting in our own isolated pools of despair, utterly alone even as we stood together.

With Sister Cecelia so close to death, where was Father Bruno for last rites? I did not wish to cast doubt on the power of our prayer and God's ability to heal Sister Cecelia, but if she died before her final confession, the anointing of the sick, and her final Communion, her soul would not be cleansed as it left her body. I looked around again, thinking maybe Father Bruno was there after all and I had simply not noticed his presence, but I did not see him. Where was he?

A dark thought entered my mind then: Were the Sisters deliberately keeping him away? Despite all his involvement in our daily lives, Father Bruno was, undoubtedly, an outsider.

Silence descended once again, and Sister Cecelia closed her eyes. I thought perhaps she would sleep, and I was about to turn away when she bolted upright in her bed, her hands flying to her throat. Her shoulders heaved, and panic filled her features as she struggled to draw in air. Sister Cecelia was clearly terrified as she clutched at her neck with claw-like fingers. She almost looked as if she were choking herself.

The Sisters around me gasped, causing several of them to begin coughing themselves. We all watched, in the dancing golden-red light, as Sister Cecelia sucked in her last, strangling breath. Her eyes rolled backward until there was nothing but empty white. She fell back against the pillow, her hands sliding limply to her sides. Her tongue lolled out of her mouth, sending a fine stream of blood trickling down her chin.

She was dead, and her soul was still stained.

* * *

We were all still crowded around Sister Cecelia's body when the bells tolled for matins. With great reluctance, we dispersed, heading for the church. Only Sister Leonella remained behind, still crouched at the dead woman's bedside. I took one last glance at the cell before I left, and I saw spatters of blood across Sister Leonella's face, caught in the crevices of her scars. The sight made me gag, and I hurried off to join the others.

What to make of such a thing? I had spoken to Sister Cecelia only a few hours before, and she had been certain of God's (or perhaps Berta's?) ability to heal her. For my part, I thought God's ability and God's willingness were two very different things, and I had the chilling thought, once again, that God was not present in our abbey—especially for a Sister who had not received last rites. The whole event of her death was so strange; we all had sensed it was near, and yet no one had called for Father Bruno.

Matins was a somber affair, complete with yet another responsory for the dead, with many Sisters sniffling in between their coughs. Sister Cecelia had been the eldest at the abbey, and had no doubt watched many of these women grow and mature. For them, it must have felt like losing a family member.

Family. My brother's death still felt remote, completely unreal, and I felt unable to conceive of an earth devoid of my bright, energetic Sebastian. Although I had not seen him in many years, we had stayed close through our correspondence, at least until his letters stopped coming. Now, I would never see his crooked handwriting splayed out on the parchment again, never smile at his jokes, his tall tales, his foibles. I felt just a small portion of the grief that must be overwhelming my parents. The others around me were surely praying for Sister Cecelia, but the name on my lips was Sebastian's. The wave of grief was surging, and I yearned to be sucked into its undertow.

Before leaving the church, all of the Sisters rose and, in silent agreement, headed for the chamber. I followed reluctantly, perpetually feeling a step behind in some dance I had not yet learned. I wondered whether that feeling would ever go away, and whether that was what I even wanted. Assimilation in this abbey was feeling less and less desirable.

The chamber felt hotter than ever before. The Sisters crowded around Berta's body, some even falling to their knees and praying as they touched her knee or held her pale but intact fingers. Next to Berta, the dead man looked even worse. His eye sockets were hollow, the tip of his nose now as black as his hands, which had curled into claws. His abdomen was so bloated he looked as if he were with child, and his smell was noxious and thick. The *drip-drop* into the bucket was now a steady trickle, and with a disgusted shiver I thought of my own woman's blood.

Prayer felt impossible in this room, but I bowed my head anyway. Exhaustion was overcoming me, and I felt my eyes start to close. If I fell asleep in the chamber, would the others leave me there?

That thought, combined with the rattling of the door, brought me back to full wakefulness. Sister Leonella thrust her head through the doorway, her figure stooped and leaning to the right. I shifted to get a better look as she crept forward, still in that same hunched posture. Before I could see what she was carrying, Mother Superior emerged into the room behind her and there was a collective sigh from the Sisters.

I rose on my toes and strained, and then I saw their burden. Between them, Sister Cecelia's body sagged slightly, wreathed in a shroud. Sister Cecelia looked withered and feather-light, her body already oozing yellow pus onto the shroud. The Sisters fell upon her in a tearful last embrace, leaving kisses and light caresses on her face and hands. As if in unspoken agreement, the Sisters took the burden of death from Mother Superior and Sister Leonella and carried the body to one of the stone chairs across from Berta, where they sat her upright, leaning her head back gently against the rough rock, the shroud draped over her shoulders.

The Sisters prayed in that chamber until the bells tolled again for us to retire. The others filed out, several with tears wetting their cheeks. I lingered by Sister Cecelia, feeling unsteady but resolute.

As terrified as I was, I needed to speak with Berta. She was, it would seem, the only one willing to give me any information.

CHAPTER EIGHTEEN

Sister Rafaela

The other Sisters' footsteps echoed in the church as they exited the chamber. None seemed to notice I stayed behind. The illumination in the chamber came from a single candle, its flame weak and quivering.

Remembering that Berta had not spoken to me before until my back had been turned, I swiveled to face Sister Cecelia. She was so thin, I was surprised her death had not come sooner. There was a spot of scarlet on her chin, and I moved forward to wipe it away with my thumb. When I touched her, a shock of cold went through me, and a despair so deep it felt endless overtook me. Was I feeling death? Was it flowing through me now? There was nothing holy, nothing good about this feeling, about this place—

"Rafaela," came the painfully familiar lilting tone from behind me. Despite her long stretches of silence, Berta's voice was smooth, like silk. Her single word ripped me away from my spiraling thoughts, and for that, at least, I was very grateful.

I remained rooted to the spot, rubbing Sister Cecelia's blood between my thumb and forefinger, feeling its tacky wetness.

"Have you seen it for yourself, Rafaela?"

She could have been speaking of any number of things, and my mind felt muddled. "Seen what?" I chided myself halfheartedly for breaking the great silence, but I had already broken it so many times in the past few days. Plus, my options were limited; the avenues open to me grew fewer by the hour. Things were getting worse, and I needed to find answers. I needed to make choices. I needed to pick a side of the fence line, once and for all.

Berta chuckled, a horrible, rumbling sound that was more like sandpaper than silk. "They have stolen your blood, I can smell it."

"No. I do not know that. They were just cleaning my rags."

"You silly girl. Of course you know what you saw," she said, her words firing out of her mouth, which I knew was upturned in that vicious little smile of hers even though I could not see it. "You saw Eugenia wringing out your rags, you saw her carrying your blood to be bottled with the rest of it. What else could it be? You know a good body must never go to waste."

"No," I breathed, a cramp gripping my abdomen fiercely. I had not even known Sister Eugenia's name.

"Deep in your heart, Rafaela, you know what they intend to do with it. You know what this is all about. You have known from the very beginning. You see things others do not want you to see. You always have."

"No," I said again, so softly I was not sure she could hear me. Hear me? Why would a corpse need to hear? I felt a mad, uncontrollable giggle burbling in my throat, and I forced it down with a ferocity I did not know I possessed.

"Remember your mother, Rafaela? All those brothers and sisters she killed? All those babies who will burn in hell instead of ascending into heaven?"

"Stop!" I cried, my heart racing. I did not want to think about the family I could have had, should have had, if only I had been brave enough to stop her. Why could I never be brave?

"Or what about the Rafaelites? You saw what they did with the animals. You knew what they were planning the second you saw that pitiful little foundling boy!"

"No! I did not see, I did not know!" I screamed in anger, in pain, but I was not sure of myself anymore. Had I not seen? Did I not know?

Berta's voice grew quiet, sibilant as a snake. "Have you tried the tincture yourself, Rafaela? Let it erase your sin? Or are you afraid?"

I thought of the half-filled bottle I had enclosed in my habit pocket, of how it had disappeared after the Sisters had carried me to my cell. "I tried," I said simply, cowering with the pain of a savage cramp. My blood was rushing, and I could feel it saturating yet another rag.

Berta chuckled again, as if she could feel my pain and was glad of it. "They stole it back, hmm? Your pitiful investigation, thwarted so easily. Did you really need that proof, Rafaela? Do you not have proof enough? Can you not trust yourself?"

"I do not know," I said weakly. Trusting others came more easily to me than trusting myself. For years, I had been told I was too caught up in my own imagination, too prone to fancy, a well-meaning liar, but a liar all the same. I had been told I did not see things, did not hear things, did not know things, even if my senses cried out in opposition. What had followed, then, when I had heeded all those people? Evil acts— infanticides, animal sacrifice, blasphemy, idolatry, murder. Even with my devotion to Him, would God really let me into the kingdom of Heaven if I continued to let things happen, simply because I had chosen to believe what others told me—that I could not trust myself?

With a newfound resolution, I squared my shoulders and straightened my body. The cramps abated for a moment, and I heaved a sigh in relief. In front of me, Sister Cecelia's eyes were half-open. I had thought they looked peaceful before, but now they appeared panicked—but maybe that was just the flicker of candlelight giving them a life they no longer carried.

I breathed deeply again, Berta's sickly-sweet scent mingling with the malodor of decomposition floating from the dead man and, much more faintly, from Sister Cecelia. It was time for me to get the answers I needed. "Did you kill Sister Cecelia?"

There was silence from behind me, and it lasted so long I began to doubt that I had ever heard anything, doubt that I was awake, doubt even that I was sane. Of course a dead body had not spoken to me, of course a corpse had not put insidious ideas into my mind, of course—

"Faustina tried to burn it down, you know," she finally said.

"What?" Her words caught me completely off guard.

"Their bottlery. Faustina had somehow managed to hear God in this place, I suppose, and he told her to destroy it."

A fire—of course. The first thing I had noticed about the structure was the black char that covered it like a disease. I had assumed something natural had caused it, maybe a strike of lightning or an accidental conflagration. I never thought the fire had been set intentionally, much less by a Sister.

"The bottlery was not set alight by anything natural or accidental, Rafaela," Berta said, as if reading my mind. Perhaps she was.

A low moan escaped my throat, the result more of anger than pain, even though my abdomen was rippling with anguish.

"They repaired that place to continue to carry out their nefarious deeds. Then they put Faustina in here to rot, and they sold everything that came out of her."

"No!" I yelled, and my own enraged voice echoed around the small chamber, its volume amplifying with every bounce on the hard stone, until it was so loud I clapped my palms over my ears.

Silence had reclaimed the space by the time Berta spoke again. It felt as if she were inside my head. Again, that was not something I could rule out as a possibility, and I felt my grip on reality slip further. "They want to sell parts of me, too," Berta said, a dark hilarity in the dips and falls of her voice. "But I am not going to rot, Rafaela, I am not going to rot at all, and they will keep coming, they will keep praying, they will keep touching with their greedy fingers and then they will sicken, and they will cry out to their god and he will not be listening!"

"No!" I screamed again, this time turning around to face Berta. I thought I heard her laughter chasing my scream around the room, but her face was peaceful, holding that same unspoiled, beatific look it had always displayed, ever since her death. The same mocking light danced in her golden-red eyes, and her cheeks were the healthy pink of the living.

Something had to be done, or else every one of the Sisters of Divine Innocence would die.

I heard Berta's voice speaking in my head, even though her lips did not move: *Would that be so bad, Rafaela?*

A grimace curled my features, and a half-sob escaped my throat. Given everything I had suspected, everything I had witnessed, I did not know if the death of the abbey would be so bad at all. All I knew was that I needed to take a stand, to do something. I had done nothing for far too long, and so many had paid the price for my inaction.

Not anymore.

*　　*　　*

I did not remember leaving the chamber. In fact, I had not even realized I had left that hot, stinking room until I felt the poke of straw beneath my body, and I returned to consciousness on my own mattress. The moonlight streaming through the high window of my cell was bright, and when I looked down at my body I could see the dark stain of blood on my fingertips. Sister Cecelia's blood.

I had never felt further from God, but I wanted to pray anyway. I wanted Him to fill my body with goodness to fortify the hesitant trust I was building within myself. A verse from Psalms floated to the top of my mind, 'Because I was silent my bones grew old; whilst I cried out all the day long.' I did not want to keep silent. I did not want to cry out all day long.

Dear God and Your son Jesus Christ, and Holy Mother Mary, please provide me with the clarity to discern right from wrong, good from evil. Please give me the strength to carry out Your will on earth. Lift me up when I am ailing and bring me courage when I am weak. O Lord, lead me to the right and true path and away from temptation. In Your name I pray. Amen.

Somewhere, distantly, I felt God's presence reignite like a flame, and my heart warmed. The pain in my abdomen that had been so constant I had grown used to it released, like a fist unclenching, and I cried out softly with gratitude. Weariness and exhaustion flooded through me, and I welcomed sleep. I would rest, I would recover, and tomorrow would bring a better day, another chance for me to live within God's holy light.

*   *   *

Fog collected in my cell and swirled like water in a basin. At first, the fog comforted me, like a blanket for the soul, but it quickly turned into something unfamiliar, something I did not understand.

From the fog which now was so thick and opaque I could not see the walls of my cell came the Sisters of Divine Innocence, gliding one by one toward my bed. Each Sister who joined the impossibly large crowd beside me looked sicker than the last. Finally, Sister Leonella emerged from the cottony mist. Her map of scars and the ferocity of her eyes were her only recognizable qualities; around those burning orbs was a face robbed of all humanity. Between her scars, her cheeks were spotted with holes, and her muscle was showing, gray and dead. Her lips were little more than dry crusts framing a blackened mouth. Her nose had rotted away completely, leaving a sunken, dark space in the middle of her face. She reached out a shriveled hand toward me, and her eyes were pleading. Closer and closer to my bed she came, and I wanted to throw off my blankets and run far away, escape the rotting woman who was now extending her hand to touch my face.

Somewhere in the fog, I heard that familiar choking chuckle—Berta's unmistakable laugh. Her footsteps echoed around the room, and before my eyes, all the Sisters of Divine Innocence began to decompose. Eyes deflated and leaked like broken eggs. Cheeks paled and caved. Abdomens rippled and bloated. Noses blackened and fell to the floor with wet thuds, and all around me the Sisters were crying out, breaking the great silence to voice their pain, their anguish, to me, their only listener, because God was not there, He was not there.

Their cries were quite suddenly drowned out by a *drip-drop* so loud it hurt my ears. The sound felt agonizingly close to me, as if it were coming from under my own bed. As the Sisters around me fell to their bone-and-sinew knees to pray, I finally threw off my blanket and leapt from the mattress.

My bedding was soaked through with crimson. In the cold fog, I could feel the same sticky darkness on my back, my legs. The *drip-drop* grew louder without my body on the mattress to muffle the sound. With a strength I did not recognize as my own, I flung the mattress from the bed frame and oh dear God, oh Jesus Christ in Heaven, oh Holy Mother Mary, there was the bucket beneath the slats of the bed frame, just as Berta had said, the bucket they put there to collect all my blood.

I screamed, my voice joining the chorus of groans and wails around me. Berta's laughter drowned us all out, growing so deafening I clapped my hands to my ears, but I could still sense it, and it was so abundantly clear to me then that God could never hear us in this cursed place.

I awoke wreathed in sweat, my blood beating thunderously in my veins. Never before in my life had I felt so terrified, so forlorn.

I sat up, trying to catch my breath. A chorus of hacking coughs from the other cells surrounded me, seeping through the walls. The terror I had just experienced may have originated from a dream, but all around me, the coughs sounded like a threat to turn my dream into reality. The

Sisters were growing sicker, and Berta was the cause.

Laying back against the pillow, I closed my eyes and meditated in silence.

I knew what I had to do. I had to be truly brave for once in my life. This was my chance to save this abbey, to atone for how I had failed to save my brothers and sisters, and how I had failed to save the victims of the Rafaelites before it was too late. I had remained silent then, I had done nothing, and my inaction led to doom, every time. I could not let that happen again. God may not have been in that abbey then, but I could still hear Him, if only faintly. I knew what He needed me to do.

I would have to bury Berta's body.

CHAPTER NINETEEN

Sister Rafaela

Many of the other Sisters were late to rise for morning duty when the bell tolled. I was the first in the bottlery, and the smell of char was strong in the air. Maybe Sister Faustina had had the right idea, but I shied away from the thought of setting fire to anything. I did not want to commit any acts of violence—I wanted to prevent them.

I moved quickly, before the doors opened to admit another Sister. I had missed my chance to test the tincture myself, and thank the Lord in Heaven for that. After seeing the man die in front of the grate, I felt very fortunate that the sample of tincture in my habit had been stolen. Drinking that tincture meant death.

I had yet to learn how the Sisters communicated what this product was to the outside world. All those pilgrims, all those villagers and laypeople, they must see the connection between the tincture and death, or at the very least severe illness? Was it possible they welcomed the fatal bottle, believing the death it conferred to be holy, somehow, a final erasure of all sins?

Ruminating on such questions would only heighten my confusion, so I shifted my attention back to the bucket in front of me. I repeated my clandestine theft, filling a bottle half-full with the tincture before corking it and shoving it deep in my pocket.

I needed to find a way to communicate to my father without the possibility of interception. It would likely not be possible to send him the whole bottle now sloshing in my pocket, but I could at least get him a sample. Dipping the edge of the parchment in the tincture would carry the smell of death, and perhaps that would provide evidence enough that something was wrong at the abbey. If the worst happened to me, my father might have an inkling of what had happened.

When a handful of other Sisters entered the blackened doors, I was busily pouring tincture in accordance with my duty. The coughs were even worse today, creating an almost constant discordant music. I missed the silence; their coughs set my heart to hammering.

Before long, the bells tolled for morning prayer. In the church, I only affected the posture of praying; bowing my head in that lonely place felt almost sacrilegious. Trying to pretend God was there would cause more harm than good.

After prayer, all of the Sisters went to the chamber. I guessed their growing sickness would propel them toward the chamber even more often, in hopes that Berta would perform a miracle and cure them of their illnesses. Could they not see the connection between their ailments and Berta's presence? Could they not feel the darkness emanating from her devilishly pristine body?

These were the same questions I had about the tincture and its buyers, I realized. Perhaps people were often blinded by what they wanted to believe; instead of listening for the voice of God, they listened to their own internal voices and shone a bright light upon them to make them feel holy.

I entered the chamber last, and, as I had come to expect, the dead man's body had decomposed even further. He was now almost desiccated. Behind me, Sister Cecelia was decaying more slowly, but decaying nonetheless. Berta, as always, looked fresh, her golden-red gaze staring at us all, laughter dancing in her eyes.

Mother Superior led us in prayer, and she had to nearly shout to be heard over the coughs, which were amplified a hundredfold in the echoing chamber. Just as she finished and we offered an "Amen," I heard a loud thump and felt the floor beneath my feet shiver. Gasps outnumbered the coughs arising from the other Sisters, and I saw several of them fall to their knees. The crowd was thick in the tight room, and I had to shift and duck to see what was happening.

Finally, I found a sightline. On the floor, a Sister was convulsing in pain, her coughs growing softer and higher pitched as she tried to suck in air. Her eyes had the same wild, panicked look that Sister Cecelia's had had in her final moments. Her cheeks hollowed, and I thought she would surely collapse back against the stone, dead.

Somehow, after what felt like an eternity, she managed to find her breath again. She did indeed fall back against the stone, but her eyes were open, the panic slowly draining from them. Her mouth was open wide, pulling in as much air as she could get.

Wordlessly, the other Sisters pulled her from the ground as gently as possible and carried her from the chamber. The action had a strange contradictory quality to it; instead of a dead body arriving in the chamber, the Sisters were carrying a living body out of it. Uneasiness filled me to the brim as if I were a goblet.

How could the Sisters think Berta might be a saint? I still could not understand it. There was far more to sainthood than incorruptibility. The Sisters were too obsessed with corporeality at the expense of their immortal souls, and their sin would doom us all.

I was the last one to leave the chamber, and I lingered before exiting through the low doorway. How would I move Berta's body? Unlike Sister Cecelia, who had been feather-light yet still required two Sisters to move, Berta looked hale and hearty; plus, she had not drained. The bucket beneath her stone chair remained empty.

If I could obtain a wheelbarrow, perhaps I would be able to transfer her without assistance or much trouble. A frown creased the corners of my mouth as I stood there, considering. Even if I did find a form of ready transportation, where would I take her body for burial, where no one would find it? How would I escape notice?

Even more importantly: If I were caught, what would the Sisters do to me?

No, I would not be able to move her immediately, even though the opportunity was present. I needed a careful plan, an escape route, a burial place. The disappearance of Berta's body would cause quite a stir. They would go looking for her.

They would probably also come looking for me.

I needed to make some sort of record of my actions and their motivations, and make them known to someone of influence who could disclose what really happened here if I failed.

I needed to write another letter to my father. I needed to tell him everything, and I needed to make sure it got to him, somehow.

I left the chamber and sat in one of the church pews, the velvet as red as blood. My head was bowed, but I was not praying; I was plotting. It was then that Father Bruno appeared in my mind's eye, his resemblance to Jesus even more pronounced. I wondered, not for the first time, if he could be the answer to all of my problems. Could he help me save the abbey, or, at the very least, convey my letter safely to my father? Confession was not far away; only the hour or so of Mass separated me from a private moment with Father Bruno. I had told him so much already, what was one more secret? So far, he had earned and kept my trust. Now, I needed to see if he was willing to do what was necessary to save the Sisters' souls.

With a renewed sense of energy and purpose, I scurried from the pew and headed for my cell. I only had a short time to write my letter to father if I wanted to enlist the help of Father Bruno during my confession.

*　　*　　*

There were so many things I needed to tell my father—about the tincture sickening people, something of which I was now certain, about the chamber of divine decomposition and the origin of the bodies therein, about Berta and what I needed to do. Plus, of course, I needed to give him some answer about my continued life at this abbey. I was not yet sure in my own mind; if I managed to remove Berta's body and restore God's holy presence to this dark place, would it not be the right thing for me to stay? Or would it be best to play my part to bring this tragic drama to its conclusion and then gracefully take my leave to serve my family? I wished I could at least have an inkling of God's one true plan for me.

Whether I reached a decision or not, father needed to know of the turmoil in my heart.

As I neared the dormitory, I could hear the great, wracking coughs coming from within, no doubt from the sickest Sister, the one who had collapsed. Poor thing, how wretched and excruciating her suffering sounded. I wondered if Berta had felt the same, and a spark of compassion kindled inside my heart for the dead woman in the chamber, the woman who was not rotting.

What if I had it all wrong?

No. No, I could not think that way. To think that way would be akin to colluding with the Great Deceiver, for Berta was surely on his side.

Was she not?

I pulled open the door and entered the dormitory to the music of coughs echoing off the stone walls. I would check on the gravely ill Sister first, then pen my letter to father.

It was not difficult to find the source of the coughs; hers was the only door shut. When I reached her cell, the coughing stopped abruptly. The silence sounded even louder than her hacking, and I recoiled from the abrupt change in the atmosphere. With my ear pressed to the door, I hoped to hear breathing; instead, a spluttering, gulping sound limped through the heavy wood.

I knocked softly to signal my presence and then pushed gently.

The door did not budge.

From within, the spluttering sounds had turned to a gasping that alarmed me even more. The gasping sounded like emptiness, like raw need without any satisfaction.

I knocked louder and pushed harder. The door still stuck fast, which made no sense to me—our doors did not have locks. Could the Sister have placed something in front of the door to keep others out?

No, she could not have done that, not in her severely weakened state. I doubted she could stand, much less move a heavy object. Had the wood simply swollen in its frame for whatever reason, maybe because of the foggy, wet weather? If that were the case, all the doors would be sticking, but my own had done nothing of the sort.

Out of frustration and fear, I rammed my shoulder against the door, registering the pain only distantly. There was silence once again, heavy and oppressive, and I was frightened.

Finally, with a loud screech, the door flew open beneath my weight as though some malevolent force had decided to admit me at last. Losing my balance, I went tumbling to the floor of the sick Sister's room.

I stood up, brushing dust and debris from my habit.

The Sister lay upon her straw mattress, her blanket pushed to the side. Her cheeks were hollow, as if carved out by a cruel sculptor. Her eyes were open wide, and I waved my hand in front of her face, trying to draw her attention.

When she failed to respond, not even to shift her gaze or blink, my eyes drifted down, until they stopped abruptly at her hands, which were clutched into fists over her chest. She had squeezed her fingers so tightly into her palms she had drawn blood, which patterned her bedding with small scarlet spots. Her shriveled hands were tiny, except, wait—what was that tucked into one clenched fist?

With trepidation, I reached out to unfold her stiff fingers, my breath catching in my throat. I had begun to suspect what I would find in her palm, but seeing it so starkly, as part of such a desperate and dire tableaux, still shocked me.

A small glass bottle rested in the Sister's hand. It was uncorked and empty, but I knew what it had held. That sickly-sweet smell washed over me like horrible incense.

The Sister was dead.

A whirl of questions filled my mind. Had she killed herself by drinking the tincture, to stop her pain? Had someone else given it to her? Had she drunk it hoping it would erase her sin and heal her, only to realize her mistake far too late?

With a start, I remembered that an identical bottle was concealed in my pocket, and I sent a silent prayer of gratitude to God for preventing me from drinking the tincture myself not long ago. In my quest for answers, I was again reminded that I could have inadvertently brought about my own demise.

In my devastation at seeing the dead Sister I had fallen to my knees on the stone floor. I rose, contemplating my next actions. I needed to alert the other Sisters and set the funerary rites in motion—although, the thought of this Sister being stationed in the crowded chamber next to Sister Cecelia, her fists tightened into claws, made me feel ill. Death was coming in droves.

I also needed to write to my father, I could not forget that crucial task. If I did not take the time now, I did not know when I would again have the opportunity to send an uncensored letter to him. Father Bruno would leave the abbey for the village after confession, and I needed to make sure my letter went with him. I had to try, and I had to try fast. Sisters were dying, pilgrims were dying, and I had to act.

Filled with the resolve that had started to sprout during my last conversation with Berta in the chamber, I turned on my heel and exited the Sister's cell. I closed the door behind me and glanced around the hall; it was still empty. Gratefully, I slipped into my own cell, intent on writing my letter before I lost my chance at privacy. The dead Sister would not be going anywhere.

Despite the abbey's ever-present odor, the air of my cell smelled almost fresh after being in the other Sister's stuffy den of death. I walked toward my window, gazing out at the rarely seen blue sky, when my heel crunched on something slippery and flexible. Looking down, I saw a letter wedged beneath my shoe.

With haste, I picked it up and tore it open, breaking my father's seal, momentarily surprised that my incoming mail had not been violated as my outgoing letter had. Was my reception of father's unopened letter a mistake?

Whatever had happened, it was clear father must have received the censored version of my previous letter after all. How quickly the courier moved these days! With hungry eyes, I read.

Dearest Daughter,

I understand your spiritual predicament. I would not ask such a thing of you if I were not desperate. I do not wish for you to endanger your eternal soul, but please know that I have spoken with Archbishop Orriva, and he understands our family's plight. I want to assure you that your leaving the Sisters of Divine Innocence would not spell ruin for our family. With us, you would be able to live a holy life and continue our family's legacy, just as your ancestors before you have done. Please do consider it more seriously, dearest daughter.

I must also make you aware of something else that has come to my attention. In my conversation with Archbishop Orriva, he mentioned a substance the Sisters produce, a sort of tincture or potion. He has told me the tincture is widely known as a sort of healing salve, a soul-saving holy liquid that removes the stain of sin; some even say it contains relics from saints. Archbishop Orriva told me these things with some hesitation, insisting these are only rumors. The Sisters, he believes, do not advertise their tincture as reliquary but nor do they discourage the gossip. It seems as though there is much confusion around this tincture, both its provenance and its God-given purpose. I am not sure what I am telling you exactly, Rafaela. All I can say for sure is that Archbishop Orriva has grown uneasy with the Sisters of Divine Innocence, and I fear that a reckoning is on the horizon. I do not want you to be an unwitting part of such a thing, dear daughter. If you come home to us now, you may well save yourself much pain in the future.

Please, Rafaela, I entreat you. Come home to us—not only for the continuation of our family, but also for your own safety. You are my only child now, and I cannot bear the thought of losing you, too.

With love,

Your father

I fell back upon my mattress, tears streaming down my face. My heart ached for my father, for Sebastian, even for my mother. The tug of home, of family, had never felt so strong before, and I nearly began readying myself for immediate departure.

A small voice within stilled me, and I took a deep breath.

Rafaela, stay. Only you can help them now.

My brow furrowed in exaltation, because I knew that voice. God had never spoken to me so directly before, and hearing His voice was the soothing balm I needed, the fortitude I required to do what needed to be done. I must save the Sisters of Divine Innocence before the ravages of sin and darkness claimed the abbey forever.

After a few more deep, cleansing breaths, I sat down at my small table, a piece of parchment before me. My father's letter had not changed what I needed to say to him, but I now had a more clearly defined plan. After I played my part in returning God's holy light to the Sisters of Divine

Innocence, I would return home. I would be with my family, and I would create my own family as well. I would not be excommunicated, and I could keep everybody happy. An unexpected, outrageous joy filled me, and I knew my father would be delighted.

I began to write.

Dearest Father,

How your letter pains me so, but worry no longer—I have made my decision. I will come home.

Before I can begin the exclaustration process, there are a few things I must attend to here at the abbey, and I beg you to understand what I must do, in the event my plans are thwarted.

Your concerns about the tincture presage what I am about to say to you. I do not know how the Sisters speak of their goods to laypersons, but they have told me it erases sin. I do know that the tincture does not contain relics of any sort. It is, in fact, poisonous. A man died in front of me as a result of drinking the tincture. It is extremely dangerous.

I must also tell you of the strange traveler who came here not long after my own arrival. Her name was Berta, and she died of illness shortly after arriving, without receiving last rites. The Sisters put her in their chamber of divine decomposition, where all their dead go. It is more involved than that—please forgive my haste, I can explain everything in more detail later, but now, time is short. Berta's body is not decomposing as it should, and the Sisters are speaking of sainthood. I know Berta is no saint; in fact, the Sisters here are growing sicker by the minute, with ailments much like what felled Berta.

God has told me what I must do—I must remove her body from their chamber. Only her removal can restore God's holy light to this place, dear father. Somehow, I am the only one who can see what is happening, and I have to save them before I can come home.

Rest assured, father, I will be home soon.

Yours in God,
Your loving daughter, Rafaela

Just as I wrote my final word, I heard footsteps echoing in the hall. With a speed borne of panic, I folded my parchment, wrote my father's name on the outside, and sealed it with wax. I held the parchment with shaking fingers. This letter was particularly damning, I knew that, but I needed my father to know, to understand. Just in case.

Gasps and coughs were now coming from the hallway. I tucked the letter into my pocket, and felt the small bottle still within. In my haste, I had forgotten to dip a corner of the letter in the tincture. Perhaps that was just as well—I did not want to sicken my father, too, and it seemed as though he already knew something of what was happening at the abbey.

I slipped from my cell and briefly joined the growing throng outside of the dead Sister's room. A few Sisters were crying, their sobs invariably turning into coughs. I wondered how many of them were struck with grief versus fear. If I had been the one with a cough erupting from deep inside my chest, staring into the face death, fear would be my most prominent feeling.

Hail Mary, full of grace. Please bring strength and good health to my fellow Sisters, and please shepherd our departed Sister on her journey to Heaven. Amen.

My prayer felt hollow, especially since I did not know the Sister's name, but I offered it just the same.

Mother Superior and Sister Leonella hustled into the hallway just as I was turning to take my leave. I faced forward quickly once again, hoping to remain as invisible as possible. I need not have worried; Mother Superior and her ever-present companion pushed their way into the dead Sister's room, confusion and grim determination on their faces.

Amid it all, still the bells tolled. It was time for Mass.

CHAPTER TWENTY

Father Bruno

As I walked up the hill to the abbey, Sister Rafaela filled my mind. I had ministered to the Sisters of Divine Innocence for many years now, and every service, every confession, every aspect of the daily life of the abbey, so far as I could tell, proceeded as if by rote. The bells tolled, the Sisters moved, the bells tolled, the Sisters prayed, the bells tolled, the Sisters ate, the bells tolled, the Sisters worked. Like a ticking clock, the bells controlled the rhythm of their lives. Each day was nearly identical to the day that preceded it, and each would be nearly identical to the day that followed it.

The abbey's predictable rhythms had soothed me, as well. There was solace and security to be found in the sameness of each day, each prayer, each ritual, each confession. In time, perhaps I might find it tiresome, but that day had not yet come.

Now, I was no longer sure that day would come at all.

Sister Rafaela had only been at the abbey for four days, by my count. It seemed impossible that in such a short period of time, so much could change. Beyond the effect her physical beauty had on me, she was a disruptor. Before Sister Rafaela, the Sisters of Divine Innocence had never spoken of saints, or miracles, or travelers. There had been a bit of excitement after the fire and Sister Leonella's burns, of course, but even that had been minimal. The Sisters had always been impassive, at least around me. Now, even Mother Superior seemed giddy.

I knew I was being unfair; apparently, even though I had yet to see any evidence of her, a traveler called Berta had arrived shortly after Sister Rafaela. Could it be Berta who was the source of all the uproar, even—no, especially—in death?

My mind floated back to something I had learned about as a younger man, something that could, quite possibly, explain everything strange happening at the abbey without placing the blame on a single individual. A few centuries earlier, all the nuns of a French convent began to adopt the same peculiar behavior of meowing like cats throughout the day. This manifestation of mass hysteria had so terrified the surrounding villagers that they took to arms, threatening bodily harm to any nun who continued to meow. From what I had heard, the villagers' aggressive measures proved effective, not that I would condone such a threat of violence being used against the Sisters of Divine Innocence. I could not help but wonder, though, if mass hysteria was also at play here, but instead of meowing, the Sisters were convinced they had a true saint in their chamber.

As I approached the church, I thought I had solved the problem, but I could not help circling back, like the snake biting its own tail. When did the madness begin? Shortly after Sister Rafaela's arrival, of course. It seemed I could not escape placing the blame on someone, after all.

With a heavy heart, I opened the solid doors of the church, trying to prepare my mind for Mass.

*   *   *

I had performed Mass for the Sisters of Divine Innocence countless times. The Latin words always slipped off my tongue as smooth as silk, easy and mellifluous.

Not so today.

The Sisters were hunched like crones in their pews, nearly every one breathing with a pronounced rasp. I could barely utter an entire phrase without being interrupted by a backbreaking cough from one of the Sisters. When they looked up at the altar, their eyes were glazed and shiny, their cheeks red, as if with fever. A few clutched bits of cloth in their fists, to better muffle their coughs. Even with the cloths, the cacophony of the coughs nearly drowned out the service. There had been a few rattly breaths and phlegmy throat-clearings at the previous day's Mass, but this clamor was something on a completely different plane. The Sisters did not simply sound sick.

They sounded like they were dying.

I looked out on the huddled congregation as they dutifully, but with great difficulty, lined up to receive Communion. Nearly every Sister choked lightly on the Host. Nearly every Sister—save one.

When Sister Rafaela arrived at the altar, she looked more radiant than I had ever before seen her. Her cheeks were pink, glowing with health rather than fever. Her dark eyes were bright and alert, and they seemed to bore into my own with dangerous guile. She smiled at me, revealing her white teeth, and I noticed a short fuzz of rich, dark hair peeking from beneath her veil where her locks were beginning to grow back. I had seen Native women in the New World show far more flesh than Sister Rafaela, and yet I had never seen anything so seductive or provocative as that flash of dark hair threatening to creep out of its confinement.

Once again, against my will, I felt my arousal grow.

Dear God in Heaven, I prayed, *Please take this feeling away. I do not want it.*

Was she feeling it too? I slipped the Host between her lips. She chewed and swallowed lustily. I raised the goblet to her lips, and she took a small, slurping sip. When she was finished, she licked the scarlet droplets from her upper lip. I had never felt more powerless, more animalistic, or less Godly.

Fortunately, a sputtering cough from one of the other Sisters broke whatever hold she had on me, and Sister Rafaela moved back to her place in the pews. When I finally finished the service, I nearly tripped over my vestments in my haste to get to the confessional. In the booth, I felt safe—I could not see or feel Sister Rafaela, and she would be unable to see or feel me.

After I shut the door to the booth, the coughs from the Sisters seemed only to get louder instead of softer. In my next letter to Archbishop Orriva, I would mention my thoughts about mass hysteria. Perhaps there was no blame to be placed after all—the Sisters would not be the first ones to succumb to madness while in the grip of illness.

*　　*　　*

"In the name of the Father—" A cough. "The Son—" Another cough. "And the Holy Spirit." The most painful-sounding cough yet rang out, making my own throat feel raw.

"Hello, Mother," I said. In a break with protocol, I could not help but ask, "Are you quite alright?"

Her cough was muffled this time, as though she were pressing her hand against her mouth. "Fine," she said, her voice gravelly. "Nothing a bit of prayer will not fix."

"'If thou wilt hear the voice of the Lord thy God, and do what is right before him, and obey his commandments, and keep all his precepts, none of the evils that I laid upon Egypt, will I bring upon thee: for I am the Lord thy healer.'"

"Digging into the Old Testament, I see," she said appreciatively. "Very appropriate, thank you, Father."

I was about to respond, but Mother Superior did not wait for my words. She began speaking.

"Father, I am afraid I have a problem at this abbey," she said.

"Is it the incorruptible body?" I guessed, secretly hoping the Englishwoman had started rotting, just to put an end to all the fevered speculation. It was not that I did not believe in saints, or that I did not believe a saint at this abbey was possible, I simply did not feel that this woman, at this abbey, at this particular time, could be holy enough for sainthood. The Sisters' behaviors of late were baffling me, and I wanted things to return to normal, both for their sakes and, selfishly, for my own.

"No," she said quickly and firmly, as if she were swatting a troublesome insect. "Sister Berta's body remains intact. I do hope you have readied yourself for the requisite work needed to support the canonization."

"I—" I began, not at all sure how to dull her enthusiasm.

"Never mind, that is not what troubles me at present," she said. My mouth was hanging open, partly shocked, partly aggravated that she would dare interrupt me, much less during her confession. With a snap, I closed my jaw, and she continued speaking.

"Father Bruno," she said. "What shall I say? I know I have transgressed, but I believe it is in service to a greater good. You see, before it could be dispatched, Sister Leonella found a letter our newest Sister, Rafaela, had penned to her father. The letter was long—I mean, the girl has only been here for a few days, what sort of lengthy news had she to report already?—and Leonella opened it. After reading the thing, she brought it to my attention, and I thank the Lord she did. Father, Sister Rafaela rashly suggested to her father that our holy essence is sickening people in the village. Can you believe the lies? Needless to say, we cannot allow such nonsense to leave these walls, much less to a man like Alejandro de Fuentes Piedra. He is close with the Archbishop, and I am sure I do not need to explain how damning lies like Sister Rafaela's could be if they get to those powerful men. So, I did the only reasonable thing I could do. Leonella and I removed the inflammatory pieces from the letter, and we left a particularly deceitful portion of it in her cell, just to let her know such things will not be tolerated."

Mother Superior finally took a breath, having spoken at great length on what seemed to be a single exhale. Another coughing fit ensued before she composed herself.

Could what she had recounted really be true? I tried to process what Mother Superior had just told me, but it was almost too much to absorb. Firstly, Sister Rafaela thought the Sisters' tincture was poisonous—an idea that had come from the deceased Englishwoman, as she had told me in confession. Clearly, I had not done enough to dispel her concerns. Then, she had written to her father, who was a powerful and well-connected man, to share her suspicions. I was not too surprised to hear Sister Leonella had stolen the letter; although I did feel pity for the woman with her still-healing scars, it was no secret she cleaved as tightly as possible to Mother Superior. I also was not surprised to learn Mother Superior had intercepted and altered the letter; I had always thought the abbess reigned over her abbey as if she were a queen—and yet, she never confessed to the sin of pride. It was difficult for us, mere imperfect mortals, to know ourselves—but God knew. God always knew.

"So, Mother, you stole from another person and destroyed her property," I said, trying to clarify. Mother Superior had not sounded at all repentant.

"That is correct, Father. I am heartily sorry for my sins, but as I said, I acted for the greater good of the abbey. Sister Rafaela's lies could destroy us, who only desire to live in eternal light."

"Mother, have you tried to speak to Sister Rafaela, to understand the source of her... misunderstanding?" I was loath to call Rafaela's words lies, even though I knew it was highly unlikely she had heard such things from an English stranger recently arrived at the abbey. Nor would I break the seal of confession to tell Mother Superior what I knew of the situation, so I tried to tread as lightly as possible.

"I told her it was a holy essence that erases sin," Mother Superior replied, her tone imperious. "We have been cultivating this essence for far longer than Sister Rafaela has walked this earth. I do not know from where she got the rest of her hideous ideas. Not from one of my Sisters, you can be sure of that."

That was not much of an explanation, and, knowing Mother Superior, I was sure her talk with Sister Rafaela had been more of a brusque lecture than a two-sided discussion. Plus, Mother Superior's unsatisfying explanation of the tincture did not really answer the most pertinent question. Even though I did not believe it, was it not still possible that the liquid was hurting people, holy essence or not? If anything, Mother Superior's deliberate evasion may have stoked Sister Rafaela's suspicion even more, rather than cooling it. I feared for Sister Rafaela—if the Sisters were willing to destroy her letters at the mere hint of wrongdoing, what would they do if Rafaela persisted?

Stop it, Bruno, I chided myself. *They're women of God, they're not monsters.*

I told myself these things, but I could not force myself to believe them. I had the sudden urge to bolt from the confessional booth, fly out of the church, and flee to the safety of my cozy rectory in the village.

When I failed to respond, Mother Superior ended the confession herself. "Forgive me for all my sins." She did not sound repentant in the least, but she would have to reckon with God on her own for her falsity.

Reluctantly, I gave her penance and absolution, and it was only when I heard the creak of the confessional door as she left, accompanied by a wet cough, that I finally felt my muscles unclench.

Unfortunately, it was not long before tension filled my body once again.

*　*　*

"In the name of the Father, the Son, and the Holy Ghost," came the familiar voice, rich like honey and just as sticky. I could not get it out of my head.

"Hello, Sister," I said. A verse from Psalms came to me then, like a flash: "'Keep thy tongue from evil, and thy lips from speaking guile.'"

With a confidence that nearly knocked me back with its strength, Sister Rafaela quoted Ephesians, unfazed: "'And have no fellowship with the unfruitful works of darkness, but rather reprove them.'"

"Quite right, Sister," I said, sputtering despite my best efforts to sound calm and measured. I thought about what Mother Superior had said; Sister Rafaela's choice of verses seemed far too prescient. What was she planning to do?

"Forgive me Father, for I have sinned."

"Please go on, Sister," I said, hoping her confession today would give me a winder window into her thoughts, or at least offer some explanation for the alarming things I had heard from Mother Superior. One should not have to choose sides when we were all on the side of the Lord, but I could not help but feel a growing schism. If I did not choose a side, I would fall into the abyss.

"Oh, Father Bruno—" I shivered with pleasure when she said my name, then tugged sharply at my beard in an unsatisfying act of self-punishment. "Father Bruno, so much has happened since my last confession. Did you hear that Sister Cecelia has died? I know you were not called for last rites. The sickness claimed her, but there was time to call you, I know there was, and so many others are ill, I know you know this, you could hardly hear the word of God coming from your lips during Mass for all the coughing from the other Sisters."

She paused, panting, like a dog in heat. Sister Cecelia was dead? Mother Superior hadn't even mentioned it, as though another death coming so close to several others was unremarkable. Even more chilling and maddening, Mother Superior had once again failed to call me to perform last rites. I could understand, to some degree, her failure with Sister Berta—by all accounts, that death had been quick, and Mother Superior had always been prompt in calling for me before the stranger's arrival—but Sister Cecelia? Even during the short span of our previous confession, I could hear the sickness eating her up inside. How could Mother Superior keep such a thing from me? How could she let a Sister of her very own order die with her sins unforgiven? Pity filled my heart for the kindly old Sister Cecelia. At her last confession, she had told me how desperately she wanted to see a miracle before her death, which she felt was coming soon. Too soon, after all.

"Father Bruno? Are you listening?"

With a start, I said, "Oh, yes, Sister. Of course. I was considering your words carefully." Inside, despite my mixed feelings about Sister Cecelia, I grew warm again—she had said my name for a second time. What a small and private pleasure, to be recognized by a beautiful woman.

Sister Rafaela took a breath. I could not help but notice she seemed to be free of the persistent coughing that had so tightly gripped the other Sisters. Was her youth protecting her? Or was it something else?

She said, "Father, I have much to say, and I feel our time is growing short, so forgive me if I speak ineloquently. I need to make you aware of a few things, and then I must ask you for two favors."

Favors? Wariness crept over me, and I leaned closer to the grille, as if greater proximity would bring sharper insight.

"Alright, Sister, go ahead."

She took another deep breath. "Father, I have grave concerns about the Sisters' tincture, in those glass bottles they sell. I know I brought these concerns to you before, and I do not want you to think I ignored what you said, but I cannot get it all out of my head. You see, I have been working in the bottlery during morning duty, and when I asked Mother Superior what it is we are bottling, she just said it was a 'holy essence.' She said it erases sin. I wanted to believe that, I really did, but—oh, Father!—it does not smell right. It smells like the chamber of divine decomposition, like all the rotting bodies within. It smells like death. And there is so much of it! And you know, the Sisters place buckets beneath the stone chairs holding the bodies in the chamber, and they collect everything that drips out of the bodies, and I know in my heart it is this liquid that goes into the bottles. Why else would they collect it? Can you imagine? If that were not horrific enough, the Sisters sell these bottles to the pilgrims that come to our abbey, and a man died right in front of me, a man whom I know bought the tincture! And now his corpse resides in the chamber, right next to Berta! And Berta is not rotting, not like she is supposed to, and every time I am in the chamber alone with her, facing away, she speaks to me—yes, she speaks—and she says the most horrible things, about how God is not here, about how the Sisters are killing the villagers on purpose, about how darkness is coming for us like a tidal wave. And I know the Sisters have been stealing my woman's blood, too, I saw them wringing my soiled rags into a bucket, and they took it all to the bottlery, and what is going to happen next?" Then, almost gasping, she whispered, "Who is going to drink me?" A pitiful, breathy scream escaped from her throat.

She was panting again, and I had no idea what to say. A tincture made from the drippings of decomposing bodies? Surely that could not be true—the tincture must be some sort of herbal remedy. But the man dying at the abbey, and his corpse placed among the Sisters? That sounded highly irregular. I did not even want to think about Sister Rafaela's woman's blood. Then, of course, there was Berta, who was, by all accounts, quite dead, even if she was not yet decomposing. Berta had spoken to Sister Rafaela? My mouth suddenly tasted sour. These were not the well-reasoned suspicions of a sane woman, especially considering I had not performed a significantly greater number of last rites than usual. People died in the village as I had seen people die all over the world. Death was inevitable, but it was also a new beginning for those who were righteous. Perhaps Mother Superior was right about Sister Rafaela after all—but, given her omission of Sister Cecelia's passing and her failure to summon me in the event of not one, but two, deaths, I was wary of trusting her word.

"Well, Sister—" I began, completely unsure of what I could say to her. Her suspicions seemed fantastic, but where to start?

"Father!" she wailed. Her words tumbling out in a chaotic jumble, she said, "My father has asked me to leave the order and return home. You see, my brother Sebastian has died, and I am the only child left in my family, and my father is begging me to return to Barcelona, marry, and carry on our family line. I think I shall heed his wishes, too—you see, I also received a letter from my father recently, and he had spoken to Archbishop Orriva, who said he knew of the Sisters' tincture, and that there were rumors about it, that the Sisters claimed it contained the relics of saints. But it does not, Father, does it? Archbishop Orriva believes a reckoning is coming for the Sisters of Divine Innocence, and my father wants me to leave before whatever darkness lives at this abbey taints me. But I prayed about it, Father, I prayed to God to give me clarity, and He told me to save the Sisters, that once I save them I can return home having acted according to His will. God has chosen me, Father!"

Now she was talking about leaving the religious life for good? Marrying, starting a family? A completely inappropriate but nonetheless tantalizing image flitted through my mind just then—sitting down to a meal with Rafaela as my wife, her belly heavy with child, our hands intertwined across the table, our hearts filled with joy. *Stop, Bruno, stop it!*

"Sister," I stammered, trying to think of something to say to calm her down. "I too know of this tincture, and Mother Superior has not lied to you. The villagers see the tincture as a holy substance of sorts, something that is as beneficial for their souls as it is for their bodies. They use it as a healing ointment, to help cure what ails them and scrub away the stains of sin. I will grant that some of them see this tincture as a vehicle to ensure their passage to Heaven, but I have tried to disabuse them of these notions."

Sister Rafaela had calmed a bit, but she still sounded frantic. "That is not what Archbishop Orriva told my father. Did you not hear me, Father? A reckoning is coming! And I have to save them!"

Could that really be true? Did Archbishop Orriva express his doubts and misgivings about the Sisters to Rafaela's father without sharing those with me, who ministered daily to the Sisters of Divine Innocence? Could I trust anything Rafaela said, when she had claimed to have conversations with a dead woman? Worst of all, could there be even the smallest morsel of truth in her claims about the tincture—could it be doing more harm than good, and if so, how had I not recognized it?

I tried to keep my tone level, my voice steady. "And how are you going to save them, Sister?"

Her confidence had returned, and, once again, the jarring change unnerved me. "I have to remove Berta's body, of course," she said. "I told you I would ask two favors of you, Father. Helping me with Berta's body is one of them. The other—well, I ask that you deliver a letter for me. I cannot... I cannot trust another Sister with it. This letter needs to reach my father, and you are the only person I trust."

My mind was reeling. I felt warm again, almost feverish, with the knowledge that Sister Rafaela trusted me, only me. I wanted to soothe her mind, to comfort her, but... she wanted to move a dead body from the Sisters' holy chamber. That was utter madness! What was she going to do with the body? How would moving it help anything at all? I would not, could not, be party to that sort of activity, but... the letter? The letter I could help with.

"Sister..." I began, searching for the right words. "I cannot help you steal Sister Berta's body, I am sorry. You should erase such plans from your mind. The dead do not speak; have you considered you might have imagined her speaking to you? You have been under intense pressure, of course, and the stress of your new surroundings, and so many deaths, and the Sisters' illnesses... it is understandable that your mind would seek a way to cope by spurring you to some sort of bold action. But this is not right, Sister."

"But, Father—"

Now it was my time to cut off her words. "No, Sister. But I can help you with your letter. Leave it with me, and I will see it safely into the hands of a trustworthy courier."

"Thank you, Father," she said, sounding miserable. "But could you not consider what I am saying? The Lord compels me to warn you, Father, before something terrible happens. Berta is no saint. Berta is a devil, and she brings only hellfire and damnation with her."

Who was this mysterious Berta who had brought so much tumult to this abbey? How could one Sister's saint be another Sister's devil?

"I would urge you to pray for guidance, Sister."

"Father, I have prayed. All I have done is pray, and the Lord God has answered my prayers. I must move her body, take it as far away from here as I can. At the very least, I need to remove it from the chamber of divine decomposition. I believe Berta is making the other Sisters sick. She is going to kill us all, one by one. Unless I stop her."

I could not help but think of the kindly old woman who had saved me in the Albanian forest as a boy—such suspicion had been aimed at her, too, and the townspeople had brutally killed her for it. Berta was already dead, but that did not comfort me. Suspicion was the real sickness, and Sister Rafaela was spreading it. Her doubt and fear were weapons, and I feared she was placing them in the hands of the other Sisters, aiming them directly at her own heart.

"Sister, please," I pleaded. "Do not do this. I beg you to pray further on it. At least think about what I have said, and we can talk again tomorrow, in your next confession. I think you will find that a little more reflection and prayer, and perhaps some sleep, will do you good."

"Yes, Father," she said, but she sounded distant, as though she were already setting plans in motion in her mind.

"And Sister? Do not tell the others of your suspicions, or of your intentions." I thanked God for the Sisters' customary silence. Sister Rafaela would have scant opportunity to show the others just how crazed she had become.

"Of course not," she said. "Of course not. But you will dispatch the letter for me, Father Bruno?"

She said my name again. How could I deny her? "Yes. I will."

"Thank you, Father. These are my sins, and I am heartily sorry."

I gave her penance and absolution, and, just as the bells tolled, she slipped a folded piece of parchment through a crack at the bottom of the grille.

I sat there, unmoving, staring at the parchment sticking out from the grille for a long time after the church went quiet. When I finally took the letter in my fingers, I heard it in my mind again, like an echo—the snap of the old woman's neck on the gallows.

*　　*　　*

Throughout my short walk home, the letter felt as if it were burning a hole through my pocket, reaching out fiery fingers to singe my skin. Before hearing Sister Rafaela's confession, I had been horrified by Mother Superior's insistence that her theft and destruction of Sister Rafaela's first letter had been righteous. Now, after listening to everything Sister Rafaela had said, after experiencing firsthand the twists and turns her mind was taking down dark passageways I could not decipher, I was not so sure.

Perhaps Mother Superior had done the right thing after all, even if she had done so in the wrong way. I knew the Sisters' vow of silence prevented communication by its very nature, but I could not help but think the abbess could have headed off this unfortunate turn of events if only she had spoken clearly with Sister Rafaela when she had had the chance. In the shroud of silence that enveloped the abbey, Sister Rafaela could only seek her own counsel, and her flawed reasoning tinged all of her experiences with darkness. Then again, what if the mass hysteria I was beginning to suspect was plaguing the Sisters of Divine Innocence was also affecting Sister Rafaela, but in a different way? She was a newcomer, after all, unused to the abbey's customs. I had been a newcomer myself so many times, I could see how easy it would be to misunderstand new customs, new rituals. Misunderstanding, mass hysteria, silence, religious fervor—it was all mixing into one toxic brew, and eventually, I feared it would ignite.

In her own way, I supposed Sister Rafaela felt it, too—her sense of urgency to save the Sisters was earnest and came from a good place, I had no doubt, but she was misguided. In fact, I secretly thought all of the Sisters were misguided, what with their chamber of divine decomposition and their practice of praying amongst the dead bodies. Did they not understand God's word? The Bible itself told us, 'He that toucheth the corpse of a man is therefore unclean for seven days.' When I first came to the abbey and learned of the chamber, I had voiced my concerns to Archbishop Orriva. He had agreed the practice was irregular, even grisly, but the Sisters had been performing their death rituals for far longer than either of us had walked this earth. In his opinion, they were Godly in all other ways, so we should not condemn their sacred rites. I did not agree; if I had subscribed to this logic while in the New World, I would never have been able to convert so many Natives. They could not have their pagan practices and follow the Lord, too. I was not the Archbishop, though, so I held my tongue and hid my distaste. The Bible also told us, 'Judge not, that you may not be judged.'

Safely ensconced in my rooms in the village rectory, I pulled Sister Rafaela's folded parchment from my cassock. The wax seal was messy, inelegant, but the script on the outside was practiced.

What could be so important that Sister Rafaela needed me to post this letter immediately? Whatever it was, I feared it would not be good. Her state of mind was so scattered, so paranoid, I once again reconsidered my assumptions about Mother Superior's actions. Would it be wrong to read the letter, just to ensure Sister Rafaela's safety, at the very least?

Before I made the conscious decision to do so, my sinful fingers were gripping a small knife and running it under the seal. I unfolded the parchment before I could stop myself, and I began to read, praying God would forgive me for my transgression.

My eyes widened in horror as I read. Mother Superior had been right to be concerned, after all. Not only was Sister Rafaela claiming the Sisters' tincture was fatally poisonous, but she was also accusing the Sisters of, essentially, murder. As if that were not enough, she was laying her own sin bare—her plan to move a dead body.

Worst of all, she was writing these things to Alejandro de Fuentes Piedra, a powerful man who had the Archbishop's ear. I had no concerns about the abbey myself, but I yet understood the letter could not be sent. In trying to save the Sisters, Sister Rafaela would be damning them all.

Another thing was very clear to me now. Sister Rafaela would not wait until tomorrow's confession to take action. Her fervor would not cool.

I had to stop her before it was too late. She might believe she was saving the Sisters, but she would only be sealing her own fate. There was no proof behind her claims, and she sounded crazed, irrational. The letter was a window into her precarious mental state, and that window must be shut as quickly as possible. Having her father believe her claims was trouble enough; on the other hand, if he did not believe them and judged her mad, an undoubtedly grim fate awaited her.

I thought again of the old woman in the woods, the one who had saved me. The Spanish did not have *shtriga* like the Albanians, but they had their own witches, their transgressors, their traitors, their hysterics— and they dealt with such outcasts severely. I could not stand the thought of Sister Rafaela's beautiful face swelling, her neck snapping on the end of a rope—or whatever sort of termination the Spanish would inflict upon her. One wrongful death was already too much to bear.

I shoved the letter back into my cassock and ran for the door. There was not a minute to waste.

CHAPTER TWENTY-ONE

Sister Rafaela

Breakfast was a somber affair, but I had trouble keeping my body still. I was buzzing with energy, ready put my plan into action despite Father Bruno's urgings. I was not too surprised he had refused to help me move Berta's body. To him, my plan must have sounded sacrilegious, horrifying. He did not live among the Sisters like I did. He did not know the darkness that lived behind the abbey's closed doors.

I picked at the bread and almonds on my plate, thankful I was not being served another helping of red meat. Around me, the other Sisters were similarly reticent to consume. I could not be sure if it was their own illnesses or the troubling events of that morning that stilled their hunger, but I guessed it was a bit of both. Seeing the Sister collapse, her rapid downfall and painful death, must have been like looking into the future for many of the Sisters whose coughs were now so severe they had difficulty swallowing.

I prayed to God for their return to health, but I also gave a silent prayer of thanks for the distraction. With the Sisters sick and foggy-minded, whoever was keeping a close eye on me would be distracted. Perhaps I would be able to move cloaked in greater privacy, and, with luck, the letter would reach my father, if Father Bruno was true to his word.

Midmorning prayer was beset with even more racking coughs. Concentration felt impossible, and for the first time since the Sisters had started getting sick, I seriously feared for my own health. I had spent time alone with Berta in the chamber; I had been forced to touch her body. I still did not understand what made me different, why I had not succumbed to the malady like the rest. Once again, I was an outsider.

As we bowed our heads in an approximation of prayer, for nothing felt blessed anymore, my cramps returned with a sickening lurch. Instead of praying for salvation, or for an end to the suffering of my fellow Sisters, or for health, I prayed to Mother Mary, begging her to keep my woman's blood from spilling forth and marking the places I had sat with shameful stains. Thankfully, she answered my prayer.

When the service ended, we filed into the chamber of divine decomposition, where the dead man and Sister Cecelia rotted, and Berta sat in quiet, malevolent contemplation. I turned to study Sister Cecelia. Her lips had shriveled back, baring her teeth. It was ghastly.

When I turned from Sister Cecelia to face Berta, the chamber door opened and Mother Superior and Sister Leonella entered along with a third Sister, carrying the body of the one who had died just a few hours earlier. She was obviously heavier than Sister Cecelia, and the three struggled to hoist her into a stone chair next to the dead man, which was the closest open seat. When they had positioned her appropriately, they stepped back, wiping sweat from their brows. The room really was quite hot, even hotter than usual. With sweat dripping down my back, I felt feverish. Was this the onset of sickness?

All around me, the other Sisters were buzzing like a hive of panicked bees; they were not saying anything, not breaking the great silence, but between their ragged inhales, their sobs, their coughs, and their gasps, true silence was nowhere to be found. I wondered who would be the next to die, and I felt sure they were all wondering the same thing.

Hail Mary, full of grace. Please give me the strength I need to act against the

Sisters' will to save them. Please give me courage, and fortitude, and clarity. Finally, please see that my letter flies on swift wings to my father, intact. Amen.

Berta, of course, had not changed. If anything, her cheeks looked rosier, her gaze more penetrating. A newcomer to the chamber, upon seeing Berta for the first time, might expect her to stand up and walk out at any moment. The other Sisters bowed their heads in her direction, and I knew they thought her holy. I thought her dangerous—dangerous and repugnant.

A particularly severe coughing fit broke out in the middle of the cluster of adulating Sisters, effectively ending our time in the chamber. One of them, coughing so hard she bent over, managed to pull open the door. The fresh air hardly penetrated the room at all, and the Sisters exited in a great crush.

I lingered behind, as had become my custom.

I was about to exit the now-empty chamber when a sharp voice whispered, "You can try your tricks, Rafaela, but you will fail."

My shoulders hunched reflexively, and a fresh gush of blood flooded from between my legs. Ignoring her words, I fled the chamber, intent on finding a wheelbarrow, determined to prove her wrong, even without Father Bruno's help.

*   *   *

To the left of the bottlery and down a short hill lay a broad, flat plain. This ground had been consecrated, and it held a small graveyard. Directly behind it, at the edge of the slope that continued downward into the valley and to the village beyond, lay a slightly wild but still somewhat cultivated garden. A rustic shed stood watch over both the graveyard and the garden, and it was to this small outbuilding that I marched, quickly and with purpose.

I had had no reason to go to the graveyard or the garden before; the

Sisters had kept me busy elsewhere. Now, as I passed by the gravestones, I was grateful for that small mercy—for the graveyard was dreadful.

A low, malodorous haze hung over the dusty, pockmarked graveyard earth, blanketing the gravestones like filthy snow. A dying tree thrust up from the center of the rocky yard, its leaves blackened, most of its branches ending in splintered, naked points. I had never seen a place of rest that was so indescribably awful, so bereft.

The garden, in sharp contrast, was thriving. Vines carpeted the ground, and leaves and other foliage sprouted from every spare inch of soil. I could see bulbous fruits growing on trees, berries ripe and ready to be plucked.

Although the garden was teeming with life, it felt just as horrible to me as the graveyard, but in a different way. The garden felt too wild, too untamed, too uncontrollable, as if it had fattened of its own volition, commanded by neither man nor God. I felt briefly ill at the thought of eating something from that garden, and then forcibly pushed my nausea away, for I had certainly been served foodstuffs harvested from that garden since I arrived, and, despite the illness affecting those around me, I remained hale and hearty.

I refocused my attention on the garden shed, where I hoped to find a wheelbarrow to transport Berta as quickly and easily as possible. I prayed to God to give me the tools I needed, but I was not sure if He heard me.

As I stood in front of the shed, I breathed deeply and pressed my shoulders back, thinking a change of posture and fresh air might inspire confidence. Slightly more prepared, I grasped the handle of the rough wooden door and pulled.

Nothing happened.

I released the handle and bent to inspect it more closely. I noticed a small keyhole, nearly indistinguishable from the dark wood. Foolishly, I pulled again, using as much strength as I could muster. Still, the door stuck fast. At best, it was simply swollen shut, like the door to the cell of the recently deceased Sister. At worst, it was locked. Fear mingled with my consternation—why would the Sisters need to lock a garden shed?

My mind reeled. What was left for me to do if I was unable to enter the shed? I would have to devise another plan, all while rushing to save the other Sisters as quickly as possible. Weakness crept into my bones, and my breathing accelerated, as if I could huff away all of my anxiety.

To calm myself, I walked slowly around the perimeter of the shed, bringing my breathing under control, hoping to find another point of ingress. There was nothing—the shed was solidly built and windowless. The door was the only way in.

As I inspected the shed, the other Sisters' whereabouts had not concerned me. Between their illnesses and their preoccupation with Berta, they seemed to be unlikely to monitor me closely—or, at least, that was my sincerest hope. As a result, when I heard a rustle of dry grass and a harsh cough, icy terror shot through me. Someone was coming, and I was not prepared.

With a speed born of fear, I darted behind the shed and made myself small, trying to keep my breathing calm and quiet. With luck, whoever was coming toward the shed would not find me. *Dear God, please protect me.*

The footsteps grew closer until they were within whispering distance from where I crouched behind the shed. I heard another cough, this one wet and fierce, and then a metallic jingle. The unmistakable sound of a key slotting into a lock came next, then a sharp clunk as the key turned. The door to the shed creaked open slowly, the sound grating against the backdrop of eerie silence.

I listened hard, willing the Sister now entering the shed to make some noise, give some indication of what could be found within. I heard her brushing aside dust and dirt and coughing, but nothing else was discernible.

My muscles were beginning to scream from the strain of crouching motionless just as the Sister appeared to have found what she was looking for. I heard a rattle, and then the door creaked again. Now that I knew it was kept locked, I prayed for the Sister to forget to use her key, to be distracted enough to leave the door open.

As if in answer to my prayer, the Sister erupted in a coughing fit so severe I thought she would collapse. I was starting to wonder if I should come to her aid when she stopped abruptly and spat into the dirt. The footsteps resumed, receding, the sound growing dimmer until the Sister crested the hill and disappeared into the heart of the abbey proper.

With relief, I stood up straight and crept around to the door. Not only was it unlocked, but it also stood slightly ajar. Gray light filtered in through the crack, and I gave the door a gentle pull before stepping inside.

The shed, as I had guessed, was dark within, with no light source to offer even the slightest illumination. With trepidation, I pulled the door open wider so I could inspect the space in more detail. There wasn't much to see, mostly rows of shelving and a few pieces of tilling equipment stacked against one wall. The shelves were littered with small shovels, rough pairs of gloves, woven baskets, and wooden buckets. My eyes drifted downward, searching.

In the back corner, which was only partially illuminated by the weak light coming through the open door, I saw the outline of a large wheel—a wheelbarrow! At the last moment, I managed to stifle a squeal of delight.

I lunged forward to grab at the wheel and pull it farther into the light, trying to move quickly enough that the door wouldn't close behind me—I didn't want to be trapped inside. Who knew how long it would take before someone found me?

I succeeded in grasping the wheel, and with a screech, the wheelbarrow rolled into the center of the floor. I caught the door just as it was beginning to swing closed again, and then returned my attention to my prize.

I immediately wished I had not.

The wheelbarrow was not clean, nor was it empty. Gray-brown stains filled its shallow tray, and I caught a whiff of that sickly-sweet smell that was inescapable in this place. Resting in the tray alongside the residue of death was a collection of shovels, the grave dirt still clinging to the metal.

I could not be sure the shovels were caked with dirt from graves, of course, but in my heart a new realization was taking shape, a terrible picture forming out of disparate pieces. It was no wonder the Sisters kept this shed locked, the tools of their deceit snugly tucked away from prying eyes.

I had long wondered how the Sisters produced so much tincture to fill bottle after bottle, especially with the chamber of divine decomposition hosting so few occupants at any given time. Why had I not thought of it sooner? Why had the realization not come to me when I saw how undiscriminating they were regarding who they stored in the chamber, whether it be a recently deceased Sister or a male pilgrim?

Of course the graveyard looked dry and dusty, and everything within was starving—for there were no bodies interred there. It became abundantly clear to me that any bodies that found their way to this abbey atop the hill, even if they made it into the dead ground of the graveyard with a sham service for the families left behind, did not remain at rest. The Sisters dug up their graves, broke open their coffins, pilfered their bodies. Those bodies went to the chamber, and they rotted. They rotted and the Sisters collected their 'holy essence' and then bottled it, only to turn around and sell it again, possibly to the very loved ones the dead had left behind. What they did with the bodies after, I did not want to know. Did they return the drained, dry husks to their wooden coffins, wedged into their graves? Did they crumble them and let the dust fly away on the breeze?

A verse from Ephesians came to me then. 'For the things that are done by them in secret, it is a shame even to speak of.' That verse could have been written about the Sisters of Divine Innocence, for it described their rites and rituals so perfectly.

All of this had been going on for some time, clearly—Berta's arrival had not tilted the Sisters toward sin; they had been rolling in that direction for years.

Surely someone must have noticed the deaths of the pilgrims and villagers… or perhaps… perhaps the arrival of evil incarnate, Berta, had infused the tincture with certain death, increased its potency. Regardless, why had no one intervened?

My certainty was growing, but I could not help questioning these vile conclusions. Was I being too quick to judge? During confession, Father Bruno had undoubtedly been skeptical of everything I told him. Could it be that I was erring gravely in my judgment? But at the same time, had God Himself not told me to save the Sisters? He had, and so I would carry out my God-given duty.

Although I recoiled at the thought of flouting the Lord's command, I could not avoid the question: Were they really worth saving?

*　　*　　*

I knew not how long I stood in the doorway of that shed, staring at the tools the Sisters used to disinter the dead for their own selfish gain, for the lavish ornamentation of their church. Did they think God would bless them to a greater degree if they had more gilt cornices and golden candlesticks on the altar? Plusher velvet cushions on the pews? I had seen how such greed had destroyed the Rafaelites, and it had almost destroyed me, too.

I very nearly fled right then. I wanted to leave the shed and run down the hill, away from everything. My torso was twisting when something stopped me—a distant fluttering feeling, the smallest of voices. I froze, listening.

God may have been absent from that abbey, but He was not far. I would leave the abbey, that was no longer a question in my mind, but I had a holy duty to perform first. I had to save them. God could save their eternal souls, but He needed me to save their corporeal bodies from the rot that burrowed to the very core of that place.

Without further hesitation, I unceremoniously dumped the grave digging implements from the wheelbarrow. Outside, the sun was a blurred disc high in the gray sky. It would not be long now until midday prayer, and I must complete my task out of sight of the others. It would be much like a surgery—they could not bear to see it, but they would all feel better afterwards.

They would survive.

I peeked my head through the open door. I was a ways down the hill, so I could not be certain a Sister or two was not just beyond my field of vision. I was taking a risk, but it was necessary.

With significant effort, I managed to pull the wheelbarrow out of the shed as quietly as possible. I shut the door behind me, not wanting to leave a trace of my temporary pilferage. As I labored to push the contraption up the hill, I composed my face into an expression of reverence, of the rapturous joy that accompanies holy work well done. It was far from our hour of recreation, so no one would be able to ask me what I was doing, but they could follow me if their suspicions were aroused. I needed my placidity to disarm them, to keep them in their places.

It was a chilly day, but sweat was dripping down my back. I feared what would happen if one of the Sisters discovered my plan before I succeeded. They had already transgressed against me, stealing and destroying my letter to father—and that had been only words on parchment. What I was doing now was taking action, working against something they greatly valued, no less. My legs trembling, I refocused my attention on God's directive, and I pulled strength from Him. It was not easy.

I crested the hill, the wheel of the barrow making a steady creaking sound that seemed enormously loud amidst the silence of the abbey. Luckily, the cloisters were clear. The Sisters were engaged in indoor work, or otherwise indisposed. I breathed a bit easier and took a sharp right along the stone path, toward the church. Toward the chamber.

I managed to open the church door and push in the wheelbarrow without too much difficulty or noise, and I thanked God. He was clearing my path, I could feel it.

I steered the wheelbarrow down the aisle between the pews. Above the altar, Jesus on the Cross stared down at me, His expression sorrowful even though his crown of thorns was gilded and the nails through his wrists and feet were gold.

I needed to hurry. Soon, the bells would toll for midday prayer, and Sisters would come streaming into the church. The chamber had only one point of ingress or egress, so I could not make my escape through a different passage. Just as I had come in through the church doors, so would I have to leave through them, but with Berta's body in tow.

I rounded the altar, my barrow pointed at the small doorway leading to the chamber. I—

Wait. A sound was coming from the chamber. It was muffled and distant, but unmistakable. Someone was speaking.

Hastily, I tucked my wheelbarrow into a dark corner at the side of the church and tiptoed over to press my ear to the chamber door.

"…you would like that, would you not, Leonella? Pray to me, Sister, and you will surely be the next Mother Superior."

That was Berta's voice, Berta's choking giggle. Berta's words, full of insidious animosity, of deception and evil—and Sister Leonella! She was listening to it all! Berta was speaking to someone other than only me. There was my proof—I had not imagined her voice!

I concentrated hard, trying to hear her response. "You will not kill her, will you?" Sister Leonella said. Her voice had a strange dreamy quality, as if she were speaking in her sleep.

"Would you care if I did, Leonella?" Berta again, her voice dripping with malice, setting my abdomen to roiling.

"No," came Sister Leonella's reply, that single word holding so much power, a window into the sorry state of her immortal soul. I was more afraid in that moment than I had been when Berta had convulsed, when Sister Cecelia had coughed her last, when I had seen that man with the missing fingers collapse, because this was Sister Leonella. This was Sister Leonella, and she did not care if a devil killed Mother Superior. She only cared about her own advancement. Perhaps this abbey was too far gone to save.

I heard a rustling right behind the door and I jumped back just in time to avoid receiving a broken nose. I flattened myself into the corner next to the wheelbarrow, praying Sister Leonella would not see me. God must have been listening, because Sister Leonella spared me not a glance, she only glided out of the church, a blissful look on her face. Disgust boiled within me.

Was Berta taking advantage of Sister Leonella's already present simmering resentment toward authority, or had the dead woman planted such hatred in Sister Leonella's heart? I was not sure I wanted to know the answer, but I also could not afford to remain ignorant. Were the Sisters here already lost to God, or were they yet redeemable? Was Berta an amplifier of their sins or a planter of evil seeds?

I shook my head. Ultimately, the answers to those questions did not matter. God had given me a task, and I would complete it. Whether Berta injected evil into the abbey or she only nurtured what was already there, the removal of her body would be the first, indispensable step toward reclaiming the Sisters of Divine Innocence for God.

Time was growing very precious; if I waited any longer, the bells—

The bells tolled.

I had run out of time.

*　*　*

I emerged shakily from my dark corner and took a seat in the pews, awaiting the other Sisters. My wheelbarrow was concealed in the shadows—so long as no Sisters looked too closely. Moving Berta's body would have to wait, probably until after the noon meal. I would have a hard time eating, I knew. Between my woman's troubles and my ever-growing fear, hunger was the last thing on my mind.

Before long, the Sisters started streaming in around me, their coughs even worse. I silently rebuked myself—these women were in mortal danger, and every moment I wasted, every time I failed to act swiftly, put them at greater risk.

Mother Superior's cough had grown worse. My thoughts drifted back to Sister Leonella, and her admission to Berta—that she would not care if Mother Superior died, as long as Sister Leonella could ascend to her vacated position of power. With the worsening of Mother Superior's cough, it seemed Sister Leonella would not have to wait long.

We prayed, but I did not feel the presence of God. Even though He had set me on this divine mission, I felt so alone, so small, so scared. It was as if the abbey was surrounded by an invisible obsidian shield, something so strong even God could not penetrate it. Beneath that shield, we burned.

Mercifully, after midday prayer, the Sisters wandered to the refectory instead of into the chamber. The meal before us was much more modest than usual, something I did not mind, but which worried me all the same. With illness weakening their bodies, the Sisters needed to maintain their physical strength. Without adequate nourishment, they were hustling themselves to death all the quicker, whether they knew it or not.

I nibbled on boiled potatoes and bread, the food tasteless on my tongue. My foot tapped uncontrollably against the floor, a constant staccato that was inaudible against the ever-present background of coughs.

When the bells tolled again, I rose speedily and then forced myself to return to a normal rhythm, so as not to provoke suspicion. My watchers, as far as I could tell, were still distracted, and I did not want to remind them of my presence any more than necessary.

I rinsed my plate in the kitchen basin and then slipped back out the door. On my way out, I grabbed a small broom so as to appear industrious. A couple of hours remained before midafternoon prayer, and I intended to have my God-given duty completed by that time.

The air outside felt even colder, a fresh wind whipping against my habit. I wished I had worn my wool undergarments, but then I thought of the stifling heat of the chamber, and the memory warmed me plenty.

Inside the darkness of the church, Jesus on the Cross stared down at me. *Dear Lord, please give me the strength I need to carry out Your will. Please smooth my path to success. In Jesus' name, amen.*

With a curt nod of my head, I hurried past the altar and found myself, yet again, at the small door to the chamber. Unease, my constant companion, surged within me. With a start, I remembered the wheelbarrow. A needlepoint of panic subsided when I found the barrow in the same spot I had left it, ensconced in the shadows. As quietly as possible, I opened the small door and pushed the wheelbarrow through.

The chamber had changed since I had last entered, and I bit back my gasp of surprise. The bodies were all in their same places, but not in their same conditions. The dead man, Sister Cecelia, and the newly dead Sister were all displaying wild grins; their lips had pulled back into shriveled black worms, baring their yellow teeth. They had died at different times, but all three appeared completely drained, blackened, and withered. Their dead flesh had rotted, but they looked like they were still in pain, twisted and sucked dry.

Berta, of course, looked as fresh as ever. At her feet, other Sisters had placed small tokens—a loaf of bread, a small glass bottle filled with stunted, dirty wildflowers, a gilt rosary. They were making an unholy altar of her.

I pushed the wheelbarrow in front of Berta's body and began moving the tokens around her feet out of the way. I was not a small woman, but my exhaustion and woman's troubles had left me feeling weak. Moving Berta would not be easy, even with the wheelbarrow.

I tried to avoid turning my back to her, lest she speak and confuse me, muddling the word of God, but such a position became unavoidable as I twisted and turned to remove the tokens. For a brief second when I was distracted by a soot-stained candelabra token that was remarkably heavy, Berta's singular voice issued forth, clear and sharp.

"It will not work, Rafaela," she said.

My blood turned to ice, but I continued fiddling with the candelabra, pretending I had not heard her. Did the others hear her, too? Or did she only speak to me and Sister Leonella? I did not want to consider the possibility that every Sister was visiting Berta alone, that every Sister was in the process of making some sort of devilish bargain.

Berta broke the silence again when I did not respond to her taunt. "Even if you could move me into that wheelbarrow, you will not get out of the church."

I finally moved the candelabra and resumed clearing the area at her feet. I maintained my silence, for once.

Another token, a wooden crucifix, crumbled to dust in my hands, and Berta spoke again.

"I know you are listening, Rafaela. Let me tell you what will happen. You may get me into the wheelbarrow, even though I am heavy. You may even get me out of this chamber and into the church proper, but once we are headed for the church door, the Sisters will discover you."

She paused, waiting to see if I had anything to say. I did not.

She continued, "You know they have taken quite a liking to me, Rafaela? They pray at my feet as though I am a god." Berta chuckled, that choking, awful sound. "I do not think their god would like that very much. All of that drivel about false idols and such. I wonder what this is doing to their immortal souls?" She cackled again, and I felt blood gush anew, accompanied by my most painful cramp yet. I cried out in pain, and Berta took that as a sufficient response.

"Yes, Rafaela, it is painful to see women of god brought so low as to pray to false idols. But let us be clear. Were their immortal souls not endangered the very first time they put the body of a disinterred pilgrim in this chamber to rot? Or perhaps the first time they placed a bucket under one of these stone chairs, or the first time they funneled those drippings into a bottle and stoppered it. Or, maybe, the first time they sold it to an innocent traveler. What do you think, Rafaela?"

Tears rolled down my face. I was staring at Sister Cecelia, or, rather, what was left of her. She looked like little more than a grimacing skeleton.

"I think it was the first time they discovered the deaths of their pilgrims and feigned ignorance. Yes, Rafaela, they know very well what their tincture does." Berta spit the words out as if they tasted bad. "They value golden altarpieces more than the lives of innocent people." Berta chuckled again. "Well, surely not all of them were innocent people. That fellow next to me—I am fairly certain he was an ardent practitioner of onanism."

"Stop!" I finally yelled, breaking my vow of silence, having taken all of the horrible talk I could bear. "Just stop."

"Ah, there you are, Rafaela. Do you see how easy it is to break a vow? It is as simple as opening your mouth."

"What do you want?" I asked, my tears drying on my cheeks in sticky trails. Before me, Sister Cecelia scowled.

"A simple bargain," Berta said, her voice alight with dark glee. "Deceive yourself all you like, Rafaela, but we both know god and the church do not look kindly upon lapsed nuns. You may think you will save the abbey here and then quietly return home and live your life as you did before taking your vows."

I gasped. She had touched on the private desires of my heart, and it hurt to feel so exposed, so vulnerable.

"What is your bargain?" I asked, my voice shaking.

"I can ensure that your family is satisfied and so is your god," she said.

My brow furrowed. "How could you possibly do that?"

"Your brother Sebastian had a bastard child before he died. The boy is currently living with his mother in a place quite unbefitting of your family's station. If your father were to discover his grandson, I am quite sure he could use his powerful connections to legitimize the child. That would leave you free to stay married to Christ alone, Rafaela." Somehow, Berta clapped her hands. I winced. "Everybody is happy."

What? Sebastian, with a child—and an illegitimate one at that? Could that really be possible? I had convinced myself I wanted to return home to a more secular life, and maybe I did, but I still recoiled at the thought of breaking my vows to God and to the Church. Berta was right—I could try to deceive myself all I liked, but I knew in my heart that leaving the religious life would put my eternal soul in unquestionable jeopardy. Yet if Sebastian really did have a child, a child who could carry on the family legacy… but wait. What of the bargain?

"And what do you want in return?" I asked warily.

"All I ask, Rafaela, is that you push that wheelbarrow aside and leave me be." Again, the strangling chuckle. "That should be quite easy for you, I trust. You are quite used to inaction, are you not?"

I opened my mouth to reply, or to sob, I was unsure which—but nothing came out, and instead I crumpled into myself with another cramp that turned my insides to quivering jelly.

"Oh, and I can take care of that for you," Berta said, and as the words left her lips, the stabbing, excruciating pain left me in a rush. A moan of relief escaped my lips.

"See there, Rafaela? I can be a very good friend to have."

"I do not know," I said, my thoughts still turning over Berta's bargain. She was right, upholding my part would be simple—and I would be able to remain a religious. But what of my promise to God?

"Well, then, I do not know about your woman's pain," she said, and with those words the pain shot back through me more forcefully than ever, shredding everything below my heart. I fell to the floor, gasping.

Then, just as suddenly as it had come, it was gone. "I want to help you, Rafaela," Berta said, her voice gentle. "I know what you think of me, but really, I am here to help."

The ghost of the pain was still too biting—it silenced me.

"I want you to have everything you need," she continued. "With your family satisfied with Benjamin—that is the bastard's name—you will be free. You will be tethered only to your god."

"I do not understand," I finally managed, pushing myself up to a sitting position. From my vantage point, I could see the last vestige of liquid dripping from Sister Cecelia, and a wave of revulsion overtook me.

"You do not need to understand. You simply need to decide."

"I—"

The bells tolled for midafternoon prayer, cutting off my words and leaving them to die in my mouth. The Sisters would be coming soon, and I needed to rearrange the chamber as they had left it, lest they start looking for answers. I felt exposed, open, raw.

With lightning speed, I replaced the tokens as best I could around Berta's feet. I pushed the wheelbarrow into a pool of darkness on the opposite side of the room from Berta, hoping the Sisters would not notice it, just as they had not noticed it sitting in the church earlier. Berta was right—I needed to make a decision. Until I could do so, I wanted to keep my options open.

I smoothed my habit and shifted the veil on my shorn head, my back to Berta.

"Decide, Rafaela. There is nothing else to do."

Her words echoed after me as I left the chamber, slipping into a pew just as the church doors opened and the other Sisters entered, their stride considerably slowed, punctuated as it was by coughing fits.

I bowed my head. My mind roiled almost more painfully than my abdomen had only a few short moments before. Once again, certainty had slipped through my fingers, and I was left feeling hopelessly alone, lost upon a raging sea, detached. Inactive.

Dear Lord in Heaven, please help me find certainty. Please help me make the right choice, and give me the strength and fortitude I need to act upon my decision. In Jesus' name, amen.

Whatever small voice had impelled me to fetch the wheelbarrow was quiet now, its words just a faint memory fading in my mind. Berta's voice was much louder, much more insistent.

The coughs around me were louder still.

CHAPTER TWENTY-TWO

Sister Rafaela

I still felt lost after midafternoon prayer. If I did decide to accept Berta's bargain, I would have to reverse most of what I had revealed in the letter to my father.

I had been so sure about that letter, so convinced of its ability to shield me from harm by virtue of the information it contained. Now, I was unsure. Information was a liability, secrets a form of currency. I was no longer certain if I would be going home at all.

Wait—Berta had said nothing of the tincture, nothing of what she was going to do about such a poison. Would she stop its production? Further, would she take away the Sisters' sickness as she had taken away my pain?

I had been so distracted during our talk in the chamber that I had neglected to ask the right questions. I had thought only of myself, only of my needs and my troubles. *Dear Lord, please forgive me my selfishness and lead me into a more holy and generous frame of mind. Amen.*

Then again, maybe it was best if father did receive my letter in its entirety. I could always clarify things later, say my thoughts were in turmoil when I wrote it. That would not be a lie; much of what I had experienced in the abbey felt impossible, the product of sick delirium.

Plus, my father was well versed in the myriad twists and turns my imagination could take.

Either way, perhaps by the time my father received my letter, he would know about Benjamin. My shortcomings and weaknesses would be quickly forgiven and forgotten, overshadowed by the joy of discovering a male heir, a small piece of Sebastian still walking the earth. It was hard to believe a piece of my beloved brother could be returned to my family. Did Benjamin have Sebastian's unruly dark hair? His almond-shaped eyes, glittering and mischievous? What about his animal hunger for adventure? Also, who was the child's mother? Who could have stolen my brother's heart so completely that he had willingly sinned, begetting a child out of wedlock? As with everything in my life, I had far more questions than I had answers, and if I did receive any answers at all, I knew they would not come easily.

I felt mentally bruised and sore from following so many thoughts down so many char-black tunnels, only to end up in the same place: uncertainty. It was terrain I knew far too well.

With nothing better to do and my head swimming, I headed to the kitchen to chop vegetables for the evening meal.

*　*　*

There were only two Sisters in the kitchen when I arrived, a thin crowd compared to the normal bustling atmosphere of that space. One of the Sisters, whose cough was not as severe as others' I had heard, was kneading bread dough. The other, who clutched a handkerchief spotted with blood in one hand, sat on a stool near the grate.

My stomach did an uneasy flip. They were still selling the tincture, even after what had happened with that man. Perhaps, I thought, *because* of what happened to that man. They needed bodies to drain, bodies to bottle, bodies to sell to other bodies. Like the serpent biting its own tail, the larger their appetite, the more precarious their situation.

As I peeled potatoes, I listened hard, straining to hear God's voice. I knew what He wanted me to do, or at least I thought I did. Then there was Berta, and her bargain—surely reuniting my parents with a lost grandchild and preserving my eternal vows to the Lord Jesus Christ were good and holy actions. I had nothing to fear from accepting Berta's bargain… right? After all, to uphold my end, all I needed to do was nothing.

A delicate but insistent pressure began pushing on my chest, as though something was trying to enter me. I thought of God, of His difficulty residing in that abbey atop the hill, and I opened my heart to receive Him.

Dear Lord, enter me if that is Your will. Enter me and guide me to the right thoughts, the right actions, the right future. Your will be done. Amen.

The pressure eased slightly, and my heart felt fuller as it began to pump faster. God had accepted my invitation, it seemed.

God did not speak, but I felt His presence, I felt His reassurance, I felt His will, and it changed my mind, it—

I dropped my knife and fell to the floor in pain, my cramps stabbing into my insides as they had in the chamber. *Oh my God, I will give anything to rid myself of this excruciating pain, please just take it away...*

As quickly as the cramps had gripped me, they released. I stood up, earning exhausted, apathetic *What now?* looks from the Sisters. The pressure in my chest and the fullness in my heart were gone.

My body quivered as I smoothed my habit and resumed the task at hand. I felt more uncertain and more alone than ever before. I had what felt like an impossible choice before me, two forces working at odds—yet one played gently, and one fought with unbearable pain. I was caught in the middle, in a snare of my own mistakes, paralyzed on the fence line. As always.

The bells tolled for vespers, and I left the kitchen quickly. Nervous energy set my muscles to quivering even as exhaustion numbed my mind.

As I walked into the church, I expected another service so full of violent coughing that there would be no room for prayer.

I was wrong.

I took my seat in one of the pews. Around me, the other Sisters did the same. Whereas just a few hours before, nearly all of them had suffered from racking, breathless coughs, now fully half of them were rosy-cheeked and smiling, breathing in great chestfuls of air with not even a wheeze. Their transformation was more unnerving than joyous. No person as ill as they had been could be simply restored back to full health in a matter of hours.

Not, that was, without the hand of God performing a miracle.

I did not seriously consider that possibility as serene voices lifted in prayer around me, with a few coughs peppered in from those who were still ill. God still felt far from here, but...

Miracles. The Sisters had spoken the previous night of praying to Berta in the hopes of witnessing a miracle.

Hail Mary, full of grace. I had felt Berta take away my pain, even though I had not asked for her to do so. What if she had taken away their illnesses, just as easily as she had made them sick?

No, no, no. My thoughts twisted and twirled, tying themselves in knots that were impossible to pick apart. Berta, God, miracles, murders. Death and sickness, greed and renewed health. I thanked God for Father Bruno, even now spiriting my letter away to my father. I needed someone outside of the abbey to understand my turmoil.

During the scripture reading, I stared at the presumably healed Sisters from the corner of my eye. One Sister who had had a particularly terrible cough, whom I had thought would not survive past the evening meal, knelt with her back straight, her face calm. Her lips had returned to their pinkish-red hue, all traces of blue eradicated. Her flesh looked youthful instead of dry and withered. Her eyes were closed, but I felt certain that beneath her lids, they shone with a newfound brightness, the whites clear. When she opened her eyes and stood up again, I saw that my guess had been correct. Surely somebody who sparkled with such health had a strong relationship with God—or so I wanted to believe.

Nothing made sense to me anymore. I had never had the strongest natural religious compass—I had failed to stop my mother's string of infanticides, for one. Now, however, the needle of my moral compass was sprung, spinning wildly, pausing on whatever was in front of me at the moment instead of whatever was right and true. I felt dizzy.

When the bells tolled and we rose for the evening meal, a few Sisters stayed behind to enter the chamber, no doubt to pray at Berta's feet. I hoped they would not notice the wheelbarrow, but if they did, that none would divine its meaning—or wonder who had left it there. After all, the bottom of the barrow had been caked with dried liquids and graveyard dirt; it had likely made many an appearance in the chamber, whether to ferry in the freshly dead or cart out their withered husks.

The rest of us, which included all of the newly healthy Sisters and a few less severely ill stragglers, flowed into the refectory. Sisters who had only picked at pieces of bread for the past two days suddenly devoured plates full of rare red meat, letting the scarlet juices drip down their chins. The sight was so jarring, so out of place, that my mouth dropped open in surprise. The Sisters who still endured coughs had bowls of thin soup before them, which they slurped at weakly. My own plate held a small tureen of soup and a juicy hunk of meat, as if even the kitchen was presenting me with a choice. Eat the meat and grow strong, or sip the soup and suffer. I did not feel hungry for either.

Instead, I drank my cup of barley tea, wishing for something stronger, small beer perhaps, and watched the newly healthy Sisters wipe their wet mouths on the sleeves of their habits, something so out of character, so uncouth, that I nearly choked on my drink. It was as though someone had replaced each sick Sister with a healthy, feral animal that had a taste for blood.

Before the bells tolled to signal recreation and the brief break from our great silence, Mother Superior and Sister Leonella, who, of course, now glowed with fresh health—even Sister Leonella's scars had started to fade, I noticed—picked up their plates and glided off to the kitchen together, a lightness in their step that had been absent mere hours before. When they left the refectory in a gust of cold air, I thought of Sister Leonella's conversation with Berta. She had been outplayed, or so it seemed from Mother Superior's newfound health, but the Sister did not look disappointed. I felt grateful to be rid of their disturbing presence as a bone-deep weariness stole over me. With feverish relief, I cleaned my plate and headed for the refectory doors.

Later, when I found Mother Superior and Sister Leonella in my cell, I wished I had stayed to speak with the others instead.

CHAPTER TWENTY-THREE

Father Bruno

My lungs were sore by the time I could see the abbey atop the hill. I had run nearly the whole way, tripping several times in my haste. At knee-level, my vestments were smudged with dirt, and my palms were raw where bits of stone had bit into the flesh. The swift journey had undoubtedly bruised me, but I felt no pain. I felt only a deep, poignant urgency to put a stop to Rafaela's plans before she caused damage too severe to repair—to the abbey and to herself.

As I approached the abbey, I heard a chorus of voices lifted in song coming from the church. The Sisters were at vespers, I presumed. I had not memorized the ebb and flow of their schedule beyond confession, so all I could do was guess at where they would be going after prayer ended. The evening meal, perhaps? Or would they have a free hour for quiet meditation?

I was painfully aware that I was well out of my element. During Mass and confession, I had a God-given right to enter the abbey, to stand within the gilt-covered church, to gaze upon the cloistered Sisters. However, at this time of day, my presence was unexpected, inappropriate; if I were spotted, I would no doubt be met with disapprobation. I was an intruder, and I could not forget it.

The voices were still raised in prayer as I crept down the cloistered path, feeling like an animal stalking its prey. The unreality of my situation hit me at once, as though I had been slapped by a rough open palm. What was I doing here? What was my plan? Did I think I could swoop in, talk some sense into a Sister who would be unable to answer by virtue of her vow of silence, convince her of what was good and true, and then leave, having saved her? As I crouched in the dark outside the church doors, I felt immature and ridiculous. As a child, I had been unable to save the old woman who had nursed me back to health. What made me think I could save Sister Rafaela now?

All I knew was that I had to try. I had not tried hard enough with the old woman, and I had been harboring the guilt and shame for my cowardice ever since. I could not suffer the destruction of another innocent soul—it would be too much to bear.

In the dark, I took several deep breaths, steadying myself, trying to formulate some sort of workable plan. Considering the sheen of normalcy I observed around me, I thought it unlikely that Sister Rafaela had already removed Berta's body from the chamber. All I would have to do was wait. Eventually, if I could be patient, Sister Rafaela would break from the group to carry out her gruesome task. When she did, I would be there to put a stop to it.

*　　*　　*

Before long, the bells tolled. I stayed hidden, waiting for my opportunity, accepting that I might have to wait for a long time before Sister Rafaela detached herself from the group. There was only one entrance to the church, and, therefore, one entrance to the chamber of divine decomposition. She would have to pass by me.

The church doors opened, disgorging a convoy of Sisters. Even in the dim light, I could see the pink of health in the cheeks of many, nothing like the feverish faces I had seen just hours before at Mass. I knew I should believe that God had restored their health, but something about the unnatural shine of their cheeks and the alert glossiness of their eyes unnerved me.

My heart fluttered when I glimpsed Sister Rafaela in the crowd, her dark eyes downcast. Her skin was paler than usual, and I longed to reach out a hand in comfort. Instead, I backed further into the darkness, enhancing my concealment. She was safe for now; she had not yet done anything that could not be undone.

The doors closed with a thud as the last of the Sisters exited the church, heading down the cloistered path. Almost gone was the shuffle of the infirm; most of these Sisters of Divine Innocence now strode with purpose. Within a few seconds, they had disappeared into the gloom. Alone once again, I breathed deeply, forcing myself to relax. I was not too late.

"There you are, Father Bruno," came a familiar, gravelly voice from behind me. My hands flew to my mouth and I let out a thready gasp, my terror sifting through my fingers to taint the night air.

I felt an unnaturally cold hand on my shoulder, its iciness almost painful. With my jaw clenched in fear, I turned to face Sister Leonella.

Before I could stop it, another gasp escaped my lips—because this was not the Sister Leonella I knew. The Sister Leonella who had been coming to me for confession ever since I took up my post was meek, if a bit too eager to curry favor with Mother Superior. She was quietly heroic, as her attempt to save Sister Faustina from the fire showed, and she wore her scars with grace. She had her faults, yes, as all of us sinners do, but she was earnest, always striving to be better, to do more for the Lord.

The woman now facing me was recognizable by her scars, but only just. The angry red welts had paled until the only evidence of her burns was a faint tracery of white, which, incredibly, seemed to be fading even more before my eyes. There was nothing meek or mild in her gaze as she stared at me; her eyes had a curious dancing quality to them, as though she were mocking me. I did not know what to say.

"You do not need to say anything, Father," she said, as if reading my mind. "Sister Berta told me you would be here."

What was happening? Another Sister claiming a dead body had spoken? Was this further evidence of the mass hysteria that seemed to be overtaking this abbey?

"I—" I began, but Sister Leonella cut me off.

"No, no, you can keep quiet, Father," she said, laughing. "Or should that be me? I suppose I am breaking a vow, speaking to you, but maybe if you stay silent it will even out, what do you think?" She laughed again, the sound like glass breaking. Whatever strange transformation had come over her had not yet affected her voice, which was as distinctive and grating as ever.

Sister Leonella squeezed my shoulder before removing her hand, and I fought the urge to shiver.

"Now, now, Father Bruno, you have been quite a naughty priest, have you not? Sister Berta told me all about it, how you have taken an unholy interest in our Sister Rafaela." When she said Rafaela's name, she nearly spat it out, so venomous was her dislike for the newest addition to the abbey. "She told me how… attentive you are when Sister Rafaela sips from your cup at Communion, when she takes the piece of the host you put in her mouth. How you touch yourself when she sits in the confessional booth next to you."

My face contorted in shock and disgust. "How could you—I have not—"

Sister Leonella slapped a finger to my lips, silencing me. "Ah, ah, ah, Father, what did I say? Now is the time for your silence. I will tell you when you may speak."

My lips felt bruised where she touched them, and I shrank away from her reflexively. What could I do? Sister Leonella was not herself, that much was clear; what of the others? All those pink-cheeked Sisters, were they becoming as monstrous as Leonella? Regret filled my throat like bile. Why had I not taken Sister Rafaela's confession more seriously—I had assumed I knew best, even though Rafaela lived with these women, prayed alongside them, broke bread with them every day. She saw everything I could not, and now, I could not help but feel I would pay a price for my own ignorance and hubris.

I had seen clues—Mother Superior's failure to call me for last rites, her theft of Sister Rafaela's letter, and dozens of other tiny infractions—and I had ignored them, or explained them away, not realizing they were all leading to the same conclusion. The Sisters had fallen away from God. Ironically, the one thing I had tried so hard to excise from my life—suspicion—would have saved me, helped me see the truth.

My last thought before a terrible pain bloomed in my skull and blackness overtook me was, *Perhaps this is exactly what I deserve.*

*　*　*

Although I had never seen it before, I knew exactly where I was when I awoke—but that did not lessen my shock. My undergarments had been removed, and my cassock and vestments had been pulled up around my hips. The stone beneath my bare bottom was hard and cold, except for a round hole into which I sank, ever so slightly. The air of the room was cloying with a wet heat and the singular stench of the abbey was so strong I fought the urge to gag. It should not have surprised me, but when I noticed it sitting next to me, the withered body still made me jump.

Ropes bound my wrists to the arms of the stone chair, but they were unnecessary—I was not going to run. I was frightened, of course, but I was also filled with a profound sense of weariness, as though I had known something like this was inevitable, ever since the day I let my fellow villagers in Albania kill an innocent old woman out of their ignorance and stupid cruelty. I had spent my whole life striving to be a man of God, one long atonement for a single grave sin, and now, it appeared, was the time for the ultimate penance.

"Welcome to the chamber of divine decomposition, Father," Sister Leonella said, her crackly voice alight with glee. "As you can see, you will not be lonely here."

Besides the body next to me, a man missing most of the fingers on one of his hands, I could see poor Sister Cecelia, barely recognizable now that decomposition had done its harsh work on her. My eyes roved around the room, until finally, they rested on the woman whose name kept spewing from the Sisters' mouths like vomit.

Berta.

I had never met the woman, but there was no denying it was her. She sat still as a statue, but her flesh was glowing, almost livid, her eyes bright and a curious shade of red-gold. As I looked into those hellfire irises, I thought, *The old stories were wrong. Shtriga do not have pale eyes at all.* I swallowed, gulping down the excess saliva in my mouth. If God really had allowed such creatures to roam His earth, then I was certain I was staring right at one.

My body was overtaken by convulsive shivers. It was unthinkable, beyond belief. There was not even the smallest indication Berta was dead. For a moment, I thought this was all an elaborate trick, and Berta had been alive this whole time. I wanted to believe anything other than what I was coming to understand: evil was very real, and it walked among us, even in what should have been the holiest of places.

Then, as if to mock the folly of my small human mind, a blowfly that must have been feasting on one of the other bodies buzzed over to Berta. Without pause, it landed directly on the white of her open eye.

She did not blink, or gasp, or try to swat it away.

I looked quickly away in horror. I had seen objectively worse things than that—Native children dying of disease, sailors rotting from the inside out with pox, and, of course, the torture of a poor innocent woman—but for some reason, the blowfly's casual landing on Berta's open eye filled me with so much revulsion I felt my bowels loosen. I had seen horrible things, yes, but they were all comprehensible. What I was seeing now, in all its unreality, was not.

Moving in front of me, Sister Leonella wrinkled her nose. Impossibly, her scars looked even more faded than before. "Had a little accident, Father?" She giggled, the sound like the crackle and pop of a pile of twisting maggots. "Fear not, it is the body's natural tendency. Everything will be leaking out of you soon enough."

I could not even muster the will to fight against the ropes at my wrists. I did not want to struggle anymore; I was ready to let it all go. If I left this chamber alive, I knew I would spend the rest of my life with that same awful image in my mind, taunting me as I tried to sleep: the blowfly landing on Berta's open eye.

There was just one thing I had to do before I surrendered completely.

"Where is Sister Rafaela?" I finally managed to say, but as I said it, I realized I was not so sure what it was I needed to do anymore. Now that I had seen Berta with my own eyes, felt the aching malevolence of her presence, I no longer knew if Rafaela was wrong in wanting to move the body from the chamber. Berta exerted an undeniable pull, an unholy gravity. Maybe Rafaela had been correct all along.

Sister Leonella giggled again. "Oh, Father, who knew you were such a lecher? Standing up there at our altar, leading our prayer, and all the while fostering that sinful tumescence within your vestments. And you dared to think you were superior to us! Do not deny it, we all know the truth. Father Bruno, the New World missionary, the learned foreigner, the man of God." From her habit, she pulled a familiar piece of parchment, the seal broken and falling apart—Rafaela's letter to her father. She waved it in front of my face. "So, Sister Rafaela was sending you on a little devil's errand? Spreading even more lies about us to her father? What a silly girl. We found the first one, did she really think we would fail to find the second? Do not look so surprised, Father. Sister Berta told me all about it, of course. Now you need not worry! I will take care of this little missive for you."

Oh God, I thought. That letter was damning—spelling out not only Rafaela's suspicions, but her plan to remove Berta's body. Now that it was clutched in Sister Leonella's viselike grip, Rafaela was not safe. No one was.

"No!" I yelled. I no longer cared about myself; I only cared about the innocent woman who would be punished because of my carelessness. I had sought to do what I thought was best for her, yet I had failed her so disastrously. I had failed them all. How could I be so stupid? "Leave her alone!" I spluttered.

Sister Leonella grinned wickedly. "Of course we will," she hissed. "After we do what we must."

I screamed in frustration, throwing my head back, trying to find God in the veined stonework of the ceiling. "Oh God in Heaven, please protect those who need you most!"

Sister Leonella brought her healed face very close to mine, her nose almost touching my own. "Your god cannot save you now."

In a flash of almost supernaturally speedy movement, Sister Leonella produced a small glass bottle from her habit. I knew what it was, of course I did. Greenish liquid sloshed inside. With deft fingers, Sister Leonella uncorked the bottle.

"Open wide, Father," she said. "Trust me, it tastes better than it looks."

That, of course, was a lie. Without waiting for me to unhinge my jaw of my own accord, Sister Leonella darted her quick fingers between my teeth, wrenched my mouth open, pulled my head back, and poured the liquid straight down my throat. When she finally released me and stepped back, I choked and coughed, dry heaving into my lap. I could feel death coming for me; at least it would be quick.

Sister Leonella sauntered toward the door. She looked back over her shoulder, merriment dancing in her eyes. "Oh, and one other thing, Father," she said. "It will not be quick. Not quick at all."

With another laugh, she swept out of the room, barely stirring the fetid air as she left.

As my insides began to burn from the liquid, and small tendrils of fire shot through my veins, all I could hear was the snap of the old woman's neck on the gallows. All I could see was Sister Rafaela's dark eyes, her full lips.

All I could think was, *This is what I deserve.*

CHAPTER TWENTY-FOUR

Sister Rafaela

As I exited the refectory, the sharp contrast between the bizarre cheeriness of the healthy Sisters and the pathetic weakness of those still suffering from coughing fits left me unsettled. Perhaps, once I was back in my cell, I would write another letter to father, or maybe just rest. I was mentally and physically exhausted, even though my cramps had released their hold for the time being. The memory of their pain still haunted me.

Outside in the cloister, cold air gusted into my face like a slap. The sky was clear, and a bright sliver of moon stared down at me almost mockingly, a silver grin as sharp as a knife. I walked slowly, even though I eagerly anticipated the quiet of my cell. My feet dragged; I felt as though I were trudging through mud.

When I finally reached the dormitory, it was silent when I entered. I assumed the other Sisters were still contentedly engaged in recreation, or, in the case of the ones still sick, huddled together trading ideas for remedies. The air was thick with ghastly joviality, and I prickled against it.

It quickly became clear that I would have no hour of privacy. Cold shock hit me like a wave when I opened my cell door to find Mother Superior and Sister Leonella sitting at my table. Their heads snapped up when the door squeaked open, and their faces were hard as stone. A queasy quake rattled my stomach.

"Sister Rafaela," Mother Superior said, her voice as cold and distant as her expression. "I hoped we would find you here."

I opened my mouth to respond, but no sound came out.

"Sit," Mother Superior said, gesturing to my straw mattress. Resting atop my blanket was a set of rags, newly clean and folded.

I had no choice. I sat down, limply pushing the rags aside.

"Sister Rafaela," Mother Superior said again, her tone imperious, all traces of her cough vanished. "Are you content here?"

I was, again, at a loss for words. How could I even begin to answer such a question?

Mother Superior took my silence for insolence. "Sister, answer me."

"Um," I stammered, "I suppose so, yes." I could not lie to Mother Superior, but I felt that giving an answer closer to the truth—that I felt terrified, ill, and exhausted, and I feared much of what the Sisters were doing was wrong—would have been extremely dangerous. I had not yet completed my God-given task of removing Berta's body, and I could not afford to arouse even the smallest sliver of suspicion.

"Really?" she said, her gaze piercing mine. Fire burned bright within those eyes, and I noticed with a start that her irises were a familiar golden-red. They had not always been that color, I was sure of it.

"Yes," I said, my voice little more than a dry croak.

"You could have fooled me, Sister," she said.

I was about to ask a question, deny her claim, anything—but Sister Leonella slapped a folded piece of parchment on the table, her face a mask of disgust. I craned my neck forward to get a better look; I could see the faint tracery of handwriting. My handwriting, and a broken wax seal.

I slumped back, feeling defeated, anxious, and more than anything, terrified. My watchers had not lost interest in me, after all. I had left that letter safely with Father Bruno. What did it mean that it had fallen into Sister Leonella's hands? Had Father Bruno given it to them, breaching my trust? Or… or had the Sisters taken it from him? My back began to sweat.

"Can you explain this to us, Sister?" Mother Superior purred, her tone gentle but her eyes hard and fiery, like coals.

My stomach flipped. For a brief moment I thought I would vomit—that would be an admission of guilt if ever there was one. I took a deep breath and prayed for the right words to come, the words that would protect me, the words that would assuage their anger. In the back of my mind, I could not shake my concern for Father Bruno. I did not believe he would willingly betray me. *Father Bruno*, I thought, *what have they done to you?*

"Well?" Sister Leonella prodded, her gaze just as ferocious as Mother Superior's. With a start, I noticed that her eyes also had that golden-red tint—like Berta's eyes. As I looked closer, I saw that the skin of her face was now as smooth and unmarred as an infant's. I shivered despite my sweat.

"My brother Sebastian has died," I began. "My father has asked me to return home, as I am now his only living child."

Mother Superior smirked. "You would break your vow to me? To your god?"

"I do not think of it as breaking my vow, I suppose, I seek to honor my father, and—"

Mother Superior stopped me with a sharply raised hand. "Nonsense, Sister." She paused, traded a meaningful glance with Sister Leonella, and continued. "You have written much in this letter, Sister, and made many dangerous accusations."

"I—"

"You think our holy essence is poisonous? You think we would knowingly poison innocent pilgrims?"

My hands started to shake, and I clasped them more tightly in my lap. "Well, I did see—"

Mother Superior's expression became even fiercer, hellfire in her eyes. I recoiled as she hissed, "You have no idea what you saw. A man happened to collapse on the grounds of our abbey, and you assume we killed him? How you defame us, Sister." She spat out that last word as though it tasted bitter in her mouth, as though I did not deserve the title. Fear gripped my spine, paralyzing me.

Mother Superior continued. "And what is this about Sister Berta? Do you think us mad, that we pray to her as though she could be a saint? What do you know of incorruptibility, Sister? Have you ever looked a saint in the face?"

A beat of silence passed. "No."

"I thought not. You judge us madwomen as well as murderers. It is no wonder you are struggling here. I should not have listened to Archbishop Orriva. You know he interceded on your behalf, even after everything that happened at your Rafaelite abbey? I did not want to take you in, I thought you might be a poisonous influence. The Archbishop convinced me otherwise." She paused and looked down, tapping the letter with one pale finger. "Now it seems I was right all along. The Bible tells us 'And the tongue is a fire, a world of iniquity. The tongue is placed among our members, which defileth the whole body, and inflameth the wheel of our nativity, being set on fire by hell.' You would do best to remember that, Sister."

"Mother—"

"No," she said, the word forceful and heavy. "You are finished speaking." Then, after a weighty pause, she said, "And to think you also planned to steal the body of a saint from our chamber? You wanted to rob your fellow Sisters of the chance to witness miracles? Look around you, Sister. Despite your plan, we are thriving. I know you have seen those Sisters who were ill, what miraculous recoveries they have made. In fact, I myself have been the beneficiary of such a miracle, as has Sister Leonella. We were wallowing in illness, and now we have been healed."

I clenched my eyes shut, as if blocking them from my view would make them disappear. I was not so fortunate.

"Look at me when I am speaking to you, Sister," Mother Superior snapped. I opened my eyes to find her golden-red ones boring a hole into me. It burned.

"You had a choice to make, Rafaela, and you chose poorly," Mother Superior said, once again imperious. "Repent. Go to Sister Berta, and repent to her." She paused, and a dark smile lifted the corners of her lips. I had never seen anything so frightening. "If you do not, even your god cannot help you."

A trickle of warmth seeped across my legs, and it was not blood this time. I was petrified.

Seeing the shameful stain spreading across the blankets beneath me, Mother Superior chuckled—a dry, choking sound. I knew it well. She stood abruptly, and Sister Leonella followed suit.

"One more thing, Rafaela," Mother Superior hissed. "How dare you involve Father Bruno in your schemes? He came to us, you know, straightaway. He handed us this letter. The seal was already broken—he had read it, of course. No doubt he was as horrified by its contents as we are. What did you think he was going to do, Rafaela? Let your madness spread itself throughout Spain like a disease?" Mother Superior laughed, and Sister Leonella joined in.

"Then there was how she was always looking up at him," Sister Leonella said, speaking about me as though I were not present. "You could hear those unclean thoughts of hers as clear as if she were speaking them aloud."

"Be a good girl, Rafaela," Mother Superior said, tutting in disapproval. "Be a good girl, repent, and stay out of trouble."

"Or else face the consequences," Sister Leonella spat, her venom nearly twice as poisonous, as if she were trying to impress her superior. The ploy appeared to work; Mother Superior flashed her a radiant smile, and Sister Leonella nearly melted in response.

"Be very careful, Rafaela," Mother Superior said. "We are watching. We are always watching."

With that, she swept out of the room, Sister Leonella at her heels. I sat rooted to my bed until I heard the squeak of the door leading into the cloister, and then I slumped onto my stomach, burying my face in my thin pillow. I was well and truly alone.

I wept.

CHAPTER TWENTY-FIVE

Sister Rafaela

When my tears stopped flowing, I rose and cleaned myself, rinsing the urine from my legs with water from my jug. Shame rose and crested over me in waves, intermingled with an almost unbearable fear.

Why was I the only one who could see the evil hiding beneath Berta's lacquered, waxlike shell—the one that made all the others think she was a saint, a Godly woman come to lift them up through her holiness? What was so different about me? Further, how could I have been so wrong about Father Bruno? I had thought him trustworthy, and believed he trusted me in turn. Apparently, I could not have been more wrong—once again, I would be the victim of my own ineptitude, my own inability to make the right choices.

As I changed my habit, I discovered the bottle of tincture still deep in my pocket. It was half-full, and a sinful thought occurred to me: Would that be enough to kill me, or would I just fall very ill?

Stop it, Rafaela. Suicide is a sin.

I transferred the bottle into the pocket of my clean habit before I could think too much about it. Killing myself was no answer, no way out. Why had such a thought even occurred to me? There was still hope. If my father had no word from me, would he not grow concerned? He might even ask Archbishop Orriva to check in on me. That prospect offered merely a thin, remote sort of comfort, but I snatched at it anyway. I needed something, anything, to make me feel safer.

I still did not understand why Father Bruno would give Mother Superior and Sister Leonella my letter. Did they have some sort of arrangement with him, wherein his main allegiance was to the abbess? I would not have been surprised were that the case, but something about that possibility rang false. We were cloistered Sisters—Mother Superior and Sister Leonella would not be permitted to speak with the priest outside of Mass or confession.

Then again, those two had strayed far from the the normal behavior expected of a Sister. Thinking ill of Mother Superior made my head ache, but such thoughts came all the same. Both she and Sister Leonella oversaw the production of the 'holy essence,' and whether or not it was poisonous, surely there must be great evil in drinking a tincture gleaned from the body of another human being. A verse from Zechariah occurred to me then, and I wondered if the Sisters of Divine Innocence had a far different interpretation of it than I did. 'I will not feed you: that which dieth, let it die: and that which is cut off, let it be cut off: and let the rest devour every one the flesh of his neighbor.'

A shiver of nausea rolled through me again, and this time I lost the battle with my body. I pulled my chamber pot from the corner and vomited into it, a thin stream. When I was finished, I felt no better, only emptier, hollowed out.

At that moment, safety felt very far away, and God felt even farther.

* * *

The bells tolled for night prayer, signaling the resumption of our great silence. I was thankful for the cessation of words—I did not think I could bear another encounter with Mother Superior and Sister Leonella.

I walked slowly from my cell, out of the dormitory, through the cloister, and into the church. What else was there to do but lapse back into routine? Everything felt preternaturally quiet, and I realized the coughs that had become constant companions over the past few days had now ceased—all of them.

Dread filled me as water fills a pitcher, and a new horror dawned on me. It was unlikely I and Sister Leonella were the only Sisters who had been offered one of Berta's bargains, seeing Mother Superior's renewed health was proof enough of that. What if, when the others were praying for miracles, what they accepted were infernal bargains? What had they traded away?

The prayer began, and I went through the motions, their rote familiarity a balm for my troubled soul.

Then—a rift. Somehow, somewhere, the words changed; they shifted away from me. I was praying, but my lips were not mouthing the same words as the other Sisters.

I pressed my lips together in silence and observed. Where prayers had once been lifted to God, to Jesus Christ, to Mother Mary and the Holy Spirit, now strange words had replaced them—I thought I made out Berta's name, now with the epithet of 'Saint,' I heard reference to Lucifer and Beelzebub, to Amdusias and Baal. It could not be real—it simply could not...

Blood beat a painfully fast rhythm in my temples. My eyes rolled wildly, looking into the earnest upturned faces of my fellow Sisters for some hint at what was happening, at what had engulfed our secluded abbey atop the hill.

I already knew, of course. I did not want to believe it, but as I looked from face to face and saw the same set of golden-red eyes in each, fresh terror descended upon me like a vulture. While I had been wavering between two choices, unable to commit fully to either, Berta had poisoned the abbey completely.

The whole situation seemed strangely fitting, however. The Sisters had been poisoning the pilgrims with their tinctures, and now Berta had poisoned them all against God, barring their souls from eternal salvation. I thought of a verse from James: 'Be subject therefore to God, but resist the devil, and he will fly from you.' The Sisters had not resisted the devil; they had, in fact, embraced him and exalted him as if he were holy.

Of course, I could not see my own face, but I knew with certainty that mine were the only eyes untainted by that golden-red hue. The absence of that hellish color marked me more clearly than anything else could; what would happen to me now? I had been an outsider upon my arrival, but now I was an exile, a pariah—a presence the others likely viewed as dangerous.

Exodus read, 'Witches thou shalt not suffer to live.' A shudder convulsed my entire body, wavelike. I wanted to scream, but I knew that could set in motion a catastrophic sequence of events. The Sisters had all shown their secrets now, wore them proudly, in fact. They had all accepted Berta's bargains, and I was the lone Sister still bowing my head and praying to God.

What was I to do? I felt vulnerable, bereft of allies and with perils staring me down from all sides. Like a frightened rabbit, I needed to run from the fox.

Then again, what good would running do? Would I make it very far?

At the altar, Mother Superior lit the candles, and the flames billowed exuberantly, impossibly. The Sisters cooed, the fire reflected in their golden-red eyes.

Fire. That was it! Another verse from Exodus came to me: 'And the sight of the glory of the Lord was like a burning fire upon the top of the mount, in the eyes of the children of Israel.' If God was not present in this place, maybe I could summon His presence. I had to try.

Something Berta had said invaded my thoughts—what had it been?

It was about the bottlery... oh yes! Sister Faustina had tried to burn down the bottlery, and she had had the right idea. Had she seen Satan coming long before Berta's arrival? Had she already tried to cleanse the abbey?

Mother Superior was leading a prayer filled with those demonic names yet again, and I mimed adulation with the rest of the Sisters. I knew there were candles in the bottlery, those were the main source of light. If I could enter and somehow start a blaze, I might yet save them all...

"O Lucifer, thou misunderstood creature, grant us shrewdness and intelligence, and allow us to see past the barriers others would thrust against us."

What were these obscene prayers? How had everything changed so quickly? Then again, with the Rafaelites, it had been quick, too—the steep slide into horrible sin, irreparable damage...

What if I could not even make it out of the church? We had scant moments before the bells would ring for us to retire... but wait, did such a schedule even hold anymore? In a world where Mother Superior stood at the altar and prayed to Satan, did the bells mean anything? I could count on nothing, I could leave nothing to chance. I would have to act quickly and decisively, something that had never been comfortable to me.

My only chance of getting to the bottlery and setting it ablaze was to take them all by surprise. I could almost hear the thought beating through all of their brains, the thought of bringing me, the final Sister, to Berta's side once and for all. They would not wait long, of that I was certain.

I would have to be either very, very quiet or very, very quick. With God on my side, perhaps I could be both.

In the midst of the Satanic service, I prayed to the only God I knew. *Dear Lord, please give me strength as I prepare to go to battle. Please remove the barriers to my success, please keep me safe, and please give me courage. Help me to exit this church still in service to You. Please keep my mind clear and my soul clean. In Jesus' name, amen.*

Although I felt as if I were screaming into a void, the vicious beating of my blood began to slow. Somewhere, very far away, God was listening. Finally, He was listening.

I needed to go. I needed to go now.

CHAPTER TWENTY-SIX

Sister Rafaela

I had never before in my life been as terrified as I was in that moment. As the other Sisters bowed their heads in a profane imitation of prayer, I rose from my seat. Thanks be to God, I had sat at the end of one of the pews. The Sister next to me did not look up as I rose, clutching my habit in my hands to muffle any noise.

I held my breath and forced myself to walk slowly, to tread lightly, down the aisle toward the doors. Mother Superior had sat down with the other Sisters and was therefore not facing me any longer, and for that I was overwhelmingly grateful. My thin shoes made the barest of sounds on the stones, but no heads popped up to investigate. It did not take me long to reach the doors, but it felt like an eternity. Finally, when I felt the rough wood beneath my palms, I knew I had come too far to turn back now. I had made my decision.

Suddenly, the Sisters' voices rose in a chanting prayer peppered with more strange names and phrases. I risked a glance back at them, my heart pounding so hard it set my habit to quivering. Their heads were still bowed, still facing forward. I looked up at Jesus on his Cross, hanging over the altar, hoping to draw strength from Him.

Even from the rear of the church, I could see it: the Savior's eyes were golden-red, peering out at his acolytes with diabolical pleasure.

I pushed open the door with a force I did not know I possessed and fled.

*   *   *

The church doors did not creak as much as I expected. My feet slapped on the stone of the cloister as I ran, my habit flowing around me. The night was dark; even the moon was invisible in the cloudy sky. In my fear and haste, I nearly ran past the turn for the bottlery. I forced myself to take a deep breath and pivot, heading for the charred husk that should have burned to the ground long ago.

When I reached the door, I gave the handle a hard yank, expecting it to pop open.

It stuck fast.

Was it locked? I rattled the handle and pulled harder, but nothing happened. I leaned against it, feeling a desperation grip me. The only door I had ever seen the Sisters lock belonged to the shed by the graveyard. Even that was odd, because this was a place of seclusion, of isolation—who would come here to steal? Unless they were trying to keep something in as much as something out, which I could understand, after all—

The door creaked open under my weight, the shock nearly making me scream. Of course, I had forgotten the door opened inward, not outward. Fear was making me stupid, a state of mind I could not afford. I filled my lungs deeply, hoping to reduce the tremor that had overtaken my hands. I must be steady.

The darkness of the structure yawned before me. The sickly-sweet smell of the tincture wafted out like an evil miasma, dark and cloying. I did not want to enter, I almost felt I would die where I stood if I went in, but I pushed ahead anyway. There was nowhere else to go, nothing else to do but move forward.

Once inside, I glanced around frantically for a candle. After a few short moments, my eyes adjusted to the darkness enough that I spotted the tiny glint of a dying flame on one of the tables. I rushed over to find a small, stubby candle.

It would have to do.

I must finish Sister Faustina's work, to destroy the Sisters' means of poisoning people, of spreading destruction and death. I needed to bring the cleansing flame of the Lord down upon this hillside, and I needed to do it immediately.

I grabbed the candle just as the bells tolled to signal our time of retirement. I froze in terror, my bowels turning to water. Would the Sisters come for me now? Would they see the open door of the bottlery and stream inside, their hands grabbing at my habit and tearing at my flesh?

Move, Rafaela, I said to myself. *In Jesus' name, move.*

If I wanted to start a blaze, I needed fuel. I breathed hard as I flitted about the room, looking for a bottle of oil, a stick of kindling, anything that might serve to feed a blaze.

My eyes fell on the buckets pressed against the wall. The buckets of 'holy essence.' The buckets of corpse drippings.

Would such a thing burn? I had to try, and there was so much of the stuff—rows upon rows of buckets.

Breathless, I hustled over to the buckets, the candle flame flickering in my clenched fist. With one foot, I tentatively kicked at the nearest bucket. It tilted back and then settled again, and I could hear the drippings and the ladle sloshing and knocking around within. It was now or never.

More decisively, I shoved the bucket over with my toe. The strength of that sickly-sweet scent tripled, quadrupled, as the liquid ran greedily over the floor. With that task accomplished, breathing became the tiniest bit easier. I moved to the next bucket, and tipped that one over with a swift kick—then the next one, and the next, and the next. Before long, the floor was a veritable sea of drippings. At the very least, I had succeeded in destroying some of their poison.

In my hand, the flame of the candle was spluttering, the stub of wax so small I was surprised there was any light at all.

With a rapid *Hail Mary*, I dropped the candle into the sea.

CHAPTER TWENTY-SEVEN

Sister Rafaela

The small flame from my candle touched the wet floor, hissing. A bolt of dread shot through my chest. What if the fire would not catch? What had I been thinking, after all? Why would bodily fluids even catch fire? The small flame became even smaller, plunging the room into near total darkness, and a sob-drenched cry rose in my throat.

I squeezed my eyes shut, praying hard for the cleansing fire. When I finally opened my lids, I rejoiced that my prayer was answered.

A small blue flame was dancing on the surface of the sea of drippings. My mouth stretched into a smile as the fire danced, rippling into an ever broader expanse.

Thank You, God, thank You dear Lord, praise be to God—

The door to the bottlery burst open with a bang, and Mother Superior and Sister Leonella strode in, the fire in their eyes burning far hotter than my small conflagration.

"Sister, now!" Mother Superior said, and for the first time I noticed the bucket in Sister Leonella's hands. I had no time to stop her before she held the bucket aloft and threw the gritty contents onto the fire, which was the only chance at redemption—for any of us.

The flame burned bright orange-red for a moment, and then the smell of iron filled the air as the flame was extinguished. The room plunged into darkness.

I heard Mother Superior's mocking voice, "Does that smell familiar, Rafaela? A little blood mixed with grave dirt—nothing works as well. " Her choking, garbled laugh was quickly joined by Sister Leonella's.

I felt rooted to the spot, immobile, horrified. I did recognize that smell, that iron-hard scent of blood. Of my blood.

"Faustina was foolish, but you are a far bigger fool, Rafaela. Did you really think you could burn anything down? And even if you succeeded, we would do the same thing we did after Faustina's ridiculous betrayal. We would repair, we would rebuild. We will not stop."

Sister Leonella chimed in, "We will never stop. And Faustina certainly got her due reward." The smirk on her newly healed face was ghoulish.

"But," Mother Superior said, her voice echoing through the utter darkness, "You, dear Rafaela, will stop. It has been decided, and now you must suffer the consequences of your actions."

"Your silly letters cannot help you now," Sister Leonella said. "And your father will never know the difference."

At the mention of my father, I finally managed to speak. "What have you done?" I said shakily.

"Fear not, Rafaela," Mother Superior said. "We have merely written to your father of your decision to stay here, with the Sisters of Divine Innocence, for the remainder of your days. Oh, and we told him of your desire to terminate all contact outside of our abbey."

They had told my father I would stay here and that I would never write to him again? What madness was this?

"He will not believe it!" I cried, panic rising in my throat like bile.

"Oh, I think he will," Mother Superior said. "For I also wrote to Archbishop Orriva, explaining the situation. If your father needs more information, surely he will trust his good friend the Archbishop."

"You cannot do this," I breathed, so softly I did not think they could hear. "Father Bruno knows, too!"

Of course they heard, though. Sister Leonella answered, "Father Bruno will no longer be a problem." She paused, letting that sink in. "Oh, and we also informed your father of his bastard grandson. What was his name? Benjamin?"

I had no capacity left to be shocked anymore. A deep, empty abyss yawned in my chest, swallowing my heart whole. I had seen their golden-red eyes, heard their Satanic service. I knew what they were.

"You have given yourselves to Satan," I said, with more force than I anticipated, given my weakened state.

"No, Rafaela," Mother Superior said. "You do not understand." She cackled again, and the sound sent icy shards of dread into my heart.

"'And they may recover themselves from the snares of the devil, by whom they are held captive at his will,'" I quoted from Timothy.

"Snares?" Mother Superior chuckled. "You think healing us of our illnesses and bringing wealth and glory to our abbey is the devil's snare at work?"

I quoted again, "'Be sober and watch: because your adversary the devil, as a roaring lion, goeth about seeking whom he may devour.'"

Rapid footsteps echoed through the cavernous room, growing louder and louder until they stopped directly in front of me. Fear gripped my lungs, stopping my breathing. In spite of the darkness, I could see two golden-red pinpricks of light directly in front of my face.

Mother Superior spoke, "It is you who will be devoured, Rafaela."

I had no time to scream, or protest, or lash out before I felt a swift, hard blow to my temple. The blackness enveloped me, and I sank into it.

CHAPTER TWENTY-EIGHT

Sister Rafaela

I was dimly aware of being dragged, my back sliding along uneven stones. There was a firm pressure at my throat, as though a strip of hide or canvas was pulling me by the neck. There were also tight knots of heat at my ankles and wrists. My eyes fluttered open long enough to see the outlines of four Sisters. I could not see their faces in any detail, but all four stared down at me with fire-bright golden-red eyes. The blackness reclaimed me, and I felt unspeakable relief.

* * *

Dear Lord, how I wished you had kept me asleep forever.

When I once again came back to myself, the first thing I noticed was the heat, which made my skin erupt in sweat like it never had before. The feeling was like standing too close to a hearth; I thought my flesh would crisp like a roasting chicken, and I began to struggle to remove my heavy habit.

I could not move. My wrists, which had been gripped in the burning hands of the Sisters as they dragged me, were now bound to the arms of a stone chair with scratchy lengths of rope.

My breathing came to a halt, and it was then that I opened my eyes. I knew where I was.

In front of me, the Sisters, now nearly aflame with ill-begotten health, knelt. A sea of golden-red eyes bored into me. At the head of the group, Mother Superior began a chant. After a while, the others joined in—they knew the words by heart.

"O Saint Berta, continue to grant us good health and wealth, gild our church that we have rededicated to you, flood the surrounding country with our tincture, bring us power untold, and we will worship you until we ourselves are placed here in this room. We will worship you even beyond death, taking our seats next to you, the pleasant burn of the afterlife keeping us warm."

I felt sure my ears were deceiving me. These women, these Sisters, who had formerly been devout and penitent acolytes of the one true God, had been so easily led astray by a false idol. Why was I the only one spared?

I wiggled my wrists in their restraints, and realized I probably was not being spared, after all.

A scream rose at the back of my throat, but I swallowed it down. I did not want to give them the satisfaction of knowing they had broken me.

I was sweating so profusely I felt slippery in my stone seat. Perhaps if I could use that slipperiness to my advantage, I would be able to pull my hands from their restraints…

I looked down, and only then did my eyes wander over to my left. The seat next to me was far from empty.

Held upright by his bonds was an elegant man with a thick black beard. No. No. My mind would only repeat that one word: No. His eyes had begun to hollow, and white jelly oozed from the sockets. His cheeks were papery and white, and his hands were curled into claws. Lengths of rope bound his wrists, too.

No. No, no, no, no.

Why had I been foolish enough to tell him all that I had suspected and feared? I had thought I would be safe when I slid my letter through the confessional's grille to Father Bruno. I had thought I would be able to tell my father what he needed to know.

Instead, my father would never know what really happened to me, and I had condemned a man of God to the horrors of the chamber in the process. I still did not know whether Father Bruno had really betrayed me as Mother Superior and Sister Leonella had insisted, but it did not matter now. Whether he had been trying to help me or stop me, he had walked unwillingly into his own doom.

Apparently, so had I.

A screech erupted from my throat; I could no longer hold it in. The sound echoed around the small room, growing ever more amplified.

If they had killed Father Bruno, a priest and man of God, with impunity, surely they would not suffer me to live.

Each pair of golden-red eyes was now trained firmly on me, and they all glittered with madness and malice.

O dear Lord, God in Heaven, Mother Mary, Jesus Christ, please free me from these bonds and spirit me away from this awful place, please let me see my family again, please please please—

"God cannot hear you, Rafaela," came Mother Superior's voice.

"He is not here!" Sister Leonella added.

A Sister I had washed dishes with spat on the ground and said, "A pox on your god!"

The rest of them cackled like harpies, throwing their heads back as gales of that choking laughter ripped the atmosphere to shreds. I could feel Berta's hellfire presence burning throughout the chamber.

Mother Superior moved in front of me, her eyes, now completely red, glinting. "We are not completely unmerciful, Rafaela."

I could not respond, for no sound would escape my mouth. My throat was raw and painful from screaming, and my tongue felt dry and useless.

Mother Superior leaned over me, even going so far as to place a hand on my shoulder. I winced; her fingers were unnaturally cold, and I could feel their prickly iciness through the layers of my habit. For a moment, I felt a queasy relief from the abominable warmth of the chamber.

"Rafaela," she cooed, "You have one last choice to make."

Still, I remained silent, panting. Her wintry fingers gripped my shoulder hard enough to bring fresh tears to my eyes. She leaned even closer to me, and when she spoke, her breath smelled foul beyond compare.

"My dear Rafaela," she said, "Saint Berta has asked us to give you an opportunity." She paused, looking around at the group of kneeling Sisters, a sharp grin plastered on her face. She turned back to me, and her eyes darkened to a deep scarlet—the color of blood. "Be wise, Rafaela. Join us."

She stepped back and resumed her position at the head of the group. Her face held an expression of deep, smug satisfaction. I struggled to comprehend what opportunity she could possibly be offering.

Join them? What would such a choice even look like? Would I fall harder than Lucifer himself and crash into a lake of fire? Would I emerge with Satanic prayers on my tongue and that golden-red flame in my own eyes? Would I burn from within?

No, I could not. I had come this far for my Lord God, I had been a devout follower of Jesus Christ since infancy. I had dedicated my life to the Church. I would not turn my back on the Savior.

Yet—what would my punishment be for refusing Mother Superior's— and Berta's—offer?

I shivered, my wrists straining agonizingly against my restraints. I knew the answer.

As I looked around the room at the sea of golden-red eyes, another thought struck me, sending needles of hot panic into my flesh: Death was far from the worst punishment they could inflict.

"Well?" Mother Superior said, her tone impatient. "Have you made your choice, Rafaela?"

I opened my mouth to speak, but nothing more than a mousy squeak issued from my lips. I swallowed and tried again. "I…" Where were the words? I had always assumed that if I had been in Peter's position, I would have the strength and courage to affirm my faith in Jesus, not cower in denial. Where was my spirit now, when I needed it most?

"Speak!" Mother Superior screeched, the sound so sudden and piercing in the small room that I let out a breathy scream in response. "Speak now, girl!" Her eyes were blazing; I could feel the heat of her stare like a torch.

I blinked hard, and fat, salty tears dripped down my feverish cheeks. "I… I will not betray my God!" This sentence came out so quickly it almost sounded as though it were one long, incomprehensible word.

Unfortunately, the Sisters understood me quite well.

Mother Superior's eyes blazed even hotter, and a malicious sneer twisted her features.

"Very well," she said.

"Tell her, Mother!" Sister Leonella cried suddenly, making me jump as much as I was able in my stone chair.

"Hush," Mother Superior hissed, but a smile had replaced her sneer. She walked toward me once again, and I found it difficult to breathe. Her fetid odor assaulted me as she spoke. "You should know something, Rafaela. It may even give you some peace of mind, which I am sure you yearn for at this moment."

I said nothing, only continued staring up at her, willing everything around me to disappear, as if the whole situation were nothing more than a particularly vivid nightmare.

Mother Superior purred, "Before we had disposed of your dear Father Bruno here, we made quite sure a special delivery was sent to the de Fuentes Piedra household, in addition to our letters."

A sharp gasp ripped through my terrified catatonia, and I found the breath to speak. "No!" I cried. Whatever they had sent to my father and mother would carry with it the evil rotting the Sisters from the inside out.

Mother Superior smiled, her sharp little teeth biting into her lips. One of them pierced the red skin, and a drop of blood beaded up before sliding slowly down her chin. "Yes, Rafaela. Do you want to know what it is we sent?"

"No!" I cried again, feeling that was the only word I was capable of forming in my parched mouth.

"Oh, I think you do, Rafaela. You see, we could not allow the family of one of our own go without the benefits of our special holy tincture. And from what we understand, it would do your murderess of a mother a world of good."

I screamed yet again, for what she was suggesting was so awful, so inhuman, so evil, that I felt for sure this must be a nightmare, and I would be able to awaken myself with the force of my agony. It was not to be.

If the Sisters had truly sent my parents the tincture, would my father and mother drink it? I knew from my father's letter that he had his doubts about the Sisters of Divine Innocence and their product, but what if the Sisters had signed the letter accompanying the tincture with my name? If they had indeed drunk it, then… then—

"Yes, Rafaela," Mother Superior said, seeing the realization dawning in my eyes. "Even if you had managed to dispatch that damned letter of yours, there would have been no one left alive in the de Fuentes Piedra household to read your filthy accusations."

"Damn you!" I cried, shaking with rage and despair. "Damn you all to hell!"

Mother Superior only smirked. "My dear Rafaela," she said, "we are already there."

"And soon, you will be, too," Sister Leonella added, stepping beside Mother Superior.

"Leonella, the tincture," Mother Superior commanded, opening her palm. In turn, Sister Leonella placed one of the small glass bottles I had come to know far too well into Mother's hand.

"No," I moaned, "No, no, no, no, no."

"Yes, Rafaela," Mother Superior said. "Remember, my sweet—it was you who chose this. We gave you an opportunity. You made the wrong decision. And now you must suffer the consequences. But at least your sins will be erased!"

The other Sisters cackled as, with one swift motion, Mother Superior uncorked the bottle of tincture, filling the room even more fully with that horrible sick-sweet odor of death. The grin was consuming her face again, and her eyes were burning brighter than ever before—miniature doorways to hell. "Open wide, Rafaela."

I clamped my lips shut and struggled with ferocity against my restraints, but to no avail.

"Do not make this difficult," Mother Superior said. When I continued to struggle, hoping and praying to God that He would release me from this inferno, Mother Superior snapped at Sister Leonella, "Leonella, now."

Sister Leonella's fist connected with my stomach so quickly I had no time to prepare, and the wind burst from me in a painful whoosh. With my mouth open, Leonella seized my jaws in her sticky hands and pried me open.

"Ah, that is better," Mother Superior said.

Before I could even attempt to clench my teeth once again, Mother Superior shoved the neck of the bottle onto my tongue and tilted its bottom upward, sending the revolting contents sliding down my throat. Without having to be prodded this time, Sister Leonella swiftly removed her fingers from inside my mouth, instead clamping them around my chin and forcing my jaws closed. She pulled my head roughly back and yelled, "Swallow!"

I wanted to fight against it, I wanted to hold the vile human drippings in my mouth so I could spit them out immediately, but I could not.

The fire in my spirit was snuffed out like a candle, and I knew my first impression of this awful place was correct: God was not here. He could not hear me. He would not save me.

I swallowed.

Mother Superior nodded in satisfaction. "It is time to go," she said to the other Sisters, and they all rose as one and glided out of the room with an uncanny speed. Only Mother Superior remained hovering over me.

"Fear not, Rafaela," she breathed. "One day, one day soon, your body will fill our glass bottles."

I hardly noticed when she left the chamber, shutting the door with a firm thud behind her. Blackness enveloped me, and screams I barely recognized as my own ripped from my blistering throat. Over the sounds of my own torment I could hear Berta's choking chuckle, the sound so irritating to my soul that I felt sure madness was waiting for me in the dark, ready to pounce.

I did not stop screaming until I felt the tincture boiling within my insides, reaching a fever pitch. I felt aflame.

I was left to burn alone.

AUTHOR'S NOTE

No historical horror novel is complete without a bit of grounding in the true story that ignited the spark of inspiration. The concept of a 'rotting room' isn't fictional. In the 17th century, the Poor Clares of Ischia, Italy, kept their dead in an underground room ringed with stone chairs, where the bodies would slowly mummify. Often, the living Sisters who came to pray near the corpses fell prey themselves to the same diseases that ravaged their dead Sisters. Terrifying, huh?

On to the thank yous! I must profusely offer my sincere gratitude to the village that props me up, supports and encourages me, and keeps me going: Mom, Dad, Ryan, Camille, Wyatt, Aunt Bevy, KC and Grant, all of my in-laws, nieces, and nephews, and all of my extended family. Huge thanks as well to Katherine Vantosh and Beth Horowicz, who are excellent beta readers and even better friends. Joe Haward ensured the accuracy of this book from a religious perspective, which I appreciate immensely.

Thanks also to Clay McLeod Chapman, Nick Roberts, and Mona Kabbani, who graciously agreed to give this book an early read. To my DreadPop Magazine team—thank you for helping me find my home in the horror community!

Last but certainly not least, thank you to you, my wonderful reader, for taking a chance on an indie author!

VIGGY PARR HAMPTON

is an epidemiologist, content marketing strategist, host of the podcast "Horror Humor Hunger," and the author of *A Cold Night for Alligators* and *Much Too Vulgar*. She is a graduate of Georgetown University and Emory University's Rollins School of Public Health. She is also a member of the DreadPop Magazine team, producing the popular YouTube segment "Tag Team Tales of Terror," where she challenges fellow horror authors to create a progressive story with her.

Connect with her at her website, www.viggyhampton.com or on Instagram @viggyparrhampton

www.ingramcontent.com/pod-product-compliance
Lightning Source LLC
Chambersburg PA
CBHW070525310726

48976CB00002BA/539